HOGG

HOGG

BY SAMUEL R. DELANY

TUSCALOOSA

First hardcover edition: 1995
First paperback edition: 1996
Second edition 2004

Originally published by FC2 and Black Ice Books, Normal, 1995. *Hogg* is
printed by permission of the author Samuel R. Delany and his agents Henry
Morrison, Inc.

FC2 is an imprint of the University of Alabama Press

Inquiries about reproducing material from this work should be addressed to
the University of Alabama Press

Book Design: Tara Reeser
Cover design: Katrina Ferguson

Library of Congress Cataloging-in-Publication Data is available from the
Library of Congress.

ISBN: 978-1-57366-119-5

FOR MICHAEL PERKINS

INTRODUCTION
BY ROB STEPHENSON

"...Hogg is like that, another country. If you were to live there, just like it is, for real, you wouldn't live long. And maybe that's your choice. It's also a great place to visit, a vacation. And then the odds for your survival improve. It's been difficult for me to find such a vacation spot. I've never read anything that does it quite so well for me as Hogg does. Maybe because no one will print the manuscripts, and you don't get to see them..."

—Dragon E, from a letter to Samuel Delany in 1992

"In a sense, pornography is the most political form of fiction, dealing with how we use and exploit each other, in the most urgent and ruthless way."

—J. G. Ballard, from the introduction to
the 1974 French edition of *Crash*

"The distinctions between them, already vast in all their other manias and tastes, are even more excessive in the case of passions, and whoever could assess and give details of these perversions might well produce one of the finest imaginable works on human mores, and perhaps one of the most interesting."

—D. A. F. Sade, from the introduction to
The One Hundred and Twenty Days of Sodom.

THOSE READERS WHO HAVE HEARD OF SAMUEL DELANY before picking up *Hogg* will almost certainly know him as a science fiction writer. Science fiction writers go to all kinds of extremes to invent other worlds that inevitably end up revealing things, hopefully profound, about our own world. *Hogg* is no exception, though it is not a science fiction novel. *Hogg* manages in just over two-hundred-fifty pages to sculpt a world that is not at all futuristic, but fantastically unfamiliar in the most disturbing ways.

Samuel Delany wrote *Hogg* in San Francisco in 1969 and finished it just days before the Stonewall riots in New York City. Over the next four years he rewrote it, while working on several science fiction novels, including the internationally acclaimed *Dhalgren*. It took over twenty years for *Hogg* finally to be published in 1995 as a limited hardback edition of five hundred copies by Black Ice Books/ Fiction Collective 2. A small paperback edition followed.

Over the years many book publishers, some eager to publish a Delany novel, would still not accept *Hogg* for publication after reading it. Maurice Girodias of Olympia Press, famous for first publishing Nabokov's *Lolita* and the novels of Sade, told Delany it was the only novel he "ever rejected solely because of its sexual content."

According to Walter Kendrick in *The Secret Museum: Pornography in Modern Culture*, concurrently with the rise of the novel in England, there was a fear that young women, reading the new "sensation novels," would not be able to distinguish reality from fiction, causing them to give in to vice. Similar views were propounded by writers such as Charles Dickens, Samuel Johnson, and Anthony Trollope. Kendrick suggests that these views eventually culminated in the obscenity trials of Émile Zola and Gustave Flaubert.

The idea of the corruptible child, a dangerous young person illuminated by knowledge he or she shouldn't be able to access, grew to a frenetic pitch during the nineteenth century in America, where this dangerous child was imagined to be either female or male. Fanatics like Alan Comstock went around the country burning books and invoking the judgments of the Almighty.

The unnamed boy who narrates *Hogg* is deliberately fashioned as the opposite of the "corruptible child." He is corruption itself. In contrast to all the rape that Hogg initiates towards women in this novel, he never has to force this boy to do anything. Anything Hogg wants him to do, he relishes. He wants to experience everything that comes his way. He craves all of the nastiness that Hogg dishes out. He doesn't have to learn to be a slave. There is even a second boy in the novel who is drawn to Hogg in the same way the narrator is, but Hogg rejects him.

The fact that *Hogg* is hardcore pornography may make it difficult, at first, to see the beauty of Delany's language, the poetry and elegance in his descriptions of bodies, objects, and places. The same magical style that sweeps us through much of Delany's writing is there, sharp and peculiar, lovely and vivid, holding everything together in a river of bloody, filthy, and downright evil sex and murder, which is occasionally punctuated by some illuminating dialogue.

Nothing is gratuitous in this novel. The excess of radical sexuality and violence in *Hogg* is reminiscent of Sade's novels, but without Sade's humorous and continual obsession with repetition and counting. Sade's characters are rarely more than two-dimensional cartoons, though at times he makes them utter remarkable philosophical musings. Delany's monstrous characters (Hogg and his gang of rapists) become uncomfortably fleshed-out humans. They elicit our sympathy. By the book's end, they seem far less distant than they do at the beginning.

Aware that I may begin to look like I'm writing the CliffsNotes for *Hogg*, I list below a few questions that might enhance a reading of this novel:

What is the most disturbing thing about this novel? In the world of this novel, what actions of the main characters can be seen as good or moral? How do the main characters change at the very end of the story? Is there any way in which this is a feminist novel? How is race important in this novel? Who loves in this novel? How does humor operate in *Hogg*? How is the media portrayed? What viewpoints on violence are expressed?

In closing, I implore you to bring to this book the rigor necessary to enjoy it. Dig deeply beneath its deceptive, gritty surface and find the riches waiting there in one of Samuel Delany's most rare and difficult gifts.

— January 2004, Ridgewood, New York

HOGG

THIS STORY IS MOSTLY HOGG'S.

But first I have to tell you some about me.

That summer, by the blistered radiator behind the landing of the steps down to the basement, I used to suck off a sad looking thirteen-year-old spic named Pedro, who wore his dad's baggy pants I don't think he ever changed and a white short-sleeved shirt he put on Sunday mornings. Saturday nights it was gray. With shiny hair bumping the underside of the stairs and their drips of dirt, he would grind his sneakers on the rusty boards by the radiator's metal feet and rub the heel of his hand on the hard place above his groin where his dad's belt was tied. (The buckle had come loose.) His knuckles were red from gnawing. "You want it?" He'd glance around, scared. "Come on, take it now. Go on, take it." His zipper was always half open.

Squatting, I'd nose between the brass teeth to smell his sweat. He would push penis, both testicles, and the two little fingers of his left hand into my mouth. Holding his thin hips, I troweled my tongue inside his foreskin till, leaning and grunting, he would spurt his greasy juice and, quickly limp, a tablespoon of urine.

Once he told me, when I stood up, "You look funny down there. You really look funny."

Though I was eleven, I was half a head taller than him. People who didn't talk to us always thought I was the older.

There were two mattresses in the cellar already.

I helped him carry the third one down. Then he got his fifteen-year-old sister, Maria, made her lie on her back, pulled her new skirt up, her stained panties down, and wedged his chin between her thighs, blinking his eyes over her cunt hair. "Look at her." (There was powdery gray on his head: I'd already done him once that morning.) He lifted his face. "She giggle all the time like that. Anybody fuck on her and she giggle. You suck my dick while I eat it out her pussy, huh?" Later he made her take all her clothes off and crawled on top, while she clawed the back of his shirt, big thighs shaking outside the sweaty cloth of his pants, big tits flattened beneath the wadded Saturday gray.

"Tickle my nuts!"

I put my hand between them where they rocked. His penis was very hot and slipped against the side of my palm. I tried to get some fingers into her. Then I tried to put my face down there and lick at her, but I couldn't.

He shot.

"Hey…" He panted, rolling off. "You didn't tickle my nuts." But he was grinning. His belt was still tied but the top button on his pants had come loose. His crotch hair was wet and his cock— a wrinkled nozzle with a vein up the side—shone. "You wanna fuck on her now?"

Maria had her forearm over her mouth. She watched me across it, blinking. She was making hiccuppy sounds.

"Come on, come on." Pedro hit her thigh with the back of his hand. "Open it, huh?"

She opened her legs for my face. Rough hair cut my mouth, till I got to the cunt, spreading around my chin. I sank in the double taste. My tongue went up against a fold in the roof where a nut, hooded in wet flesh, made her thighs clap my ears. I jabbed deeper, holding her buttocks while a mattress button on a loose thread dug the back of my hand.

She dribbled down one side of my chin.

"Fuck on her!" Pedro insisted. "Don't you know how to fuck?"

He leaned on my back with one hand, while his other reached between my legs, caught my fly. "Buttons...!" he said, before he found there were only two left. "Shit, man!" He put his hand inside and pulled my cock out. Stiff, it hurt on the edge of the denim. I almost came. "Oh, Christ," Pedro said. "You better put that thing up her pussy, cocksucker!"

I crawled up Maria and ground my wet face in her neck. She *Shisss*ed beside me.

For a while I tried just to poke it in while I held onto her shoulders. But somebody has to use hands. I got the head in— and pushed. She just stopped breathing, then went, "*Uhhhh....*" With one hand I held her shoulder and rubbed the side of her squashed tit with the other. Every third or fourth push, she'd shake her head and gasp. Her legs flapped against my sides. She lifted her feet off the mattress; and when I'd relax after a hunch in her, her ankles hit my hips.

Once I felt Pedro's fingers, like curious mice, play in the plunging juncture. But he took them away.

When I was coming, the place right above my knees got hot. The heat went on up my legs. The skin between my balls and my ass tightened. I wanted Pedro to tickle *my* nuts now, but he didn't. So I thought about his scum in there, around my dick. The slow explosion in the groin pushed all the air out of my lungs.

"Shit..." Pedro drawled. He reached between us again. I was so sensitive it hurt. So I rolled off.

Maria tried to grab me. As I got free, she said something in Spanish. Pedro hit her—he hit for her chin, but she twisted away and he just got her shoulder. He laughed. "Big, dumb cocksucker," he said. Maria sat up and pulled her skirt into her lap over her pussy. First I thought she wanted to cover herself, but she kept her fist there, as though it felt good. Or maybe it didn't.

She looked at my cock and sucked in her bottom lip.

She ran one hand to her knee, like she might reach and pick it up. Most of her nails were flecked with pearl-colored polish.

"What you doing?" Pedro asked.

"It don't look like yours," she said.

"A lot of guys, Polacks and Jews and stuff, they cut off the front part. He's circumcised, is what they call it," Pedro explained. "It's still pretty fucking big, ain't it."

"Not that." Maria arched her fingers on her knee, like a kitten on new jeans.

"He's like a fucking mule," Pedro said.

"The hair," Maria said. "Yours is black and his is yellow. On your head, I mean, yours is curly like a nigger almost, and his is all soft. But down there—"

"What?" Pedro said.

"His and yours, it's tight and rough on you both."

"So's yours," Pedro said. "I ain't no fucking nigger." He pulled up his cuff to scratch the place behind his ankle. He didn't wear socks with his sneakers. His heel was like a pole of dirt. He stopped and frowned. "Would you fuck with a nigger?"

But Maria had picked up her skirt and was shaking it out in her lap.

The next day Pedro met me in the street. "Hey," he said, "you suck it good, you know? And Maria, she like it a lot, a big one you know, shove in her pussy? These guys around here, I bet they gimme a quarter for a piece of pussy. And we got too many, see, you suck, hey? You could sleep downstairs there anyway, instead of up on the roof. You could look out for the place when I ain't there. We could do a lot of business off that dumb cunt, huh?"

Later I was coming out the hall and saw Pedro and Maria sitting on the front steps, their backs to me. His shoulders were moving a lot as he talked. Though I couldn't see her face, I could tell she was chewing on the middle fingernail she let herself bite.

Pedro was saying: "...got three mattresses down there already. The little bastard'll do anything I tell it to him. We could do a lot of business off that dumb cocksucker, huh?"

I turned around and went back downstairs.

We *did* a lot of business, too.

Pedro hit on the older guys in the neighborhood. Somebody turned one of the bikers from Ellenville onto him—the first time the Phantoms came over I wasn't there—and they'd bring beer and just haul Maria's ass all over the cellar floor, one after the other, while the rest stood around and drank and joked, or watched and played with themselves, till one would call: "Come on over here, cocksucker, and swing on this awhile for me, before I mess myself up!"

There were three of them got so they'd come in and not pay Maria any mind but go right in on me. One was the vice president or something big in the gang. The others were just strange. They were all pretty rough. But Rat, one of the *real* strange ones, would slip me a dollar sometimes, besides paying Pedro his quarter. So I liked them.

Pedro and Maria's father, Mr. Alvarez, was the super for the building across the street. (The super for the one I stayed in had died from hepatitis three months before—I don't think the landlord even knew because there wasn't any new one yet—and he'd let me sleep in the tool shack on the roof; I used to come down and eat canned chili in his apartment. But after they found his body, they put a padlock on his door so I couldn't get in.) Once Mr. Alvarez stopped me in the hall, his black eyes narrowing, kneading his hands inside his overalls pockets.

"That little motherfucker," he said. "That little no good bastard son of a bitch, he got you and his sister making a whorehouse in here, huh?" Mr. Alvarez nodded toward the cellar steps. "Shit, everybody in the goddamn city go down there and fuck with my daughter. Shit. How you like that shit? I mean, just how you like that goddamn shit? Motherfucker!"

I thought he was going to do something or say something else. But he just shook his head, scratched, and wandered away.

On the first really hot day—it had rained that morning—Pedro brought some niggers over who usually hung out around Crawhole. They came in, big, loud, and barefoot. And they had some wine.

"You only got one pussy down here, boy?"

"But don't it look like a sweet one!"

"Here's my quarter. Lemme rip into a piece of that!"

"Look out, little girl! Look out, look out!"

Maria was giggling.

"This old blacksnake of mine got a bite, honey!"

Finally, one pushed himself away from the circle of backs. His sleeves were rolled up tight. He was bullet-headed, his arms glistened in the heat, and he was so black there wasn't no brown on him. He picked up one of the gallon winejugs off the bottom step, wrapped his big mouth over the neck, swung it high, and sucked, while the plum-colored stuff bubbled in the greenish glass. He let the jug drop, and while it was swinging from his thumb, he saw me.

He grinned, put down the jug, and came over. "What you starin' at, white boy?" He ran his callused hand through my hair. "You a cute little yellow-headed bastard. You see the way that little bitch over there goes after black meat? I could sure enjoy somebody goin' after mine like that." He squeezed the back of my neck and grinned even broader. There was a scar at the corner of his mouth that went a quarter-inch up and half an inch down. It gave the left side of his expression a crazy look. He shook me a little, so that I had to grab his hip with one hand. He had on a pair of workman's blues, torn at one knee. The cuffs and the edges of the pockets were frayed. I say they'd been blue once; but there wasn't much color at all in them now. "Gonna feel real good working it down in your face, cocksucker. Go on, take it out."

Over the edge of the steps a piece of sunlight dropped across his foot. He pulled in his toes on the cracked concrete. The troughs between the ligaments were almost purple. He spread his toes wide.

I heard his fly sing.

"Go on, boy."

I put my hand inside. His groin was sweaty. He moved one leg aside so I could get it. His legs were awfully hard.

He pushed down on my shoulder.

Half stiff, it was longer than a flashlight. The foreskin made a loose hood over the plum-sized head. He got his balls out. They were wrinkled and heavy, the skin pulled into a gray-black ridge, like his sack had been sewed up along it.

He smelled like something burning in front of a vegetable stand on a hot day.

"Suck it."

I took it in my mouth. When it went all the way in—"*Yeah...!*"—he gasped. I hugged his legs. He put a hand on each side of my head and began to swing his hips. After a while I got dizzy: I was kneeling flat on the ground, and he put his bare foot on my thigh, working his toes, each time he went in. "Suck on my balls!" which was like licking black rock-salt, with his cock flapping by my ear. I looked up once, when it raised, to see his fist fall at me, beating the black shaft. "Eat it, white boy!" He pushed his balls all the way in my mouth with his thumb and jerked harder. I held his ankle with one hand and his belt with the other. "Here it...!"

I kneeled up. He crouched down and jammed my throat full, clutching my sides with his knees, my head with his hands. Three thrusts and he swelled and spilled. I drank and sucked deep as I could.

He panted, thrusting out gout and gout.

He breathed hard and held my face against him awhile. When I finally came off him, he caught his breath. "Yeah, boy!"

I stood up.

He grinned at me, put his hand on the back of my neck again. "Where you learn that?" With his other hand, he brushed his knuckles across my cheek. "You really look good down there, white boy."

I took his cock in my hand.

It was still half hard. He laughed. "This nigger's ol' pig-sticker ain't never less than a quarter stiff." He pulled me down to sit with him on the bottom step. He closed his hand around mine around his dick. He moved his face up right in front of mine so that I could smell the wine; I kept glancing at the crazy scar that made its valley down beside his black lip. His hand behind my neck kept my face right against his. The other dug between my legs.

From behind us:

"Man, *let* me get at the bitch now!"

"Aw, come on. Shit, man, you already been there!"

Maria's high, hiccupping giggle rode on a wallow of bass laughter, till a husky hysteria cut through it all:

"I'm gonna fuck 'er! I'm gonna fuck 'er, man! I'm gonna fuck 'er *now*!"

The nigger opened his mouth over mine and dug in my throat with his tongue, breathing through his nose. I could feel the stubble on his chin and cheek against mine.

He got my fly open and his hand inside. He was fingering around for my asshole, and every once in a while he'd come up and twist on my cock. I held onto his shoulders, because he was almost pushing me off the edge of the step, under the banister.

Thinking I was going to fall, I came.

He took his tongue out my mouth, brought his hand up between us. His nails were dirty and his knuckles were black like the ground in the woods when it hasn't rained in a long time and it's begun to crack. His fingers were strung with mucus. After looking at it a moment, he said: "Get it, boy. It's yours."

I held his wrist and licked his thumb and the back of his hand.

But it was already cold.

"With that dick on you and the way that yellow hair of yours is all curly, you could have some nigger in you—one of them quadroon, octroon kids. Yeah, I can see it in your nose, there. And your mouth, a little." (A lot of niggers, their palms and their soles are lighter than the rest of them. But not his. I licked the insides of his fingers.) "You gonna remember Nigg for a long time, ain't you, cocksucker? Tell you what. Ah'm gonna stick my black dick up your ass an' we gonna tongue some more. Then I'm gonna make you suck the shit off it. An' I'm gonna bust my nut again...." His scummy hand kept working down between my legs. My top button pulled loose from the worn hole. (I wanted to chew the bottom of his foot.) He began to push my pants down. "Shit, come on and sit on this nigger dick...white boy!"

Drunk and out all night, the bikers woke us up about four in the morning. One was already on his knees at the mattress, trying to eat out Maria's pussy—while she kept trying to sit up and fold her skirt—it was torn now—saying, "Just a minute.... Come *on*; just a minute, huh?" till one guy, with his cock out, came around to squat in front of her head.

A third—Rat—leaned, one arm up on the wall and one arm down on his stomach, puking. It came out mostly wine and pizza; you could tell, where it splattered the brick or splashed the floor.

Pedro sat on the bottom step, pushing quarters with his thumb off one palm to clink them into the other.

Where I lay, watching, Hawk nudged my shoulder with his boot.

Rolling on my back, eyes still sticky with sleep, I looked up.

Two thick fingers were inside Hawk's fly, with two others and his thumb outside, all working. In his other hand, tilted to his mouth, was a can of beer. His wet neck pulsed. The black hair was flattened down his sweaty chest. He was twenty-five or so. A big crease swallowed his navel, like a hairy grin, the corners hidden behind his denim vest. He flung the beer can against the wall and dropped his thick arm. The threads where the sleeves had been ripped off were a gray fringe on the blue-black cloth up near the top of his shoulder; further down, they darkened into a moon of sweat that had set on each flank. A blurry dragon above his wrist and a jailhouse swastika on his biceps, hand and forearm were cabled in veins. He grinned at me through black stubble. Red ringed his eyes, and the place his wet lashes set looked inflamed. "Hope you were dreamin' 'bout some *big* dick in your face, boy."

I sat up.

Rat finished being sick and came over, wiping stuff off his chin with two fingers. Scrawny, redheaded, he scratched the nest of acne on his chest with black-rimmed nails. "Will you look at that sleepy fucker, there!"

Big Chico laughed. The knife sheath strapped to his boot was worn off where the tip scraped the floor. His gold earring flashed.

Hawk kneaded himself. The denim had faded where his meat filled his jeans crotch. "He was just lying there, playin' with himself in his sleep," while two more 'cycles roared up outside. Ape Townley, who was the president, followed by his kid brother, called the Monk, swaggered down the cellar steps, howling. But they were interested in Maria.

And Hawk was vice president, anyway.

Someone gave Pedro a can of beer. He took a long swallow, then, wiping his mouth on his wrist, looked at his sister and the guy who was working on her.

"Hey, man!" the Monk said. "Here you *go*! Here's my quarter! Right here, go on, take it!"

Rat squatted beside me. "What was you dreaming about, cocksucker?"

"Some dick bigger'n yours, I bet." Hawk laughed, swaying from one scuffed boot to the other. The outside of the heels were worn to the soles.

"Not bigger'n mine," Big Chico said. "Least ways not thicker," which was true.

Rat got his fly down and pulled out his dick, rubbing it first overhand then underhand.

Pedro called over: "Some big nigger was in here this afternoon humping it in his face."

Rat grinned at that and rubbed harder. The head of his cock was the color a bruise would have been on his pale skin. He always made me think of a bar of dirty soap. He liked to watch and hear bad talk, mostly. "Must of had a dick-and-a-half, huh?"

"I ain't never seen this boy *get* enough dick," Hawk drawled. Though he lived in Ellenville now, he was from someplace in the South. "Hey, Chico, take mine out and feed this cocksucker." He unbuttoned three more buttons, just by flexing his knuckles. Then he held his hands aside while Chico reached in.

Hawk had hair growing halfway down it.

"Ain't *thick* as mine." Chico hefted it. "But god*damn*...!" He pushed my head toward it. "Sucker looks hungry, don't he?"

Hawk brought his hands together, as I took it in my mouth. He slid both thumbs in beside his cock and began to chuckle with a sound that never really got above his gut. My tongue worked on nail and knuckle and hairy crank, all tasting like machine oil.

Chico was working his own fat penis now.

Still squatting, Rat reached between my legs and felt me, then went back to jerking himself, his face just about wedged between me and Hawk so he could get a good look. "Spit just a-drippin' down his chin!" He held himself up with one hand on my shoulder while he leaned forward. I could feel him shaking as he jerked.

The Monk had come up to stand behind Hawk, watching.

"Hey, come over here," Ape called. "You about to miss your turn, Monk, less you goin' in for boy-pussy tonight!"

The Monk grinned, shook his head, and walked back to where Maria was taking them on.

"Hey, cocksucker," Chico said. "Hawk wants you to go around the world on his nuts. He been talkin' about it all the way over here."

Hawk was really leaning into my face, when somebody barked:

"*Hey—!*"

Hawk lost his stroke (but not his hard).

Without letting his dick go, I looked to the side.

Mr. Alvarez stopped on the steps. He was swaying, drunk as anybody there. Suddenly he laughed. "You motherfuckers really doin' it to that bitch's pussy, huh?" He squinted at the two guys on Maria. Three more stood around the mattress.

"Hey, *Popa—!*" Pedro squealed, as Mr. Alvarez's hand went back.

I thought he was going to knock Pedro across the floor into the boiler. So did Pedro. But Mr. Alvarez staggered; his hand swung sideways, up, down. He must have thought that was funny too, because he laughed. "You got my little girl all ready for her daddy, hey, boy?" His hand moved around, hit Pedro's cheek; he patted it clumsily and came down another step.

With one hand he pulled at the gray cloth between his legs.

The bikers were looking at each other, confused, but not wanting to admit it. Ape, leaning against the wall with his palm flat, moved away, then leaned back, this time on his fist. His rings clicked brick.

Maria must have opened her eyes then—she jerked up on her elbows. The guy on her lifted his blond head from between her legs, grinning and glistening, eyes to chin.

Mr. Alvarez's fly rasped.

"Two more minutes and I'll be finished with her, Pops. Then she's *all* yours." The blond guy started to go down on her again, but Mr. Alvarez caught him by his hair and yanked his face up. "How you like my little girl's pussy, 'ey?" Mr. Alvarez bent real close. "How you like it?"

"Hey, *watch* it, Pops—!"

One biker started forward.

Another made a gesture with his chin that stopped him.

Mr. Alvarez turned him loose, staggered a step away. It took him about ten seconds to get his cock out of his pants; he grinned at it.

Rat was still beating on his dick and staring. "Is that really her old man, I mean her daddy?"

"Yeah!" Chico had his, sort of hidden, in both tattooed hands.

"Oh, *shit*—!" Above me, Hawk was grinning. He pulled out my mouth and turned to watch.

Mr. Alvarez stepped over Maria, one shoe on the mattress, one on the floor. "What you think of this, hey?" He hit his up-curved cock with the side of his hand. It swung side-to-side. "You gonna take this? You gonna take it?"

He squatted down.

"God*damn*, Pops—!" That was the blond guy. Mr. Alvarez had almost sat on his head.

The blond kneeled back on the floor, scowling and rubbing his naked chest inside his leather vest.

Mr. Alvarez was fumbling it in and trying to kiss her. His shoe kept scraping on the cement by the mattress. Maria's hands kept moving on, under, and around her father's shoulders, but you couldn't really tell if she was trying to push him off, but was scared to; or hold him on, but was scared of that too. Then, escaping between their butting faces, I heard her high, hiccuppy giggle, a moment later stifled by his tongue. Her bent knees sagged and recovered at his sides as he began to hunch and grunt.

"—shit…!" from Rat.

I got down on the floor and caught the bruised head of his cock in my mouth and five fists in the face, before Rat realized I was trying to suck him. When I took it all the way to the red crotch hairs sticking through the zipper, he nearly lost his balance.

"Oh, shit…!" he whispered, squatting, his knuckles on the floor. "Look at daddy fuck on his little spic bitch!" Seven more thrusts spilled Rat's load.

I kept sucking; but he didn't mind.

Big Chico grunted behind me. I felt something pull the seat of my pants; and rip. I looked back. Grinning, Chico pushed his knife into his boot sheath. I could feel cold air on my buttocks; then, Chico's hands.

Later, I came off Hawk (who always needed it three or four times) to see Mr. Alvarez beside us, his balls hanging from his fly. His pants were wet down one inside leg.

"Hey." Hawk reached down drunkenly and shook my shoulder. "Go on and blow him, cocksucker." (Rat had gone off to squat by the guys back on Maria, now that Mr. Alvarez had finished.) "Let's see you suck on Pops awhile."

I put my hands on Mr. Alvarez's hips and ran my nose against his balls. I could smell Maria's pussy. Mr. Alvarez fumbled his cock into my mouth. He swayed unsteadily, but when I pulled back and pushed forward, he got hard right away.

"Goddamn—!" Ape came up between Hawk and Mr. Alvarez. "Well I'll be *god*damned!" He grinned around a mouth full of small, stained teeth. He was very tall—about two and a half heads taller than Mr. Alvarez. Ape's nose had been messed up recently in a 'cycle accident: a scab still ran off it onto his cheek, with two parallel lines of stitch marks. "What you guys into with this shit over here in the corner, huh?" He was unsteady as Mr. Alvarez and kept rubbing his chin with the back of his hand, in a double punching motion. His hair was the color of wet sand. His beard stubble was red. "You guys are too fuckin' much, you know?" Ape laughed; his laugh started as high as Maria's, then trundled down to shake behind his flat, bald belly. "Oh, man—" He sucked his teeth. "I'm just about drunk enough to try some of this shit myself...." He put both hands between his legs, bent his knees, howled out, "Whooo-*peeeee!*" and staggered against Mr. Alvarez, who didn't really notice. "Oh, hey: sorry, Pops! Hey, I'm *really* sorry...." Ape patted Mr. Alvarez's arm—Ape wore a lot of rings—then looked down where I was still working out. "Oh, shit... Hey, Monk?" Over his shoulder,

Ape bawled back: "Hey, Monk! You gotta get over here and watch this—I think I'm gonna *fuck* this cocksucker!" He slid his hands back down to his crotch.

Only two of the big rings were gold. He wore three and four smaller ones on some fingers; two thick ones with turquoise; and some, plain silver. Most were just twists of iron, though. He had one big one with a chunk of what looked like red marble in it the size of a quarter, on his thumb. His hands were grit-gray. His knuckles were like walnuts grooved with grime. His nails were ringed with it—the one on his forefinger, smashed in the accident, was half black. "*Monk*...! Monk? There you go...look. You gotta watch this, man. I'm gonna show these motherfuckers how it's *done*!" He worked his hands between his legs. His fly was still open from when he'd been with Maria. I could see part of his cock inside and the hair around it, like a frayed length of dock rope, with the two, big crusted warts back near the base. (I'd seen them before, once, when Maria blew him; the biggest in the Phantoms—well, Chico's was thicker—maybe it had something to do with why he was president.) Ape leaned over again to look. "Pops is just about to do it, huh?"

"Yeah...." Hawk prodded a knuckle at where Mr. Alvarez's wet brown shaft slid in my mouth. Mr. Alvarez held my head, swaying in, and in, and in. With a hoarse, soft growl, he pumped his scum in four spurts, then (and by this I knew he was father of his son) filled my mouth with whiskey pee.

"Okay, motherfucker!" Ape got his belt open.

Mr. Alvarez pulled out, panting. Warm pee ran down my chin.

"Okay—" Ape's ringed hand hung, hooked by his thumb, from the fork of his fly. "*Get* it, cocksucker!"

"You wanna come with us?" Pedro asked. "We gonna take a walk."

"Fuck you," Maria said and turned over on the mattress ticking. "You better gimme some money." She lay with her back to us. "You don't gimme some money, I'm gonna beat the piss outta you."

"You go ask Daddy for some money," Pedro said. "He give it to you, you want some money now."

"You don't gimme no money," Maria said, "you gonna be sorry." She raised her arm up under her head, facing the wall; her hand came out from under her dark hair. "Last night—Daddy say he gonna beat you this mornin', for doin' all this shit." Her nails were like pearl-flecked beetles—the middle one much smaller than the others—in a row on her brown fist.

"Fuck *him*," Pedro said. "He ain't gonna beat me. He too fuckin' drunk. He ain't even gonna remember."

"Gimme some money."

"Ask Daddy," Pedro said, and to me: "Come on."

I followed him up the steps.

The sky was just going blue.

We walked over to where the river comes up from Frontwater.

By the time we got there, the sun was still close enough to the horizon to drip gold on the sound.

Leaves and wet paper were all over the path. It was still warm. The river lapped below the rail.

"How you like that shit, hey?" Pedro grinned and dug deep in his pants pockets. "Somethin', huh?" He squinted across the river.

Down where it widened into the bay, two tugs, either side of an old Crawhole garbage scow, thrummed on wrinkled red water.

"My daddy say he gonna come down there and mess it up for us all the time. But before, shit, he always get too drunk and go after Maria upstairs in the house. Then he don't want no more.... She don't like him none. She ain't gonna ask him for no money." Pedro thrust his tongue tip between his lips. "But she like the way he fuck her pussy, man! He go at her like a fuckin' dog, don't he?" Without taking his fists from his pockets, he leaned his stomach against the rail. Long shreds of morning pulled from the bruised sky. A breeze whipped the dirt-gray collar back from his shoulder. "A fuckin' dog..." Grinning, he still looked sad.

It was Saturday—no, Sunday morning.

I started walking up the path.

"Hey, cocksucker," Pedro called, "where you goin'...?"

I put my hands in my pockets and kept walking.

"Shit..." Pedro said. Then, with the next thing he said I could hear him grinning again behind me: "Okay, cocksucker, I see you around—hey? So long."

SHE RAN DOWN THE ALLEY, SCREAMING.

He ran after her, caught her arm, spun her around.

Her scream bit off. She backed into the wall, her mouth open and her henna hair coming forward. "Come on, mister...!" She was trying to smile, to reason; it came out pleading. "Come on, now. You don't have to hurt me none. I'll give it to you! I swear, I'll give it to you! Any way you want it, honey. You don't have to fight me for it!" Her eyes darted around the alley. There wasn't any way out except the way they'd come in. "Don't hurt me, sweetheart. Don't... We can have ourselves a *good* time!"

He took a loud breath, raised his other hand, and punched her in the stomach.

She slammed back onto brick. Her head rocked forward.

Grunting, he hit her in the face, hard, with the back of his hand.

All over her head, hair shook. It was black at the roots.

"Oh, come—" She gagged, held her forearms across her belly, sliding them up. "Come on, I got two kids. I got to go to *work*! You mess me up for a couple of days where I have to lay up and I'm gonna lose my—"

I didn't see where he hit her this time because he was right on top of her; but she jerked over to the side.

"Oh, come on, I *told* you I'll—"

I *guess* she meant it.

With one hand up under her skirt, he yanked three times, and the panties came, torn and pink, from under the dingy print. He threw them down, hard, while she tried to twist from the wall. With both hands he slammed her back. She knocked into a garbage can. It crashed over, spilling stuff. One of her heels was broken and so was the plastic strap. She had on grayish stockings that just made her legs look dirty—except for an oval tear, from her ankle halfway up her calf, where her skin was white and puffy, like a real redhead's.

He hit her again, and she sagged forward, holding her jaw. He got his hand inside his green canvas pants.

I heard her skirt rip.

When he got it in her—she was backed up against the brick, now—she screamed again. His construction shoes rasped the pavement, the muddy heels lifting. One of her arms hung over his shoulder, down the back of his green workshirt. The scream constricted in a gasp. When he hunched into her, she made a fist that quivered. But she wasn't fighting anymore. He almost hid her on the wall.

When he finally backed away, breathing hard, she just went down, on her knees, gulping, and into a heap, making a funny crying thing with no sound. He turned half around, wiping his mouth with his wrist. The late sun caught on gold stubble all over his jaw. And he frowned.

I was going to duck back down behind the boxes—

"Hey...what the fuck *you* starin' at?" His cock, hanging wet from his fly, was wormy with veins. So were his big, big hands.

His broad nails were bitten so far up they were three times side-to-side as from thickened, dirt-lined cuticle to bulging, grease-rimmed nub—which, on his thumb at least, went on another horny half inch. His fingers were immense and chiseled, the upper joints clouded in yellow. He was a big man, with the start of a gut. Yellow hair tufted between the missing buttons at the bottom of his shirt, and all up around a neck thick as a scrub pail. Watching him, I got the thought that maybe a month ago he'd been on his back under a car and hadn't bothered to wash since. His hands and forearms, under the gold fur that burned in the four o'clock sun striking up the alley, were grease-gray. His face was like sunburned brick, smeared and streaked over.

He slid one callused thumb into a frayed pocket, letting his loose, soiled fingers hang. "You lookin' awful funny, cocksucker." He stepped over the woman's feet, then laughed, short and rough, like a dog barking. "Okay, boy. You wanna come over here and get it? Or maybe I'm gonna come over there and fuck your head off…?"

I went.

I was about to squat when he grabbed my hair and wrestled me, on my knees, around into the wall. He pushed the head of his half-hard cock into my mouth. I could smell pussy all over it. His own stink came through pretty strong, too. His long foreskin bunched back on his greasy meat. I got one arm around his legs and was holding onto his wrist. He kept pushing till he found I wasn't fighting, I guess. Then he began to lean in with his hips. He almost broke my neck. My hand, around his wrist, slipped down to his forefinger. He reached into his fly with his free hand and got out his balls. With his cock plunging in my mouth, they swung like peaches inches below my chin.

I heard him grunt. He smelled like a stopped toilet-stall, where somebody had left six months of dirty socks, in the back of a butcher shop with the refrigeration on the blink, on fire. The tube under his dick filled, retreated, filled again; and spilled enough spunk for three guys. "Pissin' in you now, boy…." Not like Pedro's or his pop's shotglass leakage. I swallowed five times (he was still pumping into my face), and I couldn't hold no more. Piss spurted all over his fly—I could see pee between the zipper teeth. Piss ran down my chin. He got my head—like I saw this really big-handed nigger hold a basketball, once, and turn it upside down without dropping it—and with his other hand wiped hard around my chin and face, smearing piss. He rubbed his balls with wet fingers, pulled at them, while I leaked piss out my lower lip. "Yeah... I'm gonna drown you, cocksucker!"

And pulled out, fast. He caught his dick and peed in my eyes, first this one, then that one—which he thought was really funny, the way he laughed. And all over my shirt—aimed at the lap of my jeans. His pants were wet down the legs in dark tongues. "You gonna smell sweet, cocksucker!" He leaned back on my face, without even putting it in, just rubbing it around, till I finally caught the spluttering head, sucked it in, and finished drinking.

He still had his hand down fingering his cock. After I'd been nuzzling it and licking his fingers for a half a minute, he said: "Come on."

I looked up.

"Get up."

I stood.

He pushed his works back into his wet pants. But he didn't zip.

The woman had crawled about a yard away. Her face lay on the sidewalk, but her eyes were open. When he turned, she closed them and buried her head in her arm. "I... I can't walk," she said, muffled on concrete. "You tore something. I can't walk...." Her forearm was scraped bloody, and her bruised cheek was getting dark. "Oh, Jesus...! I can't walk!" Her hair (among the black roots I could see gray) fell over her ear onto the pavement.

From his cuff, drops spotted the dried mud on his shoe. He laughed—and kicked her stomach, hard. Her crying just got higher and higher, without breaking. Her fist dragged into her belly and she rolled on top of it, making that sound.

Beside the garbage, in the pink wad of her panties, was something dark, like blood. Or maybe shit.

He relaxed his hands, grinning. His teeth were big and yellow, except up near the gum where they were green. Some teeth on the side were broken. Greasy hair fell down his forehead. He brushed it back—yellow blades of it fell again—and said: "Hey!"

That was to me.

"Come on, I said." He pushed my shoulder and started me along with him toward the alley head. "Down here...." He got in front of me, reached a gray-splattered truck cab parked there, bobtail, opened the passenger door and hoisted himself up. He turned around on the seat, looked down at me, holding the door back with his huge, nailgnawed paw. "Open your mouth." His other hand came down, grabbed my shoulder.

I opened it.

"Keep it wide. Look up here."

I looked.

With a snuffling roar, his head went back, his lips puckered; his face came forward, and hawked out—

Some of it hit my lip. Some of it went in.

Surprised, I swallowed and pulled back.

He laughed. "No you don't!" Thumb and forefinger on the back and front of my shoulder went into my t-shirt like crate-tongs. "Climb up here, boy. I think I'm gonna keep you around awhile." He narrowed his eyes. They were close and green.

I swallowed again and climbed. There'd been some thick stuff in with it.

He slid over, got under the wheel (it had some worn carpet taped to it, top and bottom), reached across me and closed the door—he had to slam it twice. "The bitch back there was work—" he turned the key with the hank of keys hanging off it, pushed pedals, pulled one of the two gearshifts: the truck moved— "but you and me are gonna have a little fun. Yeah, she must've been a dyke. 'Cause it was a fuckin' dyke who hired me. Bundle up over here next to old Hogg. I want to be able to smell you when you start to stink. They call me Hogg 'cause a hog lives dirty. I don't wash none. And when I get hungry, I eat my own snot. I been wearin' these clothes since winter. I don't even take my dick out my pants to piss most times, unless it's in some cunt's face. Or all over a cocksucker like you. What I usually do is park the truck in the sun with the light comin' in the window and piss my pants up something terrible." The truck turned another corner; he dropped one hand from the carpeted wheel between his legs, hefted his meat around some—but I couldn't tell if he was doing it or thinking about it. His pants were too wet already. "Yeah, boy; all that nice, hot stuff, running down my leg, and squirmin' my ass around in it." He glanced at me. "When I was about your age, I used to do it in school—sit in the back row and pee all over myself. Finally, they kicked me out." He chuckled, looking back at the rolling road. "I got worms, boy—had 'em ever since I was a kid. But I won't get rid of 'em 'cause I like the way they make my asshole itch." His hand came up to pat his belly. "I gotta drink a lot of beer and eat a lot of pizza pies and French-fried potatoes to keep a gut like this and all them little fuckers fed. I got a hairy ass and it sure cakes up crusty. But I just don't believe in wipin' when I got a freaky little son of a bitch like you to eat it out for me. Now how you like that?" He laughed; and changed gears. "After I got tired haulin' fruit backwards and forwards cross country, you know what the next job I had me was? A garbage man! Got my own truck so I could specialize in shovelin' *shit*!"

I was trying to wiggle around without looking like that was what I was doing to get myself away from my wet shirt—even though I had a hard-on.

"Now that was a job I liked. But a job I liked didn't make enough to hardly eat, and dog turds make you throw up after about two days, every time." Hogg glanced at me, then settled one of the gears the other way. "So you just seen how I make my

living now, boy. Stickin' pussy. Hogg's old shit sticker is pretty
much half hard all the time anyway—bad as a goddamn nigger's.
And there's this whole bunch of racketeers and bulldykes and
bankers and big men in this county who'll give me a hundred
bucks, a hundred-and-fifty sometimes, to bust up cunt. Like you
seen me doing. She never even know'd I was alive before twenty
minutes ago, and when she found out, she was one surprised
bitch. That's my work, see? That's the kind of work I like, boy.
Nice and nasty. Can't help it." He let go the wheel with one
hand, rubbed his armpit. It was wet all down the side of his shirt
with sweat or something. "I'd do it every now and again anyway,
so I might as well get paid. Thinkin' about the way that bitch was
beggin' and hollerin' when I stuck it to her just gets me hot all
over again. Take it out and suck it, boy."

He was looking straight ahead.

He sounded like he would have just put me out on the road
if I didn't. Which made me feel funny.

I ducked down and he raised an elbow. We turned a curve
and sunlight swung through the cab. His lap steamed. He put
one hand down to hoist his meat. I began to lick his dirty fingers,
nip his knuckles. "Jesus Christ." He moved himself around through
his wet greens; I kept on, sometimes nosing in the hair between
his open fly, but mostly outside. Finally he said, "Like you doin'
that, boy. Somebody lickin' and suckin' on my fingers like that,
shit—gets me about as hot as a damn blowjob, you know? Guess
that's why I'm always bitin' on 'em myself." But finally he went
into his pants and pulled his cock out. So I went down on it.
"Shit…!" Hogg drawled; his thigh moved over; a long fart growled
out. "Just went through a red light." He chuckled. "Ain't lost my
hard yet. Keep workin' on it." Maybe ten minutes later (I took a
couple of minutes' rest—just lay there with it in my face, but he
didn't seem to mind) he came all over the roof of my mouth
again. He hauled the wheel around, the truck slowed—we were
pulling onto the highway's shoulder—then his knee jacked as he
hit the break. "Okay, let up on it a minute."

I raised my head.

When his cock fell out my mouth, he winced a little.

I looked out the window at the bushes to see where we'd parked.

"I really like the way you suck that," Hogg said, grinning.

Out the other window, a car went by on the road.

"I'm really glad you like to suck, boy. Know what I'd of done if'n you didn't wanna suck, or said no, back then?" He cocked his head, sort of smiling his dirty grin. "I would of said, all right, you just get on out of the truck and take off. Then, when you was about ten yards down the road, like over there—" He nodded out my side of the truck—"I'd of taken my shotgun out from under the seat here—" One filthy hand dropped from the wheel to pat the busted seam on the cushion edge between his legs—"and blown your fuckin' head off!" He laughed real hard, reached over, roughed the back of my head. "Not 'cause you wouldn't suck, see." His face got serious again. "But 'cause you're too much into my business now, you understand?" He frowned a little, like he was thinking about what he'd just said, maybe wondering if he really would've done it.

I believed him.

He began to gnaw on his third fingernail, then on what was left of the one on his thumb. "Come on over here. You know what I can do?" He put his arm around me, pulled me up against him. His cock lay wet and red over dirty cloth. "I can come every twenty minutes, all fuckin' day long. I done it before. Have to, sometimes, in my line of work. It gets sort of sore. After about seven or eight times the fucker just won't go down. I got to walk around with a damn hard-on till I go to sleep. And I always wake up with a hard-on anyway, but after that it goes down pretty fast. But I can do it, you know?" He ran his hand down my arm. "You're a pretty solid little motherfucker." He took my hand in his thick, nail-bitten fingers, looked at it: I don't bite mine. But they were pretty dirty. He ran his hand up my arm again. "Most

HOGG

times, you find a kid your age as freaky as you are and they're usually dim or retarded or something. But you look like you're pretty quick." I just watched him. Hogg grinned. "Son, it's gonna take a lot of piss and shit before you stink like old Hogg here." With his other hand, he reached between my legs. "Hey, you got a good crank on you, too! You colored? You look like you might be. Come on, take it out and let me see you beat it." He got the top button open. I undid the other one. "Pretty big for a kid your age." Hogg's was as big as Ape Townley's. (If you wanted to cut it off him and keep it, soft, maybe you could push it all down into a beer can. But not hard, though.) "Let's see what you can do with it." His other hand was feeling around my ass. I pushed myself up from the seat so he could slip his hand under my butt. It went right in through Big Chico's tear. He had his lips together and looked serious again. "Jerk it."

I jerked.

He pushed his middle finger up my ass; then his forefinger. I was glad he bit his nails so bad. "Shit, you could take my cock up there easy. Go on. Beat on it." His fingers moved around inside me. I pushed back against his horny palm and jerked harder. "Let's see some fuckin' cum, cocksucker. I got a fuckin' thirst on me today." His breath hit my ear, hot. His stubble rasped my cheek. "You shoot that shit right in Hogg's face." He grinned, wobbled his tongue in his open mouth, lowered his face. "Lay that hot juice in me, boy. Got a big thirst on. Shoot it right on in my mouth." When he wrapped his face around my cock, I pushed his head all the way down. My hand slid on his sweaty neck. Christ, his mouth was hot.

He began to suck. His blond head bobbed.

I shot.

"Yeah...!" He came up with wet lips; something dribbled his unshaven chin. "Pretty good!" His hard hand closed on my dick. "Let the rest of it go, boy. I'm gonna make you piss now." With his two fingers in my ass, he did something. At the same time he pressed his other hand flat on my belly.

I began to pee all over myself, surprised as hell. While I was still surprised, he yanked his fingers out my ass, which felt just like coming again. "Drink it, cocksucker," he said between his teeth and pushed the back of my head forward, while he aimed my dick straight up into my face. "Drink it..." and began to chuckle. "I like to make a cocksucker drink his own piss!" I tried to catch the stream in my mouth.

He took his hand off my head—I looked up. He was watching me and sucking shit off his fingers.

I couldn't stop pissing but I tried to push up on the seat.

"Hey—!"

He got piss in his face. His chin was beaded with it. He pushed me back against the door, got his wet mouth over mine, and shoved his tongue into my throat while I held his shoulders. He got me down on my back and my pants off one leg. He was trying to get his cock in my asshole, so I swung my legs up. I felt it go in, stinging more. I licked under his tongue. His hairy stomach slapped down on my dick (which was still spilling like a garden hose), sucked up, slapped again. His balls, which had come out his pants, swung against my buttocks. He got one hand down to finger my hole, and I tried to get a hand there to play with his nuts. He tried to dig a couple of fingers in alongside his dick. He gathered to shoot. I finished pissing—and came again.

He kept on fucking. I was pushing like I had to take a shit. That felt good.

He finished—and his tongue spilled out my mouth. When he raised his head, sweat or something dripped off his chin on my cheek. He lowered himself again, panting. "That sure was some beautiful shit I was stirring up in there." He moved his hips back; his dick slipped out my ass. I farted this time. "I want to see your little yellow head a-workin' down there and that little pink tongue just a-lappin' the shit off Hogg's old pecker." He sat up on the seat, one muddy shoe heel wedged back against his butt. His other foot was on the floor. He kneaded his meat while

I slipped to my knees onto the cab floor, got my head in there and licked his cock and knuckles and fingers and balls. He got his leg between mine, and I rubbed myself off against his pants like a dog. "Hey...hold up."

I stopped.

"Take my shoe off." He pulled loose the top laces of the high, scuffed workshoe.

I tugged it off.

The smell came out and filled up the cab.

His sock was the black that one-time white socks get if you wear them steady for more than a month. The cloth was stiff. From a hole, two toes stuck out that were pretty black too. "Shit, that stinks, don't it!" Hogg laughed. I peeled off the sock. It stuck to the sole of his foot, that was horny and cracked around the sides. His ankle was hairy. "Lick it, boy." While I licked, he twisted above me. I glanced up to see him heave the shoe and the sock out the truck window. I heard them fall in the bushes. "Go on, keep lickin'. I think I'm gonna go barefoot on the left side from now on. I step in any dogshit, you can clean it off. Damn—the way you work my toes and fingers, boy, I tell you it's about as good as a blowjob any day." His toenails were all picked way back too. "Eat that jam." His balls lay on the seat right beside his crusty heel. So I licked them.

He jerked his cock, sometimes underhand, sometimes overhand, sometimes just palming the goose-egg head, sometimes rubbing his big fingers across it, one at a time, and sometimes getting a finger under the foreskin and running it around inside. "Gonna shoot...!" he grunted, pointed it down; it spurted between his dirty knuckles. Some went in my mouth, some hit my face, some ran down over the veins crossing the ligaments of his foot. I licked that off. In the gold hair on his fingers, mucus made irregular pearls. I licked them too. "Come on up here."

Wiping my face with my hand (and licking my fingers), I sat up on the seat beside him, while he started the truck. As we pulled onto the highway again, he licked the cum off his own hand. "Here...." He wiped some off my cheek with his foreknuckle, put it in his mouth. "You wanna keep suckin' my dick while I'm drivin', maybe you can loose another load." So I got my head down in his lap, pushed his thick, scummy cock into my mouth; I was pretty tired.

But he didn't really get that hard. "Gotta run over and pick up my new job, cocksucker. You can work on it till we get there." Then he laughed and rubbed the back of my head. He let his hand slip down over my face and pushed two fingers—the two that had been up my ass, I guess, from the smell—into my mouth beside his cock. I don't think he was really all that turned on; I think he felt good having them in a warm wet place. I felt good having them there, I know.

His balls rolled from thigh to thigh as he drove.

I must have fallen asleep.

"*Get* the fuck up from there, you scummy-mouthed bastard!" I hit my head on his elbow. He yanked the hand brake. I looked out the window, while he fixed his pants.

We'd stopped in front of a big house with a hedge down both sides of the graveled drive. Hogg opened the door. "Get down."

I jumped out to follow him. With his sort of lopsided gait, his one shoe ground gravel, while his bare foot hissed in the little stones. As he rang the bell and I caught up, he put one hand on my shoulder and his gritty toes over my sneaker.

The chimes played the first four notes of *Three Blind Mice*.

It was the sort of door a maid should answer.

A man with a gray suit, a yellow tie, and a bald head pulled back the door edge and peered. "Oh. Hogg...it's you." He stepped out, nervously, in shined patent leather shoes.

"Got 'er stuck for you, Mr. Jonas."

Mr. Jonas smiled and looked uncomfortable. "Well. Yes. As a matter of fact, I just got a call from her friend—the rather masculine lady you met here—who'd been notified. The police just found the one you'd..." He coughed across a pale knuckle. "It sounded like you'd done a very competent job...very efficient. And of course she was scared to say anything to them. She deserved it, you know. That young lady that you had to work on really deserved—"

"Sure, Mr. Jonas." Hogg wiped his mouth with the heel of his hand. "You want to pay me now, huh?"

"Let me see." Mr. Jonas reached under a clay-colored lapel, fingered his inner pocket, and came out with a black plastic checkbook. "What is your right name again, Hogg? I make the check out to... Hargus? That was Francis Hargus?"

"Franklin Hargus... Mr. Jonas? Remember, we said...?"

Mr. Jonas looked up.

"We said you'd just pay cash from now on. I had to make a couple of quick moves, and I don't keep no bank account just now." Mr. Jonas obviously thought he was a lot smarter than Hogg. But Hogg explained his piece like a man who'd been working ten hours straight who still had enough patience to explain it again to his retarded kid brother. "You just give me cash now. Like we agreed."

"Of course." Mr. Jonas smiled nervously. "I forgot. Really. I just forgot, that's all."

"Yeah, Mr. Jonas."

The checkbook went back into the inner pocket.

The thick red wallet came out of the hip one. "If I *could* give you a check this time, it would be more convenient...?" The crescents of Mr. Jonas' nails were white as toilet paper. His skin looked like new, pink bathroom tile.

Hogg rubbed his belly, his fingers outside his shirt at first, then going in. "I want cash." On my sneaker Hogg's toes got heavier.

"Of course." Mr. Jonas looked in his wallet. "Since that's what we agreed on. Was that a hundred? No, a hundred-and-fifty. Yes, a hundred-and-fifty was it. I'm sure." With quick, small flicks, he snapped the corners of half a dozen twenties up out of his wallet like they were cards and he was a sharp. "Did the boy help you?" He hadn't looked at me.

"*This* little cocksucker?" Hogg laughed. "Shit…" Then I think he changed his mind. "Sure as *shit* he helped me! Didn't you, you little bastard!"

"Well, this ten—" Mr. Jonas pulled loose a bill and handed it to me—"is a tip for you…kid." He would have been more comfortable saying *young man*. "And this is yours." The bills offered between Mr. Jonas' small, pale fingers crumpled in Hogg's great, grubby ones.

Hogg shifted his weight and thumbed at his crotch, the bills clutched in a knot. I guess he was getting itchy. "You got anymore work for me to do, Mr. Jonas? I done the last job real good." Reaching up, he pushed the fistful of pale green into his dark green shirt pocket. I could see a bill's edge poking from a tear in the pocket bottom.

"Well…" Mr. Jonas stood awhile, thinking. "Now, I did tell some friends of mine about you, not too long ago, actually…. Last night, as a matter of fact. And they mentioned to me—they had come over to give them to me, actually—the names of three women that could use…well, some of your disciplining."

I felt Hogg's bass laugh down in my foot.

"Yes," Mr. Jonas went on. "I believe they could."

"Sure," Hogg said. "Just tell me where to find them, Mr. Jonas—"

"One of these women, you see, cheated on a young man of my acquaintance—he was in my employ, that is, for a while…one of my bodyguards, I believe. Anyway, this young lady, though he's lost all interest in her, not to say respect for her, he still wanted to make sure—"

"Shit," Hogg said. "You know I don't like to hear no pretty stories, Mr. Jonas. Just tell me who they are and where to find them. As long as they're people who don't want the police pryin' into anything about them, I'll stick the bitches."

"Of course." Mr. Jonas reached under the other lapel, took out an envelope. "In here is all the relevant information. I'm sure you'll find it sufficient: names, addresses, and pictures. The two of them who have jobs, it tells where they work."

"Yeah." Hogg took the envelope. "That'll be fine." After all the runaround, he didn't seem surprised.

"Hargus...eh, Hogg?"

Hogg asked: "What?"

"My friends and I—my bodyguard, and then the other two, who—well, we were talking about this, you see, and..." Mr. Jonas' mouth moved around as though he were trying to catch out a fish bone with his front teeth. "Well, we all thought—my other friends as well, you see—that given the situation, we wanted something a little special for these young ladies. A little out of the ordinary. Do you know what I mean?"

"You want me to set it up so you can watch me work 'em over? Shit, Mr. Jonas, I don't mind that. Cost you more. But lots of my customers like to watch me when I—"

"No, no! Not *watch*. Of course not watch!" Mr. Jonas' sparse eyebrows wrinkled; his hair, when he had it, must have been ash blond. "I certainly wouldn't want to watch. And I don't think my friends would want to watch either. What we were thinking of had much more to do with...well, it occurred to us that while you do your work very well, if you had some help, it might be more effective...psychologically effective. I mean I've always considered your work to be basically psychological in its...well, effect, despite the inevitable physical side; I think of you as a sort of artisan of pain, a spiritual worker whose finest points might have been honed in some cellar of the Inquisition, some—"

Hogg's blank, dumb look got through.

"Well, at any rate, we thought if you could have some help—that idea came from...but you don't want to know his name, do you? You say you already have the child here...." He frowned down at me, trying to imagine what I could have done.

"I think..." Hogg began, then suddenly guffawed loudly. "I think I know what you want, hey? I know this dago. He's worked with me on some jobs. He's real mean, Mr. Jonas. I've seen him stick a knife in a bitch fast as he'd stick his pecker in a pussy. Sometimes, when we work over a cunt together, I got to hold that boy back from slittin' the bitch open."

"Well, yes, now. That's—"

"And I got a nigger, too. Works with me a lot. Big, black, and nasty. The shit I seen that spade mother pull when he gets after a bad pussy, well, it would make a gentleman like you sick, Mr. Jonas." Hogg chuckled, shook his head. "Just sick."

"Well, now you do seem to have the idea. A big colored man? That would really amuse—but then, there's no need to mention who. A darky? Yes, that sounds particularly good."

"I can think of a couple of other guys. I know a whole bunch of rape artists, Mr. Jonas. I can get you some real scroungy types. Just plain creepy. Standin' there and watchin' those guys work over some poor bitch gets me so fuckin'—"

"Fine. Yes, that'll be fine, Hogg. We understand each other now. And you'll charge me for this...?"

Hogg hefted his crotch. His fly was half open and you could just see inside it. He was chewing something over in the back of his mouth. "Well, I got to round up these bastards and keep 'em in line. That's gonna be more work than the shag job."

"I'm not interested in stories either, Hogg—"

"For something special like this I'll have to charge two hundred for each of the bitches—"

"That's fifty more than—"

"—in cash. Plus...lemme see. I'll get four guys beside me. They gotta get at least seventy-five apiece. For each bitch. Now don't look all funny—you pay me a hundred-and-fifty for one, remember. And why don't you throw in fifty bucks for the little cocksucker here?"

"Now, what in the world could *he* possibly do? I mean, really, Hogg—"

"He's a little freak. You should see 'im work. Besides, anything that's a little different is gonna be more effective, right? A nigger, or a kid. Like you say…psychologically."

Mr. Jonas' frown was as nervous as his smile. "Are you sure I couldn't pay you with a check for this one? That's almost…let me see: two hundred plus three-hundred-and-fifty, times three is…sixteen-hundred *bucks*!" The *bucks* came pretty natural.

"I told you, I don't got no bank account no more. And I gotta pay these guys in cash. Guys like this wouldn't know what to do with no check, Mr. Jonas. Don't you worry, you're gonna like what you hear about these three jobs—and the guys who gonna be doin' them ain't never gonna hear your name. I know just the guys you want. They'll do real fine."

"I'm *sure* they will, Hogg."

"If you *do* want to sit in on one or two of these, Mr. Jonas, I won't even charge you no—"

"It will be fine just the way it is, Hogg. Sixteen-hundred dollars, in cash." He took a breath through narrowed nostrils, raised his hands against his chest. "I'll have the money for you as soon as you come back and report the job done."

"Sure, Mr. Jonas."

Mr. Jonas frowned at me again. Then he closed the door.

Hogg took his foot off mine. "How you like that bastard, hey?" He turned on the steps. Through his fly, I could see the top third of his cock hanging—which was more than the whole thing on a lot of guys. "I'm just glad he ain't the only motherfucker I work for, 'cause all his bullshit would just about turn me off the business. 'Mr. Jonas' my right nut! I wonder what his real name is. I used to think he was some sort of kinky faggot—that's why I got in the habit of always leaving my fly down whenever I was talkin' to 'im. Figured some day he'd wanna suck on it and I'd make myself another twenty-five. But he's as straight as a bee-flight from the clover to the hive. He likes his women a little on the young side—if he gets it on with a bitch more than seventeen, all his friends are gonna start thinkin' he's turnin' into a gerontophile. He's into all sorts of gamblin' and runnin' whores all over the damned country and down to the West Indies. I wished to hell he didn't know *my* real name. I guess it's just as well I don't know too much about him. Safer that way, right, cocksucker? I just wonder what these guys I got to get lined up gonna do when they get hold of you?" He laughed as we walked back down the driveway. "You're a fuckin' whore, ain't you, now? I know your kind; you're gonna be tired of my meat in a couple of days. When these guys take a break from work, it's gonna be fun to watch them work on you, motherfucker." He put his hand on the back of my neck. "Hey, gimme that goddamn ten bucks! A fuckin' tip, huh?" He cuffed the back of my head, hard enough to hurt. "I ought to really bust you one."

In the truck, as we drove away, Hogg said: "Hey, cocksucker, you know why I spit in your mouth?" He pulled the wheel around, glanced at me, and grinned. On the side, I could see the stumps of his broken teeth like bark jammed into his gum, way behind the big yellow front ones. The wheel spun back. "That's how my mom taught me to train a goddamn puppy dog. You see, when you want a puppy dog to learn who its master is, you spit in its mouth every once and awhile. And pretty soon it'd know it belonged to me forever and ever." He looked at me like he was guessing how long forever was. Or maybe how far to spit. Anyway, he said, "Shit...." again. And a little bit later: "You don't worry, cocksucker. I'm gonna take care of you, all right."

That's how I got in with Hogg.

WE STOPPED IN A DINER.

The cashier pushed the bridge of his glasses up his nose with his forefinger and said, "How you boys doing? You workin' at the c-c-c-construction site over in...?" Then he looked down through the glass countertop and saw Hogg's bare foot. He just frowned—at Hogg, at me, at Hogg again.

There were a few drivers there, but not many for five o'clock.

Hogg shouted his order to the waitress, and heaved into one side of a booth. I slipped into the other. A couple of minutes later when she came by with plates for the three drivers two booths away, Hogg reached out and pinched her ass. Hard. And twisted.

She cried out, and, with her free hand, beat at the buttocks of her blue smock, whirling—and spilled beans on our table.

"Shit, that's all right, honey." Hogg pushed the beans into his palm with his fingers and, grinning at her, began to eat out of his hand. (Two of the drivers laughed. "I'm sorry," the waitress said

to them. "I'm sorry. He made me spill...") "You know?" Hogg
said to me, and I felt his feet push down on my sneakers—
workshoe and bare. "There's some pussy you see walkin' around
that's so nice and pretty, boy, you couldn't see stickin' a dirty
old dick in it. All you can do is kneel down in front of it and
give it a little stirrin' with your tongue. Maybe chew on it a little
to let it know you care." He belched—it rumbled out for about
eight whole seconds—then squinted around the diner. The
waitress was coming back with our plates. "Too bad there ain't
none of that quality pussy walkin' around here; I'd have some
with my coffee." She threw the plates on the table, and jerked
away.

Hogg laughed. His bare foot left my sneaker—his knee
thumped the underside of the table and the plates jounced—and
settled on my seat, wedging into my crotch. I didn't look down,
but I put one hand over it. The skin felt rough and hot. He held
my thumb with his toes. "This looks like some good eatin'—
AND A GLASS OF MILK FOR THE LITTLE SHIT HERE AND A
CUPPA COFFEE FOR ME!"

That cracked the truckers up too.

Hogg didn't give the silverware a chance.

Just went right in, hands first, stuffing food into his mouth,
till he was pork chop grease to the eyes. The waitress came by
with the milk and the coffee, and scowled like she was in pain.

"Here you go, boy. Earn your keep." Hogg stuck his hand
across the table, bits of meat, gravy, ketchup, and beans all over
his fingers. I leaned forward, took it by the wrist, and began to
lick. He shoved his fingers into my throat, so that once I gagged.
He laughed. "Shit, I swear that gives me a hard-on, boy. I must
be some sort of freak."

While I drank my milk—it was hard to hold the glass because my hands were so greasy—Hogg said, "If you gotta take a
piss, better do it now." His toes moved on my crotch. "That's
what I'm doing." And then, "Here..." He scraped up a couple
more French fries from his plate and fed them to me. "Keep you

shittin', boy." His hands a knot of dirt hiding his cup, he drank the coffee down in a swig.

When he dropped his foot and stood up, it sounded like somebody poured a pot of water on the linoleum. He left a yellow puddle halfway to the cashier's counter. The seat of his pants was dark with the wet. His cuff dripped all over. I followed him, just as one of the drivers looked back, saw the floor, and said, "Jesus *Christ*...!"

The cashier's frames had slipped back down his nose so that the tops of his lenses cut his pale eyes in half. With three fingers, Hogg pushed the check, soggy with coffee, across the glass. The cashier blurted: "You take your d-d-dirty talk out of here, mister! We d-don't want your money. Now get!"

Behind us one of the drivers was saying, "Hey, you see what that big, dirty motherfucker did? He pissed all over the... I mean he went and..." The others were really laughing now.

"Shit," Hogg drawled. He grinned at me (rubbing his hand in my hair, like it was a friendly gesture, but I think he was getting some of the grease off): "Hey, cocksucker, we gotta remember this place. Looks like it's good for a free meal."

"And d-d-d-don't c-c-come back!"

"PISS UP YOUR MOTHER'S PUSSY!" Hogg bellowed, and pounded his fist on the counter. It didn't shatter, but the glass cracked side-to-side.

The cashier jumped, grabbed for his falling glasses—and missed.

I think I heard them break on the floor behind the counter, as the man disappeared to go scrabbling for them.

Outside, as we walked to the truck cab, Hogg grinned. "I don't usually pull stuff like that." On the gravel, he didn't favor his bare foot at all. "I was just showing off for you some of the funny shit it tickles me to do." Not even a little. "Them truckers sure thought it was funny."

I looked back. Through the diner window, I could see the waitress holding her sponge real tight up near her neck and frowning down beside our table. The drivers were going up to the counter now, glancing at her, snickering. One shook his head.

"People are funny." Hogg gave my shoulder a push forward. "We could come back here tomorrow, you and me, in a couple of different shirts, maybe some clean pants, the both of us, actin' halfway proper, and people would look at us. But that's all. And maybe after we got our food, somebody would come over and say, 'Excuse me. But you weren't in here *yester*day, were you...?' And I'd look at 'em and say, with a big grin, 'Whatcha mean? I was haulin' crates of peaches yesterday down near Chattahootchee.' And they'd go away just as happy. 'Cause people don't even wanna see shit like that. I mean, they'd be happier pretending it didn't even happen. But you're gonna see enough of the kind of stuff I usually do. Get in, boy!" Hogg reached up and pulled the handle down on the cab door; it swung open. "Get on in." He went around to the other side. "Let's get out of here while it's still fun. Bastard's trying to phone the cops now...."

At the wall phone, the cashier was dialing with one hand and clutching the receiver and his broken glasses with the other.

One of the drivers motioned the others; they started for the door. They were using the confusion to leave without paying.

The Frontwater industrial section we drove through was deserted.

Hogg wheeled into an alley, pulled up beside a rank of dented garbage cans, and we got out. The sky was violet and copper between buildings that looked like the rotten teeth in the side of Hogg's jaw.

Above the door across the dirty brick was a sign in which I made out a P, an I, and a T; but there were more letters in it. Behind the window, the gray glass tubing of a neon sign (off) snaked through the letters of some beer brand.

It was the back entrance to a bar, and it looked awfully still.

"In here." Hogg pushed at the door. The second time he shoved, it opened.

We entered on a cracked concrete floor. A man with short gray hair and a stained apron was dragging a cardboard carton from the top of a pile of cartons. It clanked down against his belly like beer cans.

"Hello, Ray," Hogg said.

"Well, hey there!" Ray hefted up the carton a little higher. "How you keepin' yourself, Hogg? Ain't seen you around for goin' on a few days, now."

"Keepin' pretty good. Can't complain." Hogg rubbed at his pockets and more or less ignored the way Ray glanced at me, at Hogg's bare foot. "Hey, Ray, would you look in the front for me? If Nigg and Dago are there—and they ain't too drunk—send 'em on back here. I wanna talk to them in private."

"Sure, Hogg," Ray said. "They're inside. Both of 'em was walkin' last time I looked." Ray started to turn, but got another thought. "That young guy you was talkin' to last time—Denny— he's here too." The new thought became a frown, but maybe that was because a corner of the crate was slipping. "You know, Hogg—" Ray raised his knee to prop up the carton and staggered a little on one foot—"that feller is *strange*! I let him sweep up a few times, you know? He's a nice kid, even if he is a little dim. But *five* times I've come in the back here to get something—and found him in here, jerkin' off!"

Hogg laughed. "Now that don't sound so strange. You gonna tell me you never get to pullin' on your own?"

"Sure. Sometimes I do," Ray said. "But when I come in, he didn't even try to hide it or nothing—just give me this big, funny-toothed grin he got, and goes on workin' on it like that was the most normal thing in the world; and goes *on* working on it, too. *That* ain't normal."

Hogg laughed again. "I'll tell you, Ray. I usually wait a little while before I call any man normal or not. And even with the waitin', I still ain't sure, when I get around to it, if it's a compliment. You know somethin'?"

"What?" Ray raised his knee and staggered again.

"You say he was jerkin' off back here when you come in to get something? Well you know why I started talkin' to him in the first place—?"

"Yeah, I *heard* what you was sayin' to him." Ray's chin went up, and the carton slipped lower down. "Talkin' to him about the kind of crap you're doin'. Now, I don't hold with interferin' in a man's job, don't care what side of the law it's on. But tellin' a half dim kid who jerks off all the time that—"

"Ray," Hogg said, "the first time I see him standin' at the back end of the bar, he had it out and was jerkin' on it right under the edge of the counter. I admit, I thought it was unusual. But that's why I went over and struck up the conversation you heard the last of."

I thought Ray was going to drop his carton. "You mean that son-of-a-bitch was out there, beatin' his meat in front of all the goddamn *customers?*"

"The kind of customers *you* get, that ain't gonna make no never mind. He ain't pretty, but he got a piece of meat on him. Half the toothless bums who come in here is faggots anyway. He's more likely to bring 'em in than drive 'em off."

"Jesus Christ," Ray said. "Sneakin' back here to do it is one thing, but doin' it right up in the *front* there—"

"When you go out to get Nigg and Dago, you see if Denny's at the back end of the bar. And if he's sort of leanin' forward on the counter with this very serious expression, you just take a peak on down where he's—"

"Jesus Christ," Ray said again. "I mean, if I'd *known*—"

Hogg laughed once more. "I seen that boy with his dick outside his pants more times than I seen him with it in. Hey, when you send Nigg and Dago back here, whyn't you send old Denny in too. That is, if he ain't too busy."

"Jesus..." Ray repeated, but he had to prop the crate up again, so he didn't get out the "Christ." He frowned at Hogg, then at me, then at Hogg again. "Okay, I'll send 'im back here, if just to get 'im out of the front." He started off between the cartons. "Shit, if I'd of known the crazy cocksucker was beatin' his meat right out in the goddamn *bar*—" and disappeared between the cartons.

Hogg shook his head, chuckling. "Hey, boy. Get down, take it out, and suck it. I swear, if watchin' a bastard like old Ray get all upset don't come near to givin' me a goddamn hard-on too. Besides—" Hogg leaned on one of those gray, screw-out metal columns that supported a low ceiling beam—"I want to see what them bastards do when they come in here and find you swingin' on it." He glanced up where evening blue mottled a grimy window high on the side wall. "Now that's what I should've got you doin' when Ray was in here. Would've probably taught the motherfucker somethin' useful, 'stead of wastin' my time jawin' to him. He done learned half of it from Denny. I'm probably shirkin' my duty not teachin' him the other half. I got a real strong sense of duty. You got to have one when you doin' work like I do. Come on, get down." He planted his shoe over here and his foot over there, and cupped his hand under his crotch. "Hey, what's that look—*get* on down there and suck it, boy! Get down."

I knelt.

"This gonna tickle them somethin' fierce." Hogg shouted: "Hey, you black bastard, come on in here! Where are you, you dumb wop?" His hairy belly jerked in front of my face between the swinging green cloth, hanging open out of his pants.

The echo of his shout rolled through the storeroom.

Hogg fingered his red meat out of his fly; it was hard, like the yell had pumped it up. "Shit, cocksucker," he drawled. "You know you want it…. Your face just fits my crank." The stench of sweat and stale piss had got me hot again. "Yeah, there you go. Oh, shit, that's fine. Yeah, work it, motherfucker!" He closed his fist in my hair and thrust into my throat.

Behind me I heard other voices; and footsteps.

Hogg's hand stilled on my head. He slipped easy and slow around in my face. I heard him say: "Hey, you dumb guinea, *you* sure took your motherfuckin' time!"

"Evenin', Hogg. Ray said you— *Now!* Hey, nigger, ain't that a cute little thing cleanin' up Hogg's old pecker? Must've needed it too, 'cause I know just what a cheesy bastard you are, Hogg. How you doin', motherfucker?"

There was a bass rumble from some nigger, chuckling.

"Sure looks like a hungry little pig-sucker!"

"Nigg, how'd you like to feed my boy's face here awhile—I see that look you got." Hogg was still slipping it in and out. "He been chewin' on my pecker all day."

"Whyn't you let him get after Denny, here? He's already playin' with himself."

"Hey, Denny. You got your meat ready for my sucker here?"

"Sure, Hogg." That was a voice younger than either the nigger's or the wop's.

Still sucking, I looked down when something nudged my knee. A nigger's bare foot, crossed by sunlight, pulled in its toes on the cracked concrete. The ankle went up into the frayed cuff of faded blues. Above me, I heard his laughter. The toes spread.

Somebody with a big, hard hand fingered my mouth. The nails were bitten, but nowhere near bad as Hogg's. The thumb prodded in; it tasted salty. I guess it was the wop.

Then the nigger said: "Hey, Hogg. I *know* this blond-headed little cocksucker!"

I came off Hogg's dick and looked up past a black cock fucking a black fist right by my face. Above it, the bullet-headed buck with the crazy scar grinned down:

"I done paid me a quarter already to get into that sucker's face. Got a sweet asshole on him, too. You should try it out, Hogg. Spic kid had him workin' out across town along with a girl, back when I was doin' that stint down on the Crawhole docks. Good to see you, cocksucker. Just open it up again, white boy. Nigg's about to bring it on home."

"Shit." Hogg said, somewhere above and behind me. "You think he's white?"

"He's white enough for me. He's sure whiter than I am," the nigger said. "He looks whiter than this goddamn wop."

I guess it was the wop who laughed.

So did Hogg. "Well, if that ain't some goddamn shit! You just can't get in ahead of a fuckin' nigger no how—"

Then somebody did get in ahead of Nigg and shoved his dick (something glittered at the tip) about halfway down into my chest; I squinted up at the wop who was squinting down. (I liked it when they laughed.) He had a rough, good-looking face with a lot of curly black hair. He was holding onto the nigger's shoulder with one hand and Hogg's with the other, chewing on his lower lip and swinging his hips in and out.

The nigger got hold of the wop's cock and tried to pull it out. "Come on, Dago," the nigger said. "Come on. I wanna watch him suck off Denny there. Watch it, now—" The nigger got the wop's cock loose (the wop hissed, "*Shit...*") and pushed me around on my knees. "Go on, get Denny...."

I got myself turned:

He had on real dirty sneakers. His ankles were dirty too. His pants—gray canvas—were too big, torn off too short, with holes in both knees, and tied at the waist with twine. Between the aluminum teeth of his fly his dick stuck out like an Idaho potato from a snarl of brass. He was going along it underhand, catching up the drool from his foreskin with dirty fingers, to smear it back and around. His shirt looked like one Hogg had thrown away. He was scrawny and grinning under a tangle of blond hair. His front two teeth overlapped and stuck out a little and his cheeks were chewed up with acne. He was maybe seventeen.

"Go on over there and suck it for him, cocksucker," Hogg told me. "Call him, Denny."

"*Oh*, fuck...." Denny grinned wider. He sounded like a hillbilly. "Crawl on over here, cocksucker, and I'll fuck your head off!"

I went for it on all fours.

Behind me Hogg and the nigger laughed.

Denny bobbed the sticky tip against my nose. He wanted to keep on rubbing it, I think. He was another nail-biter, and all his knuckles looked like they had blisters. When I got it in my mouth, he shoved out all his breath. It scraped my teeth by accident, but after three passes, I guessed he liked that.

"How do you dig my little cocksucker, son?" Hogg asked.

The nigger said: "Denny boy is just a-grinnin'. Aw, he really likes that little dick-freak!"

The wop said: "Seems like the little sucker was pretty anxious for it, the taste he give me."

And the nigger said, "Shit...."

Hogg chuckled.

Denny leaned deep in me, butted at me, ground his hair in my face. I held his pockets. He put one blunt finger in my ear. "Damn, cocksucker, use your teeth! I'm gonna pop my pod in there soon. Hogg, is it all right if I piss in him? I like that thing you told me about where you loose your juice right when you shoot. But I don't wanna mess him up for—"

"Hell," the nigger drawled, "I bet that boy goes after piss like it was soda pop."

I put both arms around Denny's flat, flexing butt. He liked the way he was getting it. I liked the way he was giving it.

"You just piss all over him, boy," Hogg said, coming up behind me. I heard the uneven sound of concrete under hard leather and a horny foot. Hogg's rough, familiar hand moved on my face. A rough, familiar finger slid in, alongside Denny's cock. It wiggled. Denny really began to pump. With one hand he must have been feeling Hogg's dick. The other grappled my hair. His legs were shaking against my chest. He pushed his cum out with three little grunts, and I felt his ass relax, my mouth filling with slopping salts. (It wasn't beer, either.) My cheeks filled and I swallowed, but it still leaked down my chin. Finally it got so he'd plunge, I'd spurt; all over Hogg's hand and Denny's pants. He was still grunting and slipping it way in and saying, "Jesus Christ, oh shit, oh yeah! Oh yeah, goddamn, oh shit!" I heard the others come up, laughing and joking:

"Hey," the wop said. "Watch this. Denny gets so excited, you can…" The wop grunted. Denny's pants came open. "Somebody workin' on Denny's pecker, an' *any*body can fuck 'im." Denny staggered, grunted again. "See…" the wop said, breathing a little hard. There was a secondary rhythm in Denny's shove now. I came off Denny right onto the nigger's black dick, which loosed urine against my cheek. "Hell," the nigger said, chuckling. And kept on chuckling. And kept on pissing.

I went down and licked his salty nuts. Then I came up and sucked on his cock. I don't know if he'd finished pissing, but he suddenly caught his breath, tightened his belly, and came. It was thick and bitter and there was a lot of it. I came off him to the smell of shit: the wop had his cock out of Denny's ass now and up against my face.

What had glittered was a ring in his dick.

First, as it pulled back into and pushed out his fist, I thought it just went through his foreskin. His skin pulled the brass back, pushed it out again, and I saw the metal went down into the slit of his piss-hole, out through the head and on through the foreskin—not out through the bottom where the skin is thin, either, but through the side, the thickest part of the head. The flesh around the hole was dark and puckered. The foreskin could slip back on the right, but on the left the ring, about as big as a wedding ring for a large-handed man, held it forward. The heavy, work-rough hand guided the cocoa-colored crank (it *really* smelled like shit) into my mouth. "Saved my load for the sucker here, soon as he cleans off Denny's dirt." The wop laughed. He wore a workman's jumpsuit, with the zipper open down over a chest that was a black rug. His belly was invisible behind the fur. He pushed me back against Hogg's legs, pumping like a pogo stick. The ring pulled over my tongue.

"All right, you motherfuckers," Hogg said. "All right, come on, you bastards. We got work to do—"

"Just a second, motherfucker," the wop hissed. "Just a..." He went in—I heard his shoes grind cement—and forced out briny syrup.

"I wanna fuck the cocksucker," the nigger said. He'd put his cock back in his pants. But he curved his fingers around the shape along his leg. "I wanna fuck him. That chil' fuck like a goddamn kangaroo rat!"

The wop lost about a quarter of his hard, but kept sliding. "Hey, ring on my bell, boy. I got somethin' for you." I didn't know what he meant till he slipped almost all the way out, holding it with two thick fingers by the skin, rubbing the ring on my teeth.

I bit the metal and tugged.

"You can do better than that—"

So I really yanked on it.

"Yeah, cocksucker—"

And he began to urinate, breaking the stream on my teeth, my lower lip, my nose. My chin dripped. I worried the ring like a dog.

"Make it bleed, cocksucker...." He gasped, and planted his black workshoes wide on the puddled concrete. "...Make it bleed, and I'll come all over you!"

A couple of times I really thought I was gonna rip it loose. But it was in strong.

"Hey, look at the little cocksucker go!" Hogg chuckled.

A couple of times I went after the whole length, and heard him panting above me, but he'd push me out to the end, one hand on my shoulder, his knuckles on my head, and I'd start chewing on it again. Finally, while I was yanking and growling, something sticky dribbled down my face. The wop caught both my ears between his palms to hold me still. I got my tongue under his foreskin and licked around, feeling the ring barring the full trip—the skin tight around the metal, loose and floppy on the other side.

"Goddamn..." the wop said.

I opened my teeth.

His cock fell against his pants.

From the big nozzle, drops of come rolled down the wet cloth of his thigh. Then a drop of something darker welled, staining the dark cloth black and losing its edges on the wet. He let go my head and shoved his dick back in his fly, taking deep breaths.

"Come on." Hogg ran his hand through my wet hair, closed his fingers in a fist. "Look, you motherfuckers! I got some work for you to do!" I leaned against Hogg's leg, put my arm around it. My knees were sore, so I rocked back to a squat. "I got an envelope here with the names of some bitches with some sloppy pussies that gotta be wrung out and knocked into shape."

Across the floor, a trickle of piss wormed and widened. The nigger, leaning now on the wall, moved his black foot aside. (A red bulb burned in the wall socket above his head.) The trickle changed direction. When it reached his foot this time, he just looked down and spread his big toes.

I looked down.

You could see the bulb reflected.

"You get your usual bread," Hogg was explaining. (I slipped one hand under his wet foot. The urine on the floor was warm.) "You guys with me on this job? What about you, Denny?"

Denny was sitting on a crate, running his hand, underhand and overhand, along his cock. It curved up higher than his bottom shirt button. "What...?" He looked up but didn't stop rubbing.

"I said, you wanna go along with us on the job?"

"Where?"

"In the truck," Hogg said. "To do some cunt bustin'—you can get yourself maybe forty or fifty dollars."

"I don't know how to drive," Denny said. "I can handle a shotgun pretty good—but I never did learn to drive, you know?"

Which cracked the wop up laughing.

"Now come on," Hogg said. "Shut up. You gonna come with us on this job, Denny? I told you how we do before—"

"Oh," Denny said. "That...yeah, sure. I told you before too, I'd like to see some of that."

"It's a good profession, boy," Hogg said. "Like the man says, ain't nothin' you can do in this world today—go to the pictures, buy some food, or even throw away the package it come in— that don't bring somebody closer to hurt. At least this way you know that you ain't makin' your money by makin' them pictures or packages. And when you're hurtin' someone, *you're* hurtin' 'em. You look 'em right in the eye and do it. You can't very well fuck somebody without lookin' 'em in the eye, unless—" Hogg chuckled—"you do it doggy-style. Even so, you ain't droppin' no bombs on five hundred people you ain't never seen. You ain't signin' no papers that's gonna put a thousand people who ain't never heard your name out of a house and a job. You ain't enjoyin' no benefits that come down the pike three years after you finished with hurtin' folks you didn't even know existed, much less you was hurtin' them. And you can look at any TV newscast or listen to any radio report, even if it's about somethin' you just done—and I had that happen to me three times now— and know you got more sense of duty than they do!"

"Goddamn, Hogg," the nigger said, "whyn't you quit makin' speeches to that boy? He got other things on his mind."

The wop laughed. "Or in his hand."

Which I guess was true. Denny was still beating. Actually, though, you didn't have no way to tell whether he was listening or not.

"Besides, Hogg," the nigger said, "he already said he was comin'—didn't you, Denny?"

"Huh?" Denny said, looking up again. "Yeah. Sure. If I don't have to drive none, I wanna come. But nobody ever taught me. I usually have to hitchhike."

"Hey," the wop said, "you gonna pull the fucker off if you go on like—"

"Shut up," Hogg said. "You comin' with us, nigger?"

"You takin' him?" The nigger nodded toward me.

"You just tell me whether you comin' with us or not."

The wop said, "Denny don't do nothin' but play with—"

"Shut up," Hogg said again. "Come on, Nigg. Yes or no?"

The nigger had his fists in his pockets. Even so I could see the outline of his dick.

Hogg's hand slipped down over my face so I couldn't see much of the nigger's. The nigger must have smiled and nodded, though (I thought about that crazy scar twisting a little) from the way Hogg relaxed and said, "Good." Hogg pushed his third and middle fingers into my mouth. I sucked on them and licked the salty nubs, ran my tongue among the nail rim, bitten all back from the crowns. Between Hogg's legs I felt something move under my hand: his pants got pulled forward by his stiffening dick.

"What about you, Dago?"

"Sure, Hogg." The wop laughed. "My sore old pecker's just waitin' for some nice pussy to whittle on."

"Way you do," Denny said. "it's gonna be too sore to do anything with, you dumb guinea! If you just jerked it like me—"

"The sorer it gets, the stiffer it stays," the wop said. "You talk about me, you gonna wear *yours* down to a nubbin, scumbag! Yeah, Hogg, I'm into anything you are. Maybe we can make a little trade though? You guys can give me some of your time and we can go have a party with my old lady."

"That's right," the nigger said. "You was talkin' about gettin' married a couple of days back." He laughed. "So you actually went and got yourself hooked up? Well, now, I'm downright surprised."

"Sure did," the wop said. "Legal and all, too. In a church. We been married nearly a week. She's a pretty little blue-eyed thing. Sweetest piece of pussy you ever seen walkin' around on two legs. Ain't hardly twenty. Man, I had to beat the shitheads off to get her. You guys would really like it up there in that sweet cunt."

"You ever catch anybody fuckin' with her?" Denny asked.

"Shit." The wop's shoes moved on the concrete. "Day after we got all officially hitched, I was out drinkin', right down here at Ray's place. I come in half looped and she had this mother-fuckin' spic grocery boy, about as old as you, Denny, down on his knees in front of the couch just a-eatin' out her box. Just a-eatin' and a-beatin'."

Hogg laughed and pushed his fingers deeper, rubbing my teeth. "What'd you do?"

"Well, I just coughed and said, 'Boy, you better be able to keep that up long enough to stick it up my wife's pussy, 'cause I got a few ideas.' Little bastard was scared to death. She was too. But he got to fuckin' her. And I just slipped his pants down over his little brown butt, spit on my old sore cock—when he seen my bell ringer, he was real impressed—and jammed him up the ass with it. Took it almost good as you do, Denny—"

"Shit..." Denny drawled.

"—then I fucked on her a little, too. Made him suck me off. Peed on 'em. Made him ring my bell some. Oh, man, you guys gotta come down and try her out. She just see a dick and she gets all drippy. She got some good eatin' pussy, too."

Hogg said: "You ain't payin' us, wop. Pussy is money work."

"Shit!" the wop said. "You some kind of a dirty bastard."

Hogg laughed. "You guys like money, don't you?"

"I like pussy—" the nigger chuckled—"long as it fights back a little."

"Oh, man!" the wop said. "Nigger, she sees that big, black turd you got hanging between your legs and she gonna fight to wrap her face around it. Only dick what ever been in her before I hooked up with her was her pappy's. He used to fuck on her all the time. Towards the end, the dumb bastard got sort of tooth-less and stupid, and she told me he'd about gummed her to death. Pretty soon she's gonna belly out with somebody's little bastard. Then I'm gonna put her out on the street and get her ass to work. A fuckin' cunt can really make some fuckin' dough when they're knocked up and six or seven months gone—from the freaks who really like it that way. Chances are it'll be mine, but if it isn't, I'd just as soon it was one of you guys."

"You want a boy or a girl?" the nigger asked.

"You goddamn crazy? Of course, I want a little girl! You like it fightin', nigger? I like it sweet and little and hardly no titties on it. Man, I got it all planned out. I figure I'm just about five or six years away from Heaven!"

"You bastards come on," Hogg said. "We'll talk about turnin' Dago's old lady out later. Right now we got work to do." He took his fingers out my mouth. Maybe it was getting him too turned on.

"You better put your pants back together, son," the wop said, opening the cab door. "I know it feels good, but you gonna—"

"I wish you motherfuckers wouldn't all call me 'son'," Denny said, rubbing one sneaker heel again the curb, one hand against the base of his dick. "None of you guys is my fuckin' old man."

"So who is your old man?" The wop pulled himself up on the cab seat and turned around to look down between his knees.

"I don't know *who* my fuckin' old man is," Denny said, "and I wouldn't *wanna* know if he was some cocksucker like you!"

The nigger chuckled. "Well, I guess he told *you*, motherfucker!"

Hogg stopped, his hand on the headlight, on his way around to the other side. "Hey, how old *are* you anyway?"

"Me?" The wop swung the door half closed, looked down through the open window. I could see his chin in the door mirror. "I'm twenty-three. You wanna make something of it?" I would have thought he was more like thirty-three. But I guess he was just one of those big guys who looks older than he is. He was good-looking, like a grimy, black-jawed bear.

"I should be callin' *you* 'son'," Hogg said, and went around to the other side. I heard the other door clank open.

"You know," the wop said, still leaning on the sill, "I ain't never hardly *seen* Denny with his dick in his pants."

Denny still shucked his cock. "I just like to jerk off in the goddamn street!" His face sort of twisted, almost twitched. "Hey, everybody! I'm jerkin' off *MY FUCKIN' DICK!*" he yelled the last three words so loud I jumped. He turned to look down the block, crouched, his fist speedin' up. "In the goddamn street, you see?"

We were the only ones on the sidewalk.

"Come on," Hogg said, over the wop's shoulder. "Get on up here in the fuckin' truck, will ya'?"

"He gonna get in trouble," the wop said.

Denny climbed up after the wop. I climbed up after Denny. The nigger climbed up after me, and leaned out to slam the door.

"Just don't catch his peter in there," Hogg said, turning the ignition, letting the clutch. The door slammed. Everybody laughed. Denny too.

While we drove, I sat wedged between Denny and the nigger. I watched Denny playing with himself. Once I bent over and took his cock in my mouth. A couple of seconds later, the nigger's big hand slipped in there to tickle Denny's balls and my chin.

Suddenly somebody cuffed the back of my head.

"Shit, Hogg!" Denny said. "You gonna make the little bastard bite my dick off!"

"Get up from there, cocksucker," Hogg said. "What you after another load again for? These bastards gotta save their juice for an hour or so. They gotta work. So cut it out!"

I sat up again.

"Shit..." Denny mumbled. His grubby, nail-bitten fingers closed around his wet dick, ran down to the base, ran up to the head, slipped two scrawny red knuckles across it, and slid down again.

"You can fuck around later," Hogg said, pushing forward on the shift, tugging back on the wheel, "if you want. We got to work now."

Night and street lamps rushed the window. Light filled and flushed from the cab.

"Hey, Dago, reach in my shirt pocket there and pull out that envelope for me."

Denny's swollen knuckles slid over the shiny veins.

"YES? CAN I DO ANYTHING FOR——"

The wop swung his knee against the—it was cabin "87", in copper numbers—door. The chain snapped, whipping her cheek. The door edge hit her face and the knob jammed her stomach. She let out all her air and stumbled.

Hogg chuckled.

She looked too scared to make a sound. Her pink bathrobe was all knotted in her fingers against her belly.

She opened and closed her mouth a couple of times, shook her head—her hair had been sprayed into complicated shapes; one started falling. As she swung her head back and forth, they shook like blond balloons.

The nigger, with one hand on the door jamb, drawled, "*Shit*...!" His zipper rasped.

She screamed.

Hogg stepped in and hit her, hard, in the face. Which stopped the scream. He chuckled again.

Beside me, Denny's mouth hung loose. His eyelids were crimped, squinting. His dirty knuckles creased and uncreased around his dick as he leaned around Nigg to see.

She tried to back away, shaking her head, whispering, "Look—!"

Hogg grabbed the terrycloth shoulders of her robe with both hands.

"—I don't know what this is, I really don't! But you people better get out of here! Look, I'm telling you, get *out!*"

Hogg moved her a little to one side, then a little to the other—she almost stumbled—and she kept shaking her head.

He jerked the robe open, yanking it down her arms. She stumbled again and tried to cover her tits. They were big, and the gray nipples pushed out between her fingers. She looked about twenty-four, or maybe even twenty-five; and very frightened.

"Nigger," Hogg said, "fuck this bitch."

The nigger stepped up beside Hogg, grinning, his hand in his fly.

When Hogg let go, she went right back into the wall. And kicked out. The wop dodged, caught her ankle, and yanked. She went down on her ass.

A china cat fell over on the table.

"Oh, *look*, please…"

Her slipper was that gold cloth stuff, only the sole was almost worn through and had pulled loose on the edge. The wop twisted her ankle. She pushed herself up on one hand and opened her mouth. Her slipper came off. Her toenails were apple red.

"Please—"

"Shut up!" The wop jerked her leg. She let go her robe and grabbed the table leg. The cat rolled, then rolled back.

She wore black panties.

"You ever had a barefoot nigger fuck you, bitch?"

"Hey," Hogg said. "Look at that black bastard's tool. That's goin' right up your sweet little pink pussy."

"Shit." The nigger spat on one palm, then the other, then caught his dick in both hands, going down it with one and the other fist. "I ain't goin' in no pussy. Ah'm a' asshole nigger!" He grinned. The scar wrinkled.

The wop let her ankle fall on the carpet and laughed, stepping backwards, pushing the heel of one hand down the front of his jump suit. Under the blue grease-blackened cloth, you could see his cock hardening.

Hogg said: "Get them panties off!"

"You leave that front hole open," the wop said, squeezing himself, "and I'm gonna fill it up with dick."

Hogg put his bare foot—it was black as the nigger's almost except the nails, which were just gray and ringed like someone had outlined them with a felt pen—on her panty crotch. And walked his toes—they were knuckly and sort of hammered—to her belly, denting and pinching her skin. "Come on, cunt. Pull 'em off. I want to wiggle my toes in your box." She was crying, like somebody with a cold.

"Oh shit," the nigger said. "That little blond bitch gonna get this old pole jammed up her ass. Them pretty little tears gonna make me come all over myself." (Her tears were streaking her eye make-up, which she must have been in the middle of putting on. One false, black eyelash had come half off; her real lashes under it were pale and thick.) "Get 'em off, bitch! Or I'll rip 'em off!"

She shook her head, just a little. "No—"

"Yes you will," Hogg said. "Otherwise, we gonna kill you."

Her head was still shaking, but she hooked her thumbs in the side of the black material. It slid down. The waist elastic left a pink line. Her pubic hair came over the top of the dark lace. She worked the panties down on her thighs. Some of the hair was stuck together in little blonde points. She was scared and unhappy as hell.

The nigger kicked her in the side. "Roll over!"

She turned, awkwardly.

Her buttocks shook.

"Oh shit…!" The nigger squatted, climbed over her legs

First she screamed, but Hogg got down on her real quick and got the edge of his hand in her mouth, and finally she was just gasping.

"Yeah, honey…" the nigger grunted. "Just shake that shit for me. Hey, she done it this way before! You can tell…the way it gives."

She looked like she was trying to crawl, or swim on the rug, out from between them both.

The nigger pushed up from her long enough to pull her back by the hips. Hogg got one hand between the nigger's front and the woman's ass. "Man," Hogg said, "I didn't think you were gonna be able to get all that in. Fuck it, boy!"

The nigger's ass flexed.

Hogg dropped his chin and squatted down to look. "That black crowbar of his is just pryin' that pink thing inside out each time he pulls it up," he said to the wop.

The nigger was yanking at her, now. Finally, holding his arms around her, he rolled away from Hogg, so that he went on to his back, pulling her, on her back, on top of him. His black fingers caged her tits. "Hey," the nigger grunted somewhere under her hair, "somebody get into this bitch's cunt." Each time he flexed under her, her face twisted up like somebody'd smacked her. And she was just gasping now.

Hogg sucked in his bottom lip; it slipped out of his mouth wet.

"This looks like some real good stuff!" He sucked in the top one.

The nigger was still humping underneath; her hips would rise and the blond hair pull apart over the wet pink slice.

"Goddamn…!" Leading with his tongue, Hogg dropped his face on it and began to grind his head around. She screamed. And the nigger's hand left her tit—red where he'd squeezed—and clamped her mouth. She was shaking her head and pulling at Hogg's hair. It didn't stop him.

The wop stood over them, reaching for his cock with one hand, the other still a fist in his pocket. He pulled his brown meat loose. It swung up, the ring shaking from the fork of two thin veins along the foreskin. Where the metal went through, there were brown flakes of blood.

Her eyes, between the nigger's fingers, kept flashing up— the dislodged lash finally came off against his knuckle, getting in her eye first so that she clamped the lids and shook her head; then it fell down her cheek, caught in her hair. She beat the floor with one hand, beat at Hogg's head with the other.

The wop took his hand out of his pocket, holding something backhanded, thumb down. He shook it. About eight inches of blade fell out.

She really began to wriggle, then.

The wop stepped over Hogg, squatted, and just lay—letting it rest with no more than its own weight—the point on her breast, on the grayish bulge around her nipple. Hogg's chewing and the nigger's fucking kept making the flesh dimple under the blade.

She strained, all triple-chinned, to stare down at it and keep still. Hogg and the nigger were really going.

The wop, adding maybe the weight of his thumb to the knife and turning it on edge, drew the blade down her breast—a little chain of drops sprang up—and on over her ribs. One ran red down her side.

She must have done something with her legs then, because suddenly Hogg looked up. The bottom half of his face was as shiny as when he'd been at those pork-chops. "Hey, what the *fuck*—!" He knocked the knife from the wop's hand with the side of his. It fell on the floor, its handle on the carpet, the blade over the floorboards. A single drop on the point slid down the edge.

The wop didn't even get mad. He just climbed over her, his mouth wide and gasping, shoved Hogg out of the way, and pushed his dick into her bush, all stuck with Hogg's spit; he shrugged off the shoulders of his jump suit. His back was as hairy as his chest. And there was a pink, wrinkled scar about the length of my middle finger right above his furry buttocks—they tightened on all that hair; he hunched.

"Yeah," the nigger said. "I can feel it in there, man, against mine."

After a few more hunches, the wop gasped: "You better watch it, nigger, I'm coming through." Then he managed to laugh, without breaking stroke. "'Ey, Hogg, send the little cocksucker over here...."

Hogg came over and stood between me and Denny. He put his hand on my shoulder. "Go on, cocksucker. I wanna see you eat that guinea's ass out. He likes that." Denny's elbow was still swinging.

I went over to them and, for a second, wondered how I was going to do it. Finally, I straddled them and squatted down on the wop's back. At first I tried not to put all my weight on them because of the nigger on the bottom.

One hand on each of the wop's buttocks, I pushed my face between. Sometimes I could just set my tongue in his hole. The hair was rough on my face, but the way he started moving, I could tell it was turning him on, so I really got to licking around. Then I went further on down (it was sweaty and stank down there of pussy and three kinds of shit) to lick the back of his balls; he had pretty long ones. I had my hand in there (it was like getting your nose and your fingers and your tongue inside a wet engine, everything going around and in and out and joggling), and though I couldn't see, I kept trying to get my thumb in beside the wop's dick, and licking the hilt of the nigger's cock (I could tell because of the shit), and I remember thinking, while I was prodding at the turned-out rim of her asshole, and trying to get my tongue in it, that maybe licking it for her was making it hurt less. I didn't even get a hard-on, you know, until I remembered the wop's scar, where there wasn't any hair. Then my dick went up in my pants, and I started rubbing myself against the wop's shoulder.

Some light got in when somebody moved a leg; I could see, about an inch away, the nigger's wet cock (a thin column molded along the bottom of a thick one) turning out her red ass, and then disappearing again up to his black hair, and the sweat dribbling down his thigh. I lifted up his balls to go after his asshole—that was pretty funky—and he must have felt what I was doing because he farted and I heard him laugh, between grunts, up near my knees. Somebody was opening Big Chico's tear—skinny, hot hands; so it was Denny. He got behind me and eased his potato cock in, lay down on my back, holding my shoulder and grunting above my head, while I felt Hogg's callused hand wedging between my belly and the wop's hairy backbone. Hogg got down to my pants, and in.

The callused crowns of his gnawed fingers rubbed the side of my cock, then slipped beneath it so that I could rub off in his hand.

Denny shot first, wouldn't you know.

After a while, the wop stopped moving and just then the nigger's asshole pinched the tip of my tongue. I guess it must have been the surprise; I shot the same time I jerked my head away. As I pushed myself up—the wop was hunching in her again, so I guess he hadn't made it yet—Denny got off me. Hogg kneeled back, his palm puddled with pearly mucus.

"Oh shit, man!" Denny said.

He was still hard.

He was still shucking.

"Jesus Christ, I bet I know what that is!" Denny stepped around by Hogg, grinned at me once between red, rotten cheeks, then took hold of Hogg's wrist with one hand and Hogg's fingers with the other, lowered his head, and dropped his tongue like a blond cat.

As he crouched, lapping, his cock joggled at the back of the cave his legs and belly made.

After a few seconds, Hogg said, "Okay. Fuck off!" He pulled his hand away and stood up, rubbing his fingers together. The scum on his hands turned slowly gray as snow slush and ran down his hairy knuckles.

"Goddamn!" The wop pushed his other arm back into his jumpsuit sleeve, picked up his knife, and stood.

"Shit!" The nigger stood, more on one foot than the other, buttoning his fly. "That was some good ass." With his foot, he reached over and wobbled one of her buttocks.

"I think I'm about ready to try it out for myself. You guys got it primed for me real good," Hogg said.

The woman lay still.

"Hope we didn't take all the life out of her for you." The wop chuckled. His jumpsuit was open all the way so you could see the upper half of his cock. The tip with the ring was hanging down below where the zipper came together—the threads were worn and raveled. Christ, he was hairy!

Hogg said: "I don't care if she's dead."

Her hand jerked a little when he said it.

He'd said it pretty coldly, too.

She caught her breath, and when she let it out she was crying again and turned her head away.

They laughed.

"Come on, Denny." Hogg looked like he had a king-sized beer can hanging inside one leg of his pants. "Help me fix this cunt right."

"Sure." Denny's shucking got faster. "Sure, Hogg. What you want me to do?" He hadn't lost his hard since he'd come up my ass.

Hogg pulled out his dick, got down on his knees, straddling her legs, caught two handfuls of her ass and spread her. "Hey...shit, man!" His foreskin was so long a full hard didn't come out the end. Pushing it into her rectum, skin wrinkled up around the glans' base and turned back over the shaft. He leaned forward. "Oh, fuck...." Pumping, Hogg got her rolled onto her side. He grunted, "You take her cunt, Denny...."

Denny got down on the floor and wedged himself into her pussy, bucking his butt, pushing and pushing, rubbing the edge of his sneaker on her raw calf.

It looked like they were balling a limp corpse that for some reason kept gagging every so often.

"Shit," the wop said. "Oh, shit. Shit. I *gotta* drop another load in the dirty bitch. Shit. Oh shit. I'm gonna fuck her face. Shit."

She moaned hoarsely, the sound wavering with their movements. Every once and a while, her fist came up and flapped at Denny's shoulder. The boy's blond head, rocking with his thrusts, was in her neck.

The wop's cock was dull as milk chocolate. He ran his sausage-thick fingers up to the head, pinched the ring, tugged a little, let go and ran back down to the base. Then he would pull his lips, all stubbly above and below, real thin, up from his teeth and his breath would hiss into his chest. He went around to her head; when he squatted, he knocked the table leg. The cat rolled to the edge and fell.

Ceramic shattered.

Pieces rocked on the boards and on the rug.

The wop locked his grease-blackened fingers in her hair—ruined shapes crumpled like paper. He lifted her head from between Hogg's and Denny's. Her eyes were closed tight. Eye makeup had run down her face like oil. She'd been wearing skin-colored lipstick too; it was smeared all around her mouth now.

"Shit," the wop said. "Oh, man, shit..."

"You better watch it," the nigger said. He stood with his fly half closed; his hand had gone back in it. "That bitch is near crazy, now. Watch out she don't try to bite your cock off."

The wop snorted a funny sort of laugh, looked at me—I don't know why—and looked back at her. He was hefting his knife in one hand. "I don't mind a little bridge work rubbin' up against it. Come on, baby. Chew on my pecker." With the hand that held the knife, he held his cock in three fingers and rubbed the ring on her mouth. He pushed the head between her lips. But she wouldn't open her teeth. "Oh, yes you will...." He let go and laid the knife point against her neck. So she took it.

"Oh, yeah...!" He looked at the nigger. "She really chomp down on it, shit, I'll cut her head off."

Suddenly she got one arm free of Hogg's grip and reached up to try and push the wop's genitals away, pulling back while he nearly squat-walked over her to keep it in.

"Fuck..." Hogg grunted, and his hand came up and hit at her face.

She must have bit a little because the wop grinned. "That's it, sweetheart!" He yanked her hair a little, and she just let her hand stay on his knee.

I got around so I could see better.

Her loose spit ran down the wop's balls, dripped from the hair, and made a little spot on the carpet between his workshoes.

"Hey," the nigger said. "Look over here, boy." His cock and balls were hanging out his fly. His dick was shiny. His legs were apart. He flexed his toes on the rug. He put his hands behind his sac to scratch. "Come on, boy. She don't got enough holes for all of us at once. That's what you're here for."

I glanced at Hogg's hand locked around her upper arm. His fingers had tracked my cum around her elbow; there were still wet places between his big knuckles; squeezing bunched up his nubs in front of his wrecked nails.

I went to the nigger and stooped.

His cock swung up and hit my chin.

He grabbed my hair and I took it—you could smell the shit a lot—down far enough to gag.

"Suck it, cocksucker!" His hips twisted; I was almost kneeling on his feet; his hands went around to lock behind my head so that I couldn't get back too far. He worked a long time. Which was good.

Then his buttocks went hard under my palms and he tried to get his cock into my belly. I kept his spilled scum in my mouth, though, bitter and slimy and flavored with: "Shit..." the nigger said, let go my head, and pulled out. His glistening cock fell down my chin.

Denny was standing up now (overhand, underhand; I've seen a couple of guys who could stay up that long if they had a rubber band around it or something, but not like him), and Hogg had moved around to her pussy.

The wop, holding her head up with both hands, had dropped the knife again and was grunting in her face.

"Hey, nigger!" Hogg called, lifting his sweating face. "Get over here and plug this bitch's ass again. I wanna see what your dick feels like up against mine."

"Now just a second." The nigger was mauling his black hose. "Just a second. Give me about thirty seconds, motherfucker, and I'll have it up there for you." Bobbing a little, a little bowlegged, and grinning his scarred grin, the nigger walked over to them. His dick had only sagged to about forty-five degrees before it had come up again. He sat down on the floor with them and got into position.

"You limp-mouthed bitch!" the wop whispered. "Use your goddamn teeth! Goddamn it, let's feel some teeth on my dick! *Shit!*"

"This is something, huh?" Denny said. His dick still stuck out, but he'd hooked his thumbs in the twine around his pants. "How you holding up?"

I still had the nigger's scum in my mouth.

Denny reached out and rubbed away a drop that ran down my chin with his knuckle, brought his knuckle back to his mouth, licked it. Then he must have figured out what I was holding. "Hey, boy, come here!" He put his hands on the sides of my head—his fingers were moist and hot and came toward me with his mouth open and his tongue out. I opened my mouth and some of it drooled out before his face locked against mine; his cockhead kept butting my belly, so I took it in my hand. We pushed our tongues together in the stuff. We gave it back and forth, with a lot of spit. He got one hand behind my neck and the other one around my shoulders while he rooted in my gullet—

Something hit the back of my head so hard that, reeling, I bit my tongue.

"Cut that shit!" Hogg bellowed.

I guess I tripped on the rug; and went down. I kept on trying to get my eyes focused. The back of my head hurt like hell.

Something—it was Hogg's bare foot—hit my chest hard enough to knock me on my back. I grabbed his ankle and opened my eyes.

"Get on back over there, you weasly bastard!" That was to Denny. "You got some more hots, go spill it in the bitch's cunt. You're gettin' paid for this, remember! So do some work!"

Denny nodded fast. "Yeah, sure, Hogg! Sure!" His cock was still up, and he was holding onto it with one hand like he was afraid Hogg would reach over and yank it off.

Denny scooted back to the woman.

I looked up. Hogg's balls hung out his fly; his thick cock, with its hose of foreskin, curved down left of his nuts. Above that, I could see his blond gut pushing over his belt. His shirt hung open. He stared down at me, panting a little; he looked pretty fierce. When he let up with his foot just a little, I slipped down and pulled it against my face, got the first two toes in my mouth and jabbed my tongue for the jam between. After a second, he began to flex them, pushing his foot further in, getting in two more toes, and trying to grip my tongue.

Then he grinned, and rocked my head.

I watched his cuff shaking. I licked the gritty underside of his foot, then pulled myself up his leg, brushed my face on the hot skin of his balls, pushed my mouth into his crotch's stench, rubbed his wet cock on my face. He put his hand down to adjust himself against my face. I licked his fingers, which were still tacky with halfdried pussy juice and cum. I went back and forth between licking his balls and sucking his fingers. His cock rose beside my cheek. Finally he took hold of my head and pushed his dick into my mouth. He chuckled again, began to rock, stuffing his dick deep, thrusting and thrusting while I held my arms around his rocking hips. When he came, I backed to the tip, to take it in the front of my mouth, digging inside his long, loose, cheesy crease. Finishing, he let go of his breath and his bladder. I went down to the hilt again to suck his piss. He stuck a thumb beside his cock, tickling the side of his dick and my tongue, swiveling his big hand around my face, wiping hot leakage under my chin, up my cheeks, and back against his testicles. His pants leg, soaked in urine, wet my t-shirt. I drank all I could. Which was a lot. But the rest kept blowing up my cheeks to splash out finally over Hogg's pants and hands. I tried to hold my tongue over the tip and plug him but you can't do that. Gasping and grunting, he finally stilled.

And still holding me by the face, he shouted: "Hey, you motherfuckers! Get the shit up from there! We can't haul that deadass pussy around all goddamn night. We still got work to do."

"Motherfucker...." From Denny's panting, I could tell he was fucking her again. "—you won't let me neck with the cocksucker, and...now you don't give me time to get my rocks...off in here..."

"You want to drop your cookies?" the nigger asked, drawling real slow. "Okay...here you go, boy!" I heard three loud slaps.

Denny caught his breath at each one; the woman moaned.

"You shoot?" the nigger asked.

Denny was still panting, but different. "You bet your black ass I did, Nigg!"

"Shit," the nigger said. "You mean your sore one. I know what you like, boy."

Hogg rubbed his wet hand in my hair. He had his foot in my lap and was rubbing my soaked crotch. The last of his piss dripped off my chin. He reached down and thumbed piss out of my eye, then ran his thumb in his mouth.

The nigger and Denny were standing near the woman, laughing together about something.

The wop stood, one shoe either side of her; he was closing his jumper. He wiped his knife on his hip—it made a wide smear—

and put it in his pocket. The woman was still breathing, though. And I didn't see much blood on the floor, so maybe he had only made shallow cuts.

Hogg's cock—almost soft now—fell out my mouth; and he shoved himself back into his fly, pretty fast. Yellow hairs still stuck through the fly flaps. "Come on, you guys. Get yourself together, huh?"

Drops from the edge of his cuff caught in the bright hair on the top of his dirty foot, rolled between the grimy ligaments, ran down the blacker troughs between his toes.

I put my hand around the back of his leg and pushed my fingers between his wet thighs. He shook me by the hair. "Come on, get up. Let's go." Hand on the back of my head, he walked me across the rug. "You see," he said. "Now this is more like what I usually do."

We waited at the door while the wop cut the phone wires. I stood next to Hogg, who kept rubbing the back of my neck. Piss kept dripping from my hair, running over his fingers, and down my neck.

I looked back at the woman.

I think she'd moved. Her face was straight down on the floor, which was a way I never thought you could lie because your nose got in the way. But maybe hers was broken. Her legs were wide and there was blood inside her thighs. By now, some was spreading on the rug. One arm was bent funny, so her hand lay among brown and white ceramic.

Closing the cabin door—the seven had come loose from one screw and leaned against the eight—it looked just like the other cabin doors that curved down toward the motel office. The red *Vacancy* sign blinked and blinked at the driveway entrance.

I climbed up into the truck next to Hogg. The wop slid over next to me. Hogg slid his hand under my ass without saying anything.

"This truck smells like a fuckin' latrine!" the wop said. "Nigger, this place must stink bad as the inside of your black ass! Denny, you wanna sit on my dick? There ain't hardly enough room in here anyway, and I'm damned if I can stay in a place that smells like this with a soft cock!"

"I don't want that thing on your dickhead tearin' up my insides," Denny said, squirming to get comfortable.

"Come on!" The wop leaned back and lifted his buttocks to pull over his jumper right. Then he took his cock out. "Come on, now. There ain't enough room for all of us to sit out side by side, anyway."

"All right," Denny said. "All right. Just a minute, now. Just a minute."

His pants around his knees, Denny eased himself down on the wop's cock.

"Feel good?"

"Come on, come on," Denny said. "Fuck me, huh?"

The wop hugged Denny's belly with one arm and began to grunt and hump. Hogg's other hand flexed under me. Beside them, the nigger chuckled. Below us the motor rolled over.

Denny said, "*Umph...*" a few times, but that was all. He'd given up on his dick awhile—it still stuck up like a yam—and was kneading his scrotum now.

Hogg glanced over. "Go on. Suck him off."

I bent over and took Denny's dick in my mouth. Hogg had gotten his hand inside the tear in my pants and was digging his middle fingers in me. A couple of times the wop reached over and rubbed my back. My t-shirt was cold now. But it was Hogg's piss; so I didn't care.

Sucking off Denny, I found, never took too long.

I sat up and looked at Hogg. He was just driving and looking out at the highway lights. I looked at his lap. In the light passing, I saw the stains of dried fuck at the open fly, yellow hair, and the crumpled vein across his cock, thick as a pencil. His leg moved as he went to the brake: his fly shifted.

I touched his cock.

It was half hard.

He opened his knees wider so I could get it out. It got loose from the zipper; I went under Hogg's elbow and drooled Denny's come all over it—I'd kept it in my mouth.

"Oh, shit..." Hogg said softly. I took the head in my mouth, nibbled and poked around in his foreskin. Then I swallowed it all the way; he took one hand off the wheel and scratched the back of my head. It was a long lazy suck. A few times (I kept thinking: he wants his scum back), Denny reached over to get his hands in the works. I kept waiting for Hogg to push me off and say something about us having more work to do that night. But he didn't.

Every ten or fifteen minutes—I think for a while I went to sleep with Hogg's cock in my mouth, but it was probably only for a few seconds and I'm not sure—under my slow tongue, Hogg would spurt, randomly, half a cup of piss.

He rubbed my head. "Hey, Dago, you got that envelope?"

"Right here, Hogg!"

The motor thrummed.

The nigger snored.

"I GOT 'EM——" THE NIGGER CALLED BACK TO US, rummaging in the glove compartment; he dragged out the chains.

He turned in the cab doorway—they chattered down, to swing from his fist's black knot—hefted them once, and jumped.

"Good," Hogg said; he squeezed my shoulder. "I knew they was in there, Nigg."

Denny's fist slowed at his groin—for a moment it was going at the same rate as the swinging chain.

By the light up on the telephone pole, I could see the wop moving his hand in his pocket, playing with himself in his pants so that first I could see his knife's shape and then I could see his cock's shape.

Hogg beckoned with his chin.

We walked up between the pines. There was no light on in either of the store's display windows.

"Looks like she's closed," the wop said.

"Note said she slept in the back," Hogg said. "We'll get in. She's suppose to got a daughter. Mr. Jonas' note says we don't have to do nothin' to her if we don't want." I could hear him grinning. "But it ain't gonna bother him none if we have some fun with her too."

"Shit!" the nigger said. He jarred the chains; the links rang.

Hogg rubbed his pants. "Yeah." (The drying piss was making me scratchy too.) "We don't *have* to let her alone—either."

Nigg rapped on the door.

After half a minute, he rapped again. Then again.

Finally, a woman inside said, "What you want?"

"Excuse me, ma'am," Dago called. "Can you help us out for a second?"

She opened the door with one hand, rubbing her eyes with the other. "Usually I'm up this time. But I was taking a nap. What can I do for you boys?" She had on a man's blue workshirt and jeans. "I'm not supposed to be open but I can—"

The nigger, grinning—and the grin suddenly went from all lips to all teeth—swung the chains (Christ, they hit loud!) at her face.

She snarled, reeling to the side, holding her head, shaking her head, her mouth wide, one eye closed, all crouched over. Still snarling, it was like the sound of the links going on. She backed toward the counter.

Hogg started in after her. There was blood on her face. He stepped around a spool of green hose. "Lady, first we're gonna hurt you. Then we're gonna fuck you. Then we're gonna hurt you some more."

"And maybe," the nigger said, "we'll fuck you some more, too."

Her hand, flapping back behind her, hit the counter; she grabbed for the shotgun.

But I guess the wop saw it before I did; he was already there, yanking it away from her before she could get it up; I thought he was going to shoot her from the hip like I saw once in a western on TV. But he just whapped the side of the barrel against her belly. But hard. She banged into the counter again. One eye was puffed and her cheek was bruised dark as a coal smear. She came away from the counter, hissing: "...you come here for that goddamn bastard, Jimmy! You're here for Jimmy, aren't you? Well, I don't want none of Jimmy's shit no more, goddamn it! You sons of bitches get out of my place and tell Jimmy I don't give a fuck what he—"

The wop whapped her again.

Then the girl none of us had seen, sitting in the back doorway, screamed, darting forward from the shadow; metal spokes glittered at her side, till her hands clamped the rubber rims. For a moment I thought she was going to propel the chair back into the darkness.

"Oh, shit now," Dago said. "She's about as cute a piece of pussy as my old lady!"

"Goddamn it, you leave her alone! If Jimmy's got any business, he's got it with *me*—"

Nigg's shoulders jerked with the chain's swing. His lips were back and his tongue made a peppery bulge between his teeth.

The woman staggered without a sound.

Chain flailed back the other way.

The woman went down on her knees, holding her head with both hands.

The wop took a breath, opened the rifle, saw there were no shells in it, laughed, and started to lean it against the counter; when suddenly the chair shot forward.

With sweeping strokes, the girl sent it around the pyramid of paint cans. She barreled toward Hogg, who turned, said, "Huh—?" and started back. If she'd crashed full into him, he would have been ready. But, at the last moment, she clamped her hand on one wheel so that the chair spun; the two ten-inch handles off the back—the rubber had worn half off one—raked his belly, just over his groin.

Teeth gritted back over her shoulder, the girl sent herself back into him, hard. Hogg grabbed himself and staggered.

The chair went forward again.

Hogg lunged for it and missed, going down on one knee.

"Goddamn...!" the wop said, then ducked. The paint tin hit his head anyway. "*Damn*—!" He moved back.

The second one she hurled—by the central table she had raked half a dozen pint cans into her lap—missed; but she wasn't screaming anymore. She turned in the seat and hurled the third one at Hogg. It hit his shoulder, and I don't know if it was pain or surprise, but it stopped him.

"Hey, now, little lady—" the nigger said, hefting chain.

She whirled her chair to face him.

"Hey, now—" the wop repeated.

Her hands reversed directions on the wheels and she swung back; because the wop was a lot closer.

The wop said, "Maybe we can have ourselves some *real* fun with you!"

"Fuck *you*...!" she hissed. "Fuck you, you bastards—!" Another can came up, back, then forward.

The wop ducked left; which was a mistake, because she'd figured that was the way he was going. It hit him full in the face, and from pushing around in that chair, I guess, she had a pretty good arm.

The wop held his cheek. Rubbing it and squinting, he took a step forward.

"You leave her alone!" the woman shouted. "Don't you touch her! Jimmy don't have any argument with her! You bastards keep your hands off—" which is when the nigger, chains in both hands, threw them around her neck and yanked her against him.

The girl darted the wheelchair forward, swiveled again, then backed away. The cans rolled from her lap. One landed upright. Two rolled across the floor boards.

Then Denny and the wop rushed her.

Denny went around one side of the center table. The wop pushed over the grinning man in bib overalls (cardboard) unreeling a spool of green rubber garden hose (the hose on its metal spool was real), and came around the other.

Her chair swiveled again, then backed toward me.

When it was about to run into me, I grabbed one handle and leaped aside, tugging. The chair went up on one wheel—the girl shouted and so did the woman—spun on its wheel, and crashed to its side.

The girl's shout just cut. She slid across the floor, her arms crossing over her pink sweater and her head going down and one knee buckling up, the other leg dragging. She had on funny shoes, laced high, almost like Hogg's workshoe; and the foot that dragged was leaning in the wrong direction. The wheelchair crashed on top of her ankle, tilted further, then back, the big wheel with its two-inch smaller rim spinning.

With Denny just behind him, the wop stopped. He put his hand in his pocket. I saw it moving but I couldn't tell on what.

The girl pushed herself up on her hands, tried to drag herself away, but she couldn't get her foot loose from under the chair.

The wop stepped up, dropped to a squat, and put his other hand on the girl's cheek. He pushed her hair, lighter brown than her mother's, back from her ear, bringing his dirty middle finger down her cheek, under her jaw—she blinked, opened her mouth a little, closed it again, but she must have been scared to turn her head—down her neck, and hooked it in the round, pink collar. He pulled at it, slow, down enough so you could see the top of her bra. She was maybe fourteen; and the bra was just about flat.

The woman, half limp in the nigger's grip, was crying now. It wasn't a full sound at all, but a non-stop squeak that went on at the same pitch while she shook her head, with her eyes closed tight.

The girl was taking quick breaths, then holding them a long time. I couldn't tell if that was fear or pain.

Hogg, who'd been watching with half a smile, turned to the woman. His cock made a tent of his pants. He went toward her, one hand between his legs. He got the other in the woman's jeans and yanked a couple of times at the top button. Her arm that had been swinging out limply suddenly came up in a fist, and the squeak turned into a full, white-eyed, red-mouthed growl. She tried to lunge up and knee Hogg in the nuts, but the nigger was on her, anyway, holding her. But from there on, it was all fight. They hit her a lot, and her shirt got just about torn off. Once I saw Hogg sink his yellow teeth into her shoulder; blood ran down her arm and down across one tit, as well as on her face where the chains had cut. When they hit or bumped or kicked things, they just grunted; most of it was awfully quiet, with just scrabbling and hissing and gagging and catching breath.

Kneeling beside the girl, the wop had one hand down the front of her sweater, the other around under her white plastic belt. Where the sweater was up, you could see the blue elastic along the top of her panties stretching and going back together as he worked his fingers down. He nuzzled her neck. Somehow she didn't seem to be paying attention to him anymore, though. I wondered if she was trying to just let him do what he wanted, now.

But maybe she was just tired. About every ten or fifteen seconds she would try to pull away, but she really couldn't get anywhere.

"Grab her...there, get her, nigger! Get—"

"God*damn*! This bitch is a tough—Ow!—tough pussy, Hogg!"

The wop, still in a squat, tried to make her take his cock in her hand. He jerked her wrist from the floor toward his crotch. She went down on her other elbow. Landing on your elbow hurts, too. But she didn't cry out. He rubbed her loose hand against the ringed shaft up-jutting from the fork of his jumper zipper.

Mom stopped struggling a couple of seconds, mainly to get breath.

But it gave Hogg a chance to look up. "These two must wanna get fucked *real* bad." Hogg was breathing hard. "I always figure the more they fight, the more they wanna get fucked—"

"Aw, fuck *you*—!" Mom said without even looking at him.

Hogg chuckled, looking at me now. "Course that ain't true. But I always tell 'em that, 'cause it gets 'em upset. And, after all, gettin' 'em upset is the fundamental nature of the enterprize, here." He jerked around to give her a sharp, backhanded smack. "Hey, Denny, you and the cocksucker go work on the little bitch. Do her in good."

"Yeah, sure," Denny said. I was standing just behind him and I could see his arm still moving. He grinned back at me. "Sure, Hogg!"

"Hey, Dago—get over here, you goddamn guinea. Give us a hand. Help me get this bitch—that's it… On the floor!" But the woman didn't go down yet.

The wop let go the girl, who sagged to her other elbow. He stood, sighed, zipped himself up, and went over toward Hogg and the nigger and the woman.

"That's right, on her knees—" Hogg grunted. This time he kicked her with the back of his heel behind her shin, while the nigger yanked her sideways.

She went down.

As the wop walked toward her, one hand went back in his pocket to play.

Behind her, the nigger grabbed the woman's brown hair, tight, on both sides of her head; which made her mouth open. I thought she was going to fall over on the floor, but the nigger kept her up on her knees. Her eyes were wide.

The wop came up, his hand in his pocket, working. He took another step. And another.

The nigger, standing behind her, hands still grappling in her hair, pushed her face toward the wop's crotch. She tried, but couldn't turn away.

I heard a click.

The woman froze.

The wop began to laugh.

Sticking out the thigh of his jumpsuit, tip glittering half an inch from her eye, was the blade.

She just tore her head away. And lost hair; I heard it. And saw some of it, too, in the nigger's fist.

Hogg began to laugh. "Hey, come on. You gonna fuck the bitch, you gonna fuck her. You gonna beat up on her, you gonna beat her up. You don't got to cut her none." He still thought it was pretty funny.

"Shit..." the wop whispered. He began to swing his hips in and out. Her eyes were closed and her head turned half away. But when the blade touched the side of her nose, she jumped— with her whole body, from the knees to the neck. She jerked in the nigger's grip: "Goddamn it, you tell me why that bastard sent you—why Jimmy sent you here! He's too fucking chicken shit to... Go ahead, you just say it—" The nigger yanked her hair again.

The wop's knife slid back inside the cloth.

He snarled his zipper from chest to groin, took out his cock.

She heaved up, she kicked, she hammered. Hogg came in on her again. With the nigger and the wop. It took the three of them to hold her, and none of them could really quite get on, I guess.

Denny was looking at the girl.

When she glanced up at him, her tits in the pink sweater stopped moving up and down. Her eyes flicked to Denny's hand, swiveling on his dick.

When he stooped down, she pushed herself up on both hands and drew back so far she fell again, rolling to her back. Denny took one tit in his dirty fingers and squeezed. The sweater bulged between his knuckles.

Her chin wrinkled as she stared down at his hand. Her lips got real thin. Her eyes were very wide.

"Hey," Denny said. "Can you take your sweater off?"

Her eyes closed. Tight.

She lifted her hands—one of them brushed Denny's arm and flew away like she'd been burned—and finally dropped on the belly of the pink wool. Her nails had the same pearly polish on them Maria used to wear.

She took a breath, eyes still closed, jaw still set; her fingers closed in the wool and she began to pull it up from out of her white belt. Thick, white skin pushed out between them all around. There was a scar, high as an appendectomy operation, but much thicker and without the cross cuts, slanting down under her skirt. The white ribbed bra came out, left tit then right, shallow as dessert dishes of vanilla pudding. She wriggled on the floor once to get the sweater from under her back; then her face, all close-eyed and frowning, disappeared in pink wool, her light brown hair following into the neck hole.

Denny grinned at me. Then he stuck one finger in the top of the bra and pulled. One vanilla pudding came free. Denny got it with both hands; he bent over, elbows on either side of her, and began to suck.

The woman screamed.

I looked back as Hogg—the nigger and the wop had her up on the counter, the nigger on her legs, the wop on her arms—dropped on her. Then the wop let go with one hand and pushed the side of his palm into her mouth, right by Hogg's straining face so that she couldn't scream anymore; and if she bit, she bit the inside of her own jaw. The scream chomped off; the only sound she made now came out like, "Awwwwww!" but very loud.

Hogg hunched. Hogg grunted. Hogg grinned—you could see it the way the muscles moved on the back of his jaw and neck.

The woman kicked her legs around his side, but the nigger held, grinning at Hogg's bucking blond ass; Hogg's pants were halfway down.

The girl, staring at the top of Denny's twisting head, looked up at me. Denny stretched out now, rubbing himself on her thigh. I reached between his legs to feel his balls, but I couldn't get under his pants.

"Oh shit..." Denny whispered, nosing between her dish-of-icecream tits. "Look, I'm gonna fuck on her and you can suck my nuts, okay? Then you can fuck on her and I'll give it to you up the ass so you don't lose your hard." He kneeled back from her and said, "Hey, take off your skirt."

She sort of fumbled with the belt.

"Come on!" Denny yanked it out of her hands; she rocked, grimacing. But, already half open, it came off the rest of the way. Eyes going back and forth between us, she put her thumbs in the waist and worked the stretch band down. That scar was awfully big. It went on over her hip—in fact it looked like part of the hip bone on that side was missing—then under her panties, and out and on down her thigh, halfway to her knee. That thigh was a lot thinner than the other one, too.

"—goddamn it, you tell me what Jimmy's trying to do! Leave her alone—what that bastard—" The wop hit her this time.

"She got some fight in her!" Hogg said, pushing up on his hands. He was breathing pretty hard. "Maybe we better take her in the back room there." He yanked her shoulder over, hard enough that the wop, who was holding her arm, got dragged a step around the counter end.

"Why?" the wop asked.

Hogg glanced over at us. "It's Denny's first job—and the cocksucker ain't seen too much of this sort of shit, either. We really gonna have to get rough here, so I don't want 'em seein' anything that's gonna turn 'em off the profession before they get their tastes fixed to it." Hogg's next breath got his grin settled. "Besides, I don't want 'em to think that some of these bitches fight back too hard." He winked over at Denny and me. "It might just get them all upset."

The woman's one open eye darted around. "You're goddamn right I'm fighting back!" she shouted suddenly, arching her shoulders from their grip. "You low-down filthy sons of bitches! You weak-assed, yellow-bellied scumbags! You—!" and got her hand free—"two-bit, chickenshit—" She pounded the wop a good one on the side of his neck; it made him open his mouth and gasp. The nigger hit her again with his free hand on her head, and her words suddenly got thicker. But they didn't stop coming, and she didn't stop pounding.

"You shouldn't of…" the wop grunted, trying to grin at the nigger; it didn't look like *much* of a grin: "…of done that!" He grabbed for her swinging arm and missed. "Goin' on like that, she was getting me—watch it, there!—all worked up again—" She hammered her arm into Hogg's chest, fist to elbow, so he staggered. She hit him again—at the same time kicked the nigger hard in the knee; his foot jerked up off the floor and he almost lost his balance—so that Hogg went all the way out to the end of his grip.

"Shit…!" the nigger gasped.

But Hogg came back in again.

They struggled to get her in the back room. Once she kicked over a pile of gallon paint cans that rolled, clanking and thunking one another. "Jesus…!" the nigger said and danced out of the way of one, while the wop tripped on another; they dragged her back toward the door. She was still beating on the wop—got in three good ones to his head. Hogg went in last, hefting the chains with one hand, pulling up his pants with the other. Over their grunts, I heard her suddenly scream; then chains connected— hard. The scream stopped.

Denny pulled his fingers out of the girl's pussy—the elastic of her panties snapped her belly—and licked. "Get your legs apart. Aw, come on! How am I gonna fuck you like that? Hey—" That was to me. "Lick out that cunt, cocksucker." He reached to pull her panties down, but she rocked away from him and gave him a look that was like a roar without a voice. Then she put her thumbs in the band and pushed them down herself till they were a roll on her unequal thighs.

They were blue. The panties.

I kneeled over her, wedged my face against the soft brown hair—it was pressed very flat. Once she tried to push me away with one hand. Then I felt her shake and heard Denny grunt. I don't know where he hit her. But she stopped pushing. I got in with my tongue.

Her cunt was like a small hole full of cold snot. I grabbed her buttocks with one hand. The other I kept rubbing over the scar, and tried to keep going in, nipping and tonguing in the slippery seam, tasting pee. I nosed the nut of flesh, and every time I did, her thicker leg jerked.

Then Denny was over me, one hand on my shoulder, trying to butt me aside. I felt his dick against my ear, pushing between my jaw and her leg.

I got loose and Denny crawled over her and fingered it in. His pants were down around his ankles, and one sneaker was hidden in the loose cuff. While he humped her, I licked his asshole and, down at the back of his balls, even got the tip of my tongue and a finger in her pussy along with his dick.

It only took him about a minute to shoot.

"Okay. *You* fuck her!"

I got my pants down and crawled on. Denny was slipping them further down my thighs. I lay my head on her shoulder (and felt her twist her face away from mine) and after I got it in, I put both hands on the floor.

Denny's cock, still slippery from her juice, wedged between my buttocks, missed twice, then went straight. I gasped and brought my hands to her shoulders. She tried to get out from under us. Struggling, she began to grind her cunt on my dick. I thrust and grunted on her. A few times she pushed back, but it was just to get us off her. Denny bit my shoulder and began to pump hard. I mashed my lips on her salty collarbone while she tensed and twisted her belly. Her head rocked against mine.

It was hot between them.

I sweated.

She kept catching her breath and biting it off with little hisses. Her cunt sucked and strained around me. (Somebody dumped a bucket of coals behind my groin.) Blubbering in her neck, I shot. (The gush, very slowly, put them out.)

"Shit!" Denny yanked out. That stung like hell.

I wondered if she had come too, but I don't think so. Because I remember the last hiss was more like a cry, and her nails dug my shoulder, while a muscle in her leg quivered under mine. It probably just hurt.

Denny reached between my legs to dig my dick out of her pussy. I peeled off her. She glistened with sweat, chin, neck and tits. Most of it was mine, I think.

With his tongue out, Denny dropped his face in her box. I tried to push my head under his belly to eat my shit off his dick. I could smell it as I tried to wedge my head in there, and could feel his cock butting my forehead. (Her knee hit my ear.) He pushed up so I could grab it in my mouth. I got my head around; and, all slick with juice and shit, it went right in.

In the other room the nigger was laughing.

The girl was struggling again. Maybe I was hurting her knee. But Denny was holding her wrists and lapping out her box when—

"Now what the fuck—"

—the voice came from the front door.

"—do you little bastards think you're doing?"

I jerked my head from under Denny and looked up.

Denny jerked around too.

The man took his plaid shoulder off the door jamb, shifted his weight to his other hip; he was tall, bony, with spiky brown hair. He had very buck teeth, dark gaps between all of them, some of which was decay. Chin and cheek were all patchy stubble. "Jesus Christ, ain't you into some shit here." Tattooed panthers stalked in the hair down his forearms, tails still under his rolled sleeves. With a knobby hand, he plucked at the crotch of his jeans—all those long muscles rolled: it seemed one panther took another step. "Ain't this some shit, though?" He had big black workshoes on, laced high.

"Jimmy...!" The girl pushed herself up to sitting now, put one hand over her mouth, one over her cunt.

"Where's your momma gone to, left you in here fuckin' around with these two young som'bitches?"

Why Denny said anything, I don't know. But after a second he blurted: "They got her, in the back!"

Jimmy frowned. He took a breath; something chattered way back out of his nose and he spat it out on the floor. Drops hit his shoe and made little dark spots on their dust. He walked around the overturned wheelchair, stepped across the paint cans—he was sort of stoop-shouldered and bobbed his head a little each step, like he was sneaking—and stopped in the doorway.

Denny and I looked at one another.

The girl had her face forward in her hands and was taking deep breaths.

Jimmy stood at the door just looking. For a long time. "Oh shit..." he whispered at last. You could hear the grin. He turned back. With his teeth, that grin looked pretty weird. A bulge angled the thigh of his jeans. He moved his knobby fingers to it. His nails were long and dirty. "Now ain't *this* shit just somethin' else! You guys must be up from Mr. Jonas...?" He frowned. "Yeah...? Oh, shit..." He worked his thumb into the top of his fly and got the zipper down that way. (I could see the pull tag had come off.) He walked back toward us, a long, knock-kneed man, trying to go bowlegged.

He squatted down beside us and the girl.

"Oh, Jimmy..." I guess it was because at least she knew him, but she threw her arms around his shoulders and began to sob against his chest.

He had one hand around her back. With the other, he was fooling with his belt. "Aw, there now. I'm gonna take good care of you. Good care of you, pretty honey!" Over the top of her head he looked at me and Denny and winked.

The floorboards had left red lines slanting her back.

The hand Jimmy was pulling loose his belt-buckle with came out, went round her, and pointed to her buttocks—then he lost his balance a little and caught himself on the floor with his knuckles. But Denny, kneeling behind her, got the idea.

Denny wedged both hands under her ass and lifted.

She came up squealing, "Oh, Jimmy...!" Really. She tried to fight him then, but he had his arms around her tight. So she could just scratch and punch at his sides and throw her head around.

Denny still hadn't lost his hard. He tried to wedge it into her asshole. But he couldn't get it in, till Jimmy turned loose with one hand—she was twisting Jimmy's shirt now, but maybe she had some of Jimmy in it too, because he grunted once and yanked back—spit on his palm, then reached down to fist Denny's cock.

Denny slid in, clutched her back.

"*Ohhhhhh...!*" just became sobbing; she clutched Jimmy's plaid shoulders. Her fingers would open suddenly, quiver, then clutch again.

They wrestled her around. She was too scared to fight much now. While I was holding her, once my arm just brushed her face. She jerked her head away, and got one hand loose and grabbed her jaw. Maybe she'd bit the inside of *her* cheek.

When I do that, sometimes, it hurts so much I want to cry.

Denny, pumping in her, got her on her back on top of him. She tried to pull his fingers from her breast. Once I guess she figured she could get him by raising her head and banging it back on his face. The first time she glanced off the side of his jaw.

"*Gaaaaa...*" Denny grunted.

She raised her head again. But I hit her in the mouth, hard as I could. With the back of my hand. I didn't really connect, but my front knuckles stung. So I hit her back the other way. I could feel her goddamn cheekbone. I think I knocked her out for a couple of seconds.

Jimmy was kneeling back, his cock out. It was red as the inside of a broken brick. Veins snaked to the belled head. Stroking it with just the heel of his hand, he dropped his head into her wet, winecolored cunt. You could hear him, like a pig at trough.

He got her thin leg up over his shoulder; she tried to kick his back, but I guess she couldn't do too much with that one. Every once in a while he'd do something that made her try to clap her thighs together against his ears—I guess it was those teeth—but she couldn't, really.

I went around beside him, lay down, and shoved my head under Jimmy's belly—he was still on his knees. I got the head of his cock in my mouth; and a face full of his bobbing fist. When he realized what I was trying to do, he stopped jerking himself, put his hand behind my head and pushed me down on it. I clutched his bony hips and twisted my throat on him; a couple of times I had to come off and take my head out.

Once I saw him lift his face. Wet to the cheeks, he opened his mouth to her thin spout of pee. (I've seen a cat do that when it was scared to death by another one who'd got it on its back and was trying to kill it.) His tongue came from under his teeth to break her yellow stream. Then, a hand on each hip, he fell again to rooting.

Me too.

I felt him tensing up. Once he reached down to feel around my face and his hand was wet—I guess he'd been fingering in her. His cock gave a couple of spurts, then drooled out all its mucus.

Someone chuckled.

I finished swallowing and came up.

Hogg, Nigg, and Dago were standing around us and grinning—well, the wop was standing a little off, actually. Actually, *he* wasn't grinning at all.

Hogg, one hand hanging down at his thigh, made a little beckoning gesture with his dirty fingertips.

I crawled over beside his leg and leaned against it. He scratched the top of my head. I put one hand around back and inside his leg, raised my fingers until I felt the head of his cock hanging inside the moist cloth. He slipped his hand forward through my hair, down over my face; he put his third finger in my mouth. His hand was hot and rough on my jaw. I sucked and tongued on the bitten crown and felt his cock grow.

"Goddamn," Jimmy said, sitting back on his knees.

I could only see him out one eye; Hogg's hand was over the other.

"Mr. Jonas is really on the ball, hey?" Jimmy wiped his chin. "I been lookin' for an excuse to get my face in this pussy here for so long now...." He shook his head.

Denny rolled the girl off him. She thumped onto the floor and just lay there. Denny sat up and pulled his pants back up over his knees.

"It was really beautiful to see you guys giving it to that bitch back there. You know why I wanted to get at her?" Jimmy got to his feet. "You know why I wanted Mr. Jonas to get somebody to get that bitch back there? When we was doin' work for Mr. Jonas, she and some motherfuckin' boyfriend—"

"I don't know why you wanted to," Hogg said, "and I don't want to know."

"—her motherfuckin' *boy*friend, can you imagine," Jimmy said.

"Shut up, motherfucker."

Jimmy got sort of a funny look. "Well, I mean...well, she pulled some real shit, you know?"

"She right back there," the nigger said, "if'n you wanna work her over some more."

Jimmy turned, frustrated. "Hey, nigger, you—"

"Hey, nigger, what?" the wop asked. He had his knife out. Not open; just playin' with it. He still wasn't grinning.

Jimmy shifted his weight to the other hip. He looked a little funny; the funniness turned into a smile.

A moan came from the back.

Jimmy's lips opened even wider over the buck teeth. "Yeah, I wouldn't mind that at all. I really wouldn't. 'Cause that bitch…" He looked down at the girl, then up at Hogg. His face twisted, all the lines got deeper; he brought his hand up in front of his chest. "Well, I got my reasons!"

The nigger laughed. "Come on."

He and Jimmy went into the back.

The wop was standing near the girl's head. He'd put his knife away. Now he opened his jumpsuit all the way down to the crotch, took out his dick, and frowned at it. Denny came up to him, reached for the ring

"Get the fuck out of here!" The wop knocked Denny's hand away.

"You gonna fuck her?" Denny looked down at the girl.

Hogg pushed another finger in my mouth. "Go on, you dumb guinea. Let's see you fuck her."

"Aw shit," the wop said, still looking at his cock. He got his balls out too. "I ain't gonna do no more fuckin' for five *whole* minutes—" He looked sharply up—"if it's all right with you?"

Hogg laughed.

A wet spot grew, warm, in the cloth over the head of Hogg's dick. Beside my ear, I heard gas bubbling and growling out between his buttocks as the laughter made him loose.

The wop went back to examining himself.

"If you ain't gonna fuck her," Denny said, "I'm gonna go in the back and see what *they're* doing." He walked away between overturned paint cans and red and white bags of plaster.

I looked up at Hogg, because he'd taken his fingers out of my mouth. Watching the wop, Hogg pushed his dirty thumb in his left nostril, dug around, pulled out green and white snot, and stuck it in his own. "When she tripped you on the floor back there, that foot of hers stamped down on your nuts pretty hard, huh?" Hogg chuckled; he dug in his nose some more.

"Is it gonna *kill* you if I take a five-minute break, mother-fucker?" The wop cupped both hands around his genitals, bent his knees a little, screwed his face, and hissed. "You should've let me slice the bitch. Goddamn bitch ain't supposed to do a man like that."

Hogg chuckled again. "She's suppose to if she can."

"That ain't a fuckin' bitch in there," the wop said. "She must be a fuckin' lesbian or something. Bitch ain't suppose to do like that."

"She may be. She may not be." Hogg sucked, dug. "She's just a bitch and a half." Now he stuck his thumb up the other nostril. "You know what I'd do if I was a bitch?" He looked at his finger, but there wasn't enough on it, so he dug out some more. "I'd get me a gun, go out on the street, and—bip! bip! bip!—I'd put a bullet in everything I even *suspected* had a pecker swingin' between its legs. Anything else a bitch is gonna do is just crazy. Course, bitches is crazy. But the way you know it is just 'cause they don't do the one sane thing they could: Go out and start shootin'." Hogg gnawed on his thumbnail. He said around his knuckle: "Men hate bitches, man. *All* men hate *all* bitches."

The wop looked up from his sore joint and straightened his knees. "I don't hate my old lady."

"Men hate bitches the way white men hate niggers."

"You white," the wop said. "If you hate niggers, what you got that black son of a bitch workin' with you for?" He jerked his chin back at his shoulder, toward the rear door.

"Oh, sure," Hogg said. "Long as they do like we say they're suppose to do, everything always looks fine. But let one of them get even a little, teeny, weeny bit out of line, then you watch what happens—we wanna kill. We may *not* kill, but we *wanna* kill. Well, if I was a bitch and knew what I know 'cause I *ain't* one, I'd get out there and start killin' first. That bitch got out of line with Jimmy." Hogg shrugged. "That's why we're here," and dug in his nose again—he was trying for something real high this time.

The wop had gone back to checking his nuts.

I looked up at Hogg, his face all screwed up and turning his thumb.

He glanced down at me. "What *you* starin' at, nigger?"

I opened my mouth and rolled my tongue along my lower lip.

Hogg got it, pulled it loose—it flopped down the back of his thumb—and frowned at me.

Holding his leg, I stretched my head up far as I could and opened my mouth wider.

"Aw, come *on*, cocksucker—" He batted at me with his hand— the one he'd been picking his nose with. I grabbed it and pushed his thumb into my mouth, sucking snot: some of it was crusty and bitter, some was soft and salty. He tried to pull his hand away. "Come on, you little bastard…" I licked his salty fingers. "Aw, come on…" But Hogg was laughing. "You really are some kind of fuckin' little freak. Come on, cut it out. You're givin' me a hard-on." But he let me finish licking and sucking, running my tongue over his bitten nails, on the callused flesh around them, the thick cuticles behind them, the horny knuckles above. "Yeah," he said. I rubbed his leg. "I know the kind of cocksucker you are—hangin' round the fuckin' johns, suckin' any dick you can get your face around. I'm gonna wipe my ass all over you, boy, before we're finished. You know it, too." I could still smell his fart; I liked it. "I just been pissin' in you and comin' in you till now. But when I start to shit…you better watch it!" He laughed.

The wop was taking a piss against the counter.

And Hogg was curious about what was going on in the back room since Denny had gone in there after Jimmy and the nigger. "Come on…." He pushed my head.

So I started to crawl after him toward the door.

But Denny came out, shifting his shoulders around in his torn shirt. One pocket had got ripped down the side. Where the flap fell back, the cloth under it was a lot cleaner.

Hogg stopped. "You guys about finished, huh?"

Denny ran his fingers to the head of his cock and squeezed, making the piss-slit pucker, then back into the hair tufting out his fly and squeezed there so that his dick swung sideways; then to the head again; he grinned.

"Wooooooo-whee!" Jimmy came out, bent nearly double, then threw himself back, rubbing his stomach. "Ohh*hhh* shit!" He shook his head, grinning around his buck teeth. "Watchin' that nigger pumpin' in her like that, man, I had to stick it in her face! Couldn't hold it *back*! Couldn't hold it, even if I'd just shot already—" Jimmy snapped his fingers. "That bitch deserves every busted rib and bruise she got. And the nigger's still workin' on her— You fellas do this for a *livin'*?"

Hogg nodded.

"Yeah!" Jimmy shook his head. "You bustin' up mean bitches like this one, puttin' 'em in their place. I can see that!" There was a sound behind me. I glanced back. In a trickle across the floor, the wop's piss had snaked from the puddle beside the counter till it touched the girl's face. She hadn't moved. But she had begun to cry, as though all the rest had gone through her or she had fended it off, but that was too much,

Jimmy looked at her and frowned. "I guess you don't gotta be too rough with Judy, here. I mean, I always knew she was some good pussy, and I know what her momma thinks of her. And I know how her momma gonna feel about this, and that's why I said you could mess with her too. You can fuck on her, but...well, she ain't really done nothin', so I guess—" He scratched his head—"you don't got to hurt her too much. You know?"

The wop's jumpsuit looked like parentheses around the hair from neck to crotch. He was still fingering himself, but it was like he wasn't too sore anymore. He looked at the ring.

"If you're the boss, then what you say goes—you say leave her alone, and I'll leave her alone." The wop grinned at me. "Come and get it, cocksucker."

I crawled over, got my feet under me in a squat. The wop took hold of my head and slid his wet cock in. With the first push, he jetted a final thimbleful of piss. I held his hips to steady for the come.

"You motherfuckers really work that little cocksucker," I heard from Jimmy.

"Shit," from Hogg. "Less he got a dick in one end or the other, he ain't happy."

The wop began to grunt. I felt the ring in the back of my mouth and bit hard. His hands tightened.

"You know," Hogg said, with his tongue somewhere else than in the front of his mouth, "we got another stop to make tonight. Okay, you shot it a couple of times real quick; but maybe the next one'll take a little longer. You look like a guy who could get the hang of this business."

"Huh—? Aw...no," Jimmy said. "Naw, I mean... Well, you guys can have your fun. I ain't got nothin' against it. It's a job. You gettin' paid. But I couldn't get into nothin' like that with...I mean, with that bitch *there*, I got some good reasons to get it on with her. I mean, her and her boyfriend—"

"Okay," Hogg said. "I know. You just looked, for a while, like you was gettin' into it. And I was just askin'."

The wop finally spilled; and a lot.

"Well, we gotta get out of here," Hogg said. "Hey, you dumb dago, you finished with the cocksucker?"

"I guess I better get out of here too," Jimmy said. "I walked in here 'cause I saw your truck. Maybe you guys can run me down to the mill-road and I can walk on back into Ellenville from there in ten minutes, and nobody'll ever know I was here."

"May be a little crowded." Hogg said. "But we'll try."

The wop, still breathing hard, let go of my head. I came off him chewing rough. When I rang his bell, he caught his breath and grinned down at me.

The nigger had come out by now and was standing by Denny. They were both looking over at me like they wanted their turns. But you could tell Hogg was getting restless by the way his head set between his shoulders. By his hips, his hands were still working.

In a sort of monkey crouch, I came back over the floor to him, and he rubbed my head. "I guess we can—"

Then the girl suddenly reached across the floor—she had to stretch, too, and for a moment I didn't think she'd get it—for one of the pint tins. In a movement, she rolled to her back, sat up, and hurled it, hard, at Hogg's head.

Hogg barked out, pushed me aside, and whirled on her. (The can fell down and hit my shoulder, bounced on the back of my hand on the floor—I snatched it up—and rolled away; the fucker hurt!)

The girl's hand came back against her mouth, like now she thought maybe it hadn't been a good idea. But the expression between her spread fingers wasn't fear; it was all rage.

"Oh, hey..." Hogg said slowly. "Now that's *really* fine...." A funny grin replaced his grimace. He loped towards her.

She threw herself on the floor and rolled over on her belly.

Boot one side of her, bare foot the other, Hogg bent over, raised his hand higher than his shoulder, and brought it down hard against her head—she rocked ten inches to the side—then back. "That's—" He hit her again—"fine!" He paused for breath, brought his forearms back a moment against his knees. "Go on. Do something like that again." He took another big breath. "'Cause I was gonna get some more licks in on you before we pushed off out of here anyway. But it's more fun for me, see, if I can make like I'm punishin' you for somethin' you done that you shouldn't ought to. You see? So you go do something like that again... Go on!" Once more he hit her head.

Her fists were clutched up against her ears.

He was about to hit her again when the nigger lunged forward—for a moment it looked like he was going to push Hogg away, but he was just pulling himself around him. The nigger went down on his knees, spread wide by her head and, with horny heels up—the flesh on the soles of his feet was black, creased, and cracked—and toes turned under, grabbed up her head.

She screamed.

"Goddamn, nigger—" The wop laughed. "Nigger, get *off* the bitch! What are you tryin' to—?"

Though Hogg had gone back a step, he was still grinnin' pretty wide too.

"I gotta get me some of this stuff before I go," Nigg grunted. "I mean I ain't had none of—" He yanked her face against him; he'd got her up on her elbows—"this stuff here!" His knuckles clamped her cheeks so that her mouth opened and her scream lost voice and became all breath. He got her head in the crook of one arm, hunched down over her, got his cock out; then, with his knuckles back in her cheeks, pulled her face down on it while one of her hands slipped on the splintery floor and the other beat at his hips and thighs. His lips were pulled back. His scar was all twisted up in the creases of his face.

"God*damn*, nigger!" The wop began to really laugh.

Hogg, still half crouched over them, stood up and laughed too. "Oh, shit, look at that—come *on*, nigger! Get off the bitch! She's a fuckin' cripple, now—" Hogg reached out to pull the nigger off, but he was laughing too hard; his hand came back to his stomach. Guffawing, he shook his head, wiped at his nose, then shook his head again.

I looked at Jimmy. He had a funny smile that kept drifting into disbelief, then would jerk back to a grin.

Denny wasn't smiling. He was looking back and forth between Jimmy and the nigger workin' on the girl, sort of interested, sort of confused; and sort of strange.

Jimmy began to laugh out too.

"Come on," Hogg was saying, whenever he could get his voice back. "Come *on*, nigger! Get off her… Come on!"

"I'm comin'," the nigger said, on his knees, his hips working. "I'm…" and then, suddenly, he rocked forward, grunted, let go her head, and rocked back, staggering to his feet. "I just *came*…!" Grinning, he staggered back again, and nearly tripped on a paint can. Which just cracked Hogg, Jimmy and the wop all up.

The nigger pushed his glistening cock inside his pants.

The girl lay on her face, gagging and gasping and swallowing, trying to get back her breath.

"All right, now let's get *out* of here!" Hogg said. He was still grinning and rubbing his belly. I wonder if it was from laughter or because it still hurt from when the wheelchair handles had first hit him. "We got *other* things to do this evening!"

Flat on her stomach, the girl turned her face to us, all scrunched up like a white raisin. "You motherfuckers..." she whispered; the nigger must have hurt her throat, because she was all hoarse; one side of her chin was shiny with something clear and wet—"You motherfuckers are annoying as *hell*!" Which must have taken a lot to get out, because she gasped again, and turned her face almost onto the floor. Really, I don't think she was fifteen.

Hogg looked back. Bemused surprise filled his green eyes, hollowed his unshaven cheeks, creased his dirty, sunburned forehead behind the strands of greasy blond. He raised his hands—I thought he was going to go hit her again. "Sweetheart," he said, "*that's* why we're here." His hands dropped. "Hey, cocksucker, get up and come on. The rest of you bastards come on too."

The nigger hefted himself, stepped by the wheelchair. With one finger between the spokes, he gave the wheel a spin, and started for the door. You could hear the bearings hiss around the axle.

I stood up.

Jimmy came forward. He had to step over the girl's ankles.

Denny had started shucking again.

Digging a finger in his ear, the wop turned toward the door.

Then there was a crash from the back.

I looked around. So did Hogg.

There was another one—and the woman sort of fell into the light where you could see her, clutching the door edge. It looked like she was keeping herself from falling on the floor just by her fingertips dug in the wood. She swayed, and her head sagged forward, and her shirt was swinging down from one shoulder, and there was blood in her hair and blood smeared all over her side. She pulled in her breath, loud as a broken engine, and pulled up her head too—one eye was closed and the other one, with just a sliver of gray showing, blinked—and heaved forward. The way it dragged from her hip, I figure one leg was almost as useless as the girl's, and I thought she was going to crash flat, but she caught herself on the counter edge and pulled her other leg up under her. Her face was wrinkled as a rubber mask somebody's just grabbed from behind: all bloody, it came up to look at us. Then it swiveled, and looked down at the girl on the floor.

Then it came up again.

Then the one eye opened real wide. So did her mouth—round, like the eye of a camera, I was thinking—and kept opening, and...did not scream. She rasped, a hoarse, gravelly sound, that drew both shoulders in and pulled her head, still facing us, down between them.

"Jesus..." Jimmy whispered; I wondered what he saw here he hadn't seen in the back before.

The rasp came on and, in the middle, something fell out her mouth and broke on the floor: a bridge of about five teeth. I could see the little metal wires. In the fight they must have cut up her mouth pretty bad, because they were so bloody it took me three seconds to figure out what it was.

"...Christ," Jimmy finished, in a voice that made me look at him.

He had his fist all balled up and he looked scared as hell; then the scared suddenly got all nasty in his face: he started forward, like he was going to rush her and do her in right there.

Hogg's arm just came up, and Jimmy hit right into it when he started forward. "Hold on," Hogg said. "We done finished here. Come on, boy."

Jimmy was shaking and really looked funny.

Hogg just pulled him right around. "Come on."

The woman lurched another few feet, holding to the counter.

"Shit," the nigger said, turned, real cool and easy, opened the door and ambled out. Jimmy, with Hogg leading him—Jimmy trying to glance back and not quite doing it—went next.

"Come on," the wop said and gave me a shove on the shoulder. So me and Denny went next, with the wop behind us. He slammed the door.

Through it I could hear her dragging her foot the next couple of feet.

"Jesus Christ," Hogg said, with another bark of laughter, "you bastards must have just about croaked the old lady, it looks like."

"Well, she walkin'," the nigger said. Which cracked him up laughing. The wop started laughing pretty hard too.

Hogg was grinning.

And Jimmy just looked nervous.

"Naw," the nigger went on, recovering, "she ain't nowhere's near croaked. Too much fight. You seen her—"

We were halfway to the truck. But from inside the store, that rasping roar came again, rough and loud as if she was a foot away. Hogg cracked up this time. "Hey, nigger, you got the chains—"

"Aw, man, I left 'em in the *back!*"

"You a real fuck-up," Hogg said. He turned around, went back up the driveway, went in the door. It swung slowly closed. The blade of light narrowed across the gravel.

Thirty seconds later, Hogg came out, carrying them—he came in a sort of gingerly hurry.

"What'd they *do?*" the wop asked, grinning.

Hogg looked practically surprised. "Nothin'. They wasn't in too much *shape* to do nothin'."

"Well, *she* sure didn't look like she was," the nigger said, and started laughing all over. "You guys—" That was to Denny and me—"if you guys gonna be in this profession, you got to learn to be a little rougher."

Jimmy's lips were just about covering all his teeth when we reached the truck cab. And one hand was sort of rubbing up and down on one hip.

As he was climbing into the cab, the nigger looked back at Jimmy: "Don't worry. You seen her, she ain't dead."

"If she *was* dead," Jimmy said, "it wouldn't make me shed no tears." But it sounded a little funny. "Naw, after what that bitch done to—"

"Go on," Hogg said. "Get your ass up there, man. And shut your face."

"Yeah. Sure, yeah...." Jimmy climbed up right after me.

Hogg came around up the other side.

It was pretty crowded. I sat on the wop's lap. Denny sat on the nigger's, with Jimmy wedged down between. Hogg started the motor. We were pretty quiet. I guess because there was a stranger, we didn't fool around. I really wanted to bend over and stick my head under Hogg's elbow and take out his dick and suck it. But I didn't.

While I was wondering about everybody being so quiet, Jimmy said: "Well, I guess everybody's got their reasons for what they do." He had his hands on his thighs and was looking at his lap. He still sounded nervous. "Take you guys. Now you probably got your reasons for doin' a job like that... Yeah, how'd you get into something like this anyway?"

"What you wanna know for?" Hogg asked; but he was sort of grinning.

"Well," Jimmy said. "I just bet it would be a story."

"Shit..." Hogg's thigh tensed: the clutch disengaged. He palmed one of the gear shifts back. "Me, I ripped off my first piece of pussy when I was nine. And I *ripped* it, too." Hogg suddenly laughed, as some memory returned to surprise him. "My little sister, Betsy. Bitch bled like a throat-cut nanny goat. Hollered up shit. Daddy came in and swore he were gonna beat the two of us to death. But he got to laughin' over it—Daddy had a real sense of humor—and he beat us, too. But he'd hit us twice, then he'd get to laughin' so hard he'd have to go and sit down. He'd take a drink, then he'd come back and start beatin' all over again. I guess Momma was too drunk to care. Daddy used to beat up on her too; and she'd just cuss him out and then go get drunker. First piece of pussy I had to beat up on myself—" We turned a corner and the light put a bright edge up Hogg's profile—"was when I was fourteen. *Mmmmm*, that was sweet. A couple of years older'n me, and lived down the road. I'd follow her into the woods, then knock her around until she let me fuck her. Later, I used to get my brothers and we'd all go knock her around. She used to run when she seen us comin'.... But she never told." He laughed. "Didn't run too fast, neither."

"You grow up around here?" Jimmy asked. His hands had slipped down between his knees and were working a little—but too far forward for him to be doing anything.

Hogg glanced over. "Not too far away. But it was out in the real sticks, man. I came up in the middle of some real shit. You better believe it was shit. I was tellin' you about my daddy? He was a scrawny squirt. I guess he wasn't half as big as I am. He had big feet, big hands, a nothin' head under the dirtiest hair you ever saw; he was all mean and all scrawn, from his nose to his knees, and what wasn't scrawn was dick. I know that 'cause at least once a week, when he'd get drunk—which was not a rare occurrence—he'd try to fuck just about everyone of us each. There was more girls than boys. He said that made him happy, but I don't think he really cared. He'd be givin' it to the old lady. We'd all be peekin' in the door—reach in my pants, cocksucker, and play with that thing." I did. "Yeah, that's it. My old man, he was somethin' else. Kept the old bitch pregnant all the time, I remember. He'd drink up half the relief check and she'd drink up the other. Then they'd fuck and fight—bust up the whole damn shack—and fuck some more. Once, he told my older brother, Bo, he could stick it to the old lady if he wanted, 'cause he was tired of her and by this time Betsy was old enough to take a growed-up cock. He went right over to Betsy, too, and began to fool around with her, sticking his hand in her dress and his tongue in her mouth and putting her hand in his fly—Hey, lean down there and suck my balls, boy." I did. "Well, Bo, who was about seventeen at the time, he'd been sneakin' looks at Momma in the can and like that a long time anyway. He took him a big drink out the bottle and went over to Momma, just a grinnin'. Momma was in the big green chair, pretty drunk—but maybe she done told the old man she was after Bo anyway, 'cause she just lunge off across for his pants, and pullin' them open and gruntin' 'cause she couldn't get the rope he'd got on for a belt untied at first, and he's tuggin' at her dress till one of Momma's old tits flops out. I remember they got down on the floor and was just goin' at it, right there. And by this time, Daddy—he's got Betsy laid back on the dinner table."

"What was you doin'?" Jimmy asked.

Hogg adjusted his leg and, thrusting up into my mouth, shot. But he didn't even stop his story while I tongued around the briny mouthful. "Had my hand in my pocket through the hole, workin' somethin' furious. Now my kid brother, Piper, he was something like this cocksucker here. I mean he'd get after my cock every chance he got. And Bo's. And Daddy's too, when the old man'd let him. Mary Ellen and Sweet Jo both used to make him eat out their pussies, but I just don't think it was his natural taste, you know? But he'd do it—usually the old man would try to bust Piper's head open if he found him workin' on any of us—bust him harder for the girls than for the boys, which maybe swung him in our direction—but we sort of liked it, Mary Ellen, Bo, and me especially. So Piper'd just sneak around until he'd find some other place where we could get him off to. Maybe Piper give me my taste for gettin' it sucked on—he sure got us pretty well broke in. That night he saw me playin' with myself in my pants: well, Piper couldn't let that go by. He got me back in the corner, we got down on the floor together, he got his face between my legs and just went to town—got me three times without even takin' it out his mouth. I just curled up in the corner and went to sleep, finally, with his face wedged in there, waitin' for the next show. I woke up, I remember, because Daddy, in just his old t-shirt (I don't think I never seen him take it off; it was about as gray as Friday night's coffee on Monday morning. What finally got it was that the hole under the left arm got so big there was more hole than shirt and it just fell off. So next week he got another one and wore that into next winter and right through spring), was rollin' around in bed with both Emily *and* Sweet Jo by now, but he got up to piss. There was a beer bottle he'd opened and then forgot on the side of the sink, so he picked it up and started pourin' warm beer into his craw and at the same time loosed his water. Only he missed the sink and got it all over his foot, so he was steppin' around tryin' to hit the tin and wouldn't put the beer down for nothin' 'cause that was the way Daddy was. Piper, he seen that and he scooted over, got Dad's old pecker, still spurtin', and pushed it down into his face and began to work on it. Well, it must have felt pretty good to Daddy, 'cause he let him suck on it and suck some more *well* after he'd finished his damn beer. In about two minutes, I heard Daddy grunt. After he come I figured he might bust Piper in the jaw. But he just patted Piper's head, pulled out, and staggered back to bed. And Piper come back over to me, a little grinnin' cross-eyed motherfucker, with spunk still runnin' out the corner of his mouth. He didn't like to swallow real quick, but sort of keep it around and savor it for the taste. Pretty soon Daddy was humpin' and puffin' and gruntin' in Betsy again. Sweet Jo was snoring—she always did when she slept on her back, even when she was ten or eleven. And Piper, he just slipped his face back around my peter like he was goin' home."

"Sounds like some family," Jimmy said; he shook his head. "That sounds like you come from quite a family."

"Goddamn," Hogg said. He reached down to nub my neck with his blunt fingers. "Daddy raised a real passel of little bastards. After awhile, Betsy was the first of the girls to belly out—she weren't more'n thirteen. Momma was mad as a wet she-weasel over it. But Daddy was busy takin' bets on whether it was his, or Bo's, or mine, or even Piper's—came out a little black bastard, and Momma laughed her head off and said it served Daddy right. And he yelled and screamed and ranted and raved about what goddamn nigger had gotten after his own sweet Betsy... never did find out, though. Pigmeat—that's what they named the little black son of a bitch, though he ain't never been too fat—when all the rantin' and ravin' was over, turned out to be just about Daddy's favorite. Last time I went home, there was five—or was it six?—little milk chocolate bastards around; one out of Momma, too; and Pigmeat got one off his own momma, Betsy. The little nigger ain't fifteen yet. And Daddy's just as proud; he say him and Pigmeat is the only one's what are keepin' the family goin'. Pigmeat's boy—Mincemeat there, the one he got off of Becky—is just a little darker than the cocksucker here. But they look kinda alike. Maybe that's why I cotton to 'im."

Hogg's cock was going softer. It felt big and half limp and good. I swallowed the cum a little at a time.

"What does your daddy think about you?" Jimmy asked.

"Momma and Daddy both don't got too much use for me, I guess," Hogg said. "They think I'm a faggot." Hogg rubbed my neck and laughed. "Gettin' your peter sucked on, now and then, Daddy allows that's all right I guess. But he don't really approve of nothin' else except stickin' your dick in a pussy...or maybe an asshole if you been real lonesome awhile." I could feel Hogg shrug. "Maybe they're right.... Only thing, every time I see a woman, any woman just about, it don't seem to matter: I start to think about her with a bruise under her eye, or a bloody nose, or cryin', or even lookin' helpless and scared, an' my dick gets so hard it just about hurts. I mean, I'd keep a cocksucker around, but I wouldn't go looking for it. But a bitch, I mean: it gets me so hot I think I'm gonna lose my fuckin' head!"

"Yeah," I heard Jimmy say, like he understood that. "Yeah, I guess I can see that. Things are like that: some things make you hot, some things make you happy, some things make you mad. I mean, I'm just a normal guy. But what that bitch and her boyfriend done to me when I was—"

I felt Hogg's leg tense. The truck jarred, stopping.

Hogg said: "Getup, cocksucker."

I sat up.

Hogg pushed his wet meat back in his fly. "Time for you to get out," he said to Jimmy; I guess Hogg really had no intention to listen to *none* of Jimmy's story.

"We ain't at the mill-road yet..." Jimmy leaned forward, looking out the windshield.

"Come on," Hogg said. "Get on out. We're about a couple of hundred yards up. This way, nobody'll see you gettin' out of our truck."

"Oh," Jimmy said. "Yeah, sure. I guess that's a good idea." He was twisting around to get forward on the seat.

"Just a second," the nigger said. He opened the door beside him. "I'll get out and let you down."

Hogg opened his door too. "Yeah, I think I can use a little legstretchin' too." He swung out. "Come on down, cocksucker," he said to me. "Come on, move!" Which I did while the others got out the other side.

"I guess the turnoff's just down there?" Jimmy came around the front of the truck. The headlight splashed his plaid chest and stubbly chin as he passed through it.

"That's right," Hogg said. He was standing near the cab door, one hand up on the door frame, half leaning. Denny and the wop came around too. Standing on the other side, I could hear water against the wheel. The nigger was taking a leak.

The only light on Jimmy's face now was a crescent from the road lamp on the top of one of the telephone poles a few yards down. "Well, thanks, I guess...." He looked a little embarrassed, tried to swallow his teeth a little.

"You sure you don't want to come with us and try out on the next job we got?"

"Naw," Jimmy said. "Naw. I ain't into that. Thanks... Naw, I'm gonna be goin', I guess." He took a couple of steps backwards, bobbing his head, wiping his hands on his hips; then turned and started down the road.

"*Watch* it, cocksucker!" Hogg whispered suddenly; he leaned by me back into the open door, reached under the seat, and came out with a narrow-gauge shotgun.

I stepped back, surprised.

Hogg raised the gun. His body jerked with the *crack*!

Thirty feet away, Jimmy jerked too.

Denny—or the nigger—whistled.

"Come *on*!" Hogg whispered. He grinned at me. Then he sprinted forward. I followed.

Jimmy lay on his face, trying to push himself up, going: "*Uhhhhh... Uhhhh... Uhhhhh... Uhhhh....*" Blood wet the gravel on the road's shoulder, spread to the asphalt, and began running left and right like a T, until at one point it started to roll across the topping, so that it was spreading out now in three directions.

With his shoe under Jimmy's hip, Hogg rolled him onto his back.

Jimmy's hand clawed up gravel and flopped out.

"*Uhhhhh... Uhhhh....*"

Hogg pushed my shoulder. "Go on, cocksucker! Get that fuckin' dick out of his pants and start suckin'!" He had a funny grin in his voice.

I was scared. But I got down, my knees between Jimmy's, and pulled his fly open. There was blood on his pants; it had run down from his shirt. I took out Jimmy's limp cock; as soon as I put my mouth around it, I felt Hogg's bare foot on the back of my neck; he mashed my face against Jimmy's fly. The zipper on one side scratched my cheek. The limp cock folded inside my mouth.

I could hear Nigg and Dago and Denny coming up.

"Just keep on suckin', boy! Just keep on suckin' that dick! You really gonna like this, cocksucker..."

Jimmy's next "*Uhhhh...*" was muffled. His legs moved, suddenly, like he was struggling. I twisted, still under Hogg's foot, to see. Hogg was wedging the gun barrel into Jimmy's mouth. Jimmy was pushing at it with one hand and the "*Uhhhh...*" was a single sound now that kept going on.

I could feel Hogg laugh through his foot on my neck. Then: three sounds at once—*Crack*! and I nearly bit his cock off, and hurt my neck jerking against Hogg's heel; *splat*! and a sort of *spludge*! Jimmy shook once. My mouth filled with piss.

I didn't know it was going to happen, though; and I gagged. Piss came out my nose and stung.

"Drink that stuff up, boy. You don't get a chance to get it like that too often. Drink it, boy. Drink it." Hogg chuckled; I could feel it in his foot and hear it. "A motherfucker'll piss every time if you shoot 'im in the head."

I coughed, lost the spurting flesh.

"Come on, come on, cocksucker! Don't waste it! Get it back in there!" So I pushed it back in my mouth; I tried to drink, got a lot, but lost a lot too. The night gravel was chilly to kneel on. It dug into my knees.

"Jesus Christ..." Denny said. "I mean... Oh, *wow!*"

Hogg let his foot up a little off my neck. "You finished?"

I nodded. At which point the urine actually did run out. I coughed again and got my breath. I couldn't even see because my eyes had teared up so bad when I couldn't breathe. I blinked and sat back. My whole shirt was hot and wet. Piss was running down my chest and the inside of my left sleeve. I rubbed my knuckles across my eyes.

Jimmy's chin was there. And something that might have been an ear, or might have been something just torn off his jaw. Then there was a mess with some hair one side of it. I didn't see any teeth at all, bottom or top. Blood had spurted around five and six feet.

"Christ, Hogg!" Denny said. "I mean, god*damn*...!" Denny's cock was still out his fly. But only half hard. His shoulders were scrunched up, and he kept moving his hands around on his leg a little jerkily. "I mean, the way you just... I mean, like that with the bastard... What did you...?"

"Huh?" Hogg turned, sort of surprised.

"I mean," Denny said, "*why* did you...?"

"That fucker was crazy, man!" Hogg said; he dragged the gun butt back across the gravel, toward his shoe. His fingers worked on the barrel, which must still have been pretty warm. "You heard the way he was goin' on, about his *reasons?* The motherfucker was crazy as a fuckin' jaybird!"

"Yeah," Denny said. "Yeah, but...well, you didn't have to—"

"Aw, man!" Hogg lifted up his shotgun—I saw Denny jump a little. "The fucker was crazy, didn't you hear him—hey, you guys! Get him off the goddamn road, huh?"

The nigger hoisted up Jimmy's ankles. The wop grabbed one of his arms. Gravel fell from the loose fingers.

They dragged him toward the bushes beside the road.

He was awful loud going in.

"You gotta shoot a crazy motherfucker like that," Hogg explained. "Or he's just gonna get guilty and go to the police and the next you know, they got your description and the whole thing. I mean, I seen it happen. It happened to me more'n once."

"Well, suppose *she* went to the police," Denny said. One hand, moving on his hip, had snagged two fingers in his pocket. The other pulled at his baggy crotch. "I mean you didn't kill *her*...."

Hogg considered. "Well," he said—there was more leaf chatter off the road as Nigg and Dago decided to pull Jimmy another few feet—"all these bitches supposed to be in so much trouble already, they ain't gonna go anywhere near the police. Leastwise that's what Mr. Jonas told me, see? But, now, even if she was to say, 'Fuck it, I'm goin' anyway, I don't care,' and they was to come after us—well, if it was from her, somehow that would be okay. But if it was from that loose-assed cocksucker—bet he shit his jeans, too—" Hogg jerked his chin over where Nigg and Dago were tramping around off the highway—"that would just turn my stomach, somehow." Hogg shook his head, put the shotgun in his other hand, and put a hand on Denny's shoulder. "Come on, let's go back to the truck. Hey—!" he called to me. "Come on, cocksucker!"

I followed.

"Yeah, I guess so, Hogg…" Denny said. "But, well, I just—"

"Come on, Denny," Hogg said ahead of me—the seat of Denny's pants was awful baggy and, in the roadlight, Hogg looked like he'd been sitting in black grease—"Look." The gun butt swung back by Hogg's knee as they ambled on. "The fucker is up there *with* us, beatin' on the bitch, and fuckin' on the bitch, and just gettin' into the whole thing. Then he's gonna turn around and tell us he's got *reasons* for actin' like he's doin'? Now you do somethin' like that, man, 'cause you *want* to. 'Cause you get your fuckin' jollies that way. 'Cause that's the way you like it. But can you think of a goddamn *reason* for doin' something like that, the way we done them women?—of somethin' they could of possibly done to someone else to make that all right, like he's tryin' to tell us?"

After about four steps, where he got both hands in his pockets and then took both out again, Denny said, uncomfortably, "No… But you ain't gonna go back there and kill that Mr. Jonas fella, the one who's supposed to be payin' us."

"Now Mr. Jonas wants it done," Hogg said. "And I can think of reasons for wantin' to do what we been doin'. But Jimmy was up there doin' it *with* us. And that's somethin' else. Naw, the motherfucker was crazy. He's tellin' us about some reasons… I know them reasons, I seen'em before. And lemme tell you, in three days, them reasons weren't gonna be enough for him. And when he starts to feelin' guilty, we're the motherfuckers what gonna get in trouble. I seen it, Denny."

"I don't know." Denny didn't sound so upset now, but he sounded funny in another way. "Maybe you could've done somethin' else that would have been all right, though…"

"I gave him his chance," Hogg said. "I asked him, did he wanna come along and help us on another job. You heard me, I asked him three goddamn times. If he'd come along with us, I wouldn't of harmed a hair on the motherfucker's head. Wouldn't of liked him no more than I did, but I wouldn't've of shot him. 'Cause then he would of been doin' it 'cause he wanted to do it, and maybe it would have come to him that's why he was doin' the other one. But reasons, man? I ain't got time for shit like that. I've let a couple of motherfuckers like that go—more'n a goddamn couple. And I was always sorry. So I give 'em a chance. Give 'em two or three. But I'm not gonna put my ass out for some crazy motherfucker like that to string up—with his goddamn reasons!"

Denny grunted. "You didn't ask him three times. You only asked him twice."

"Only asked him twice?" Hogg looked at Denny and frowned. "Well, goddamn, ain't *that* somethin'! I usually ask the motherfuckers three times. I really do."

The nigger and the wop came up behind me, laughing about something that must have happened in the brush. Especially the nigger.

I glanced back at them.

"Hey, cocksucker," the wop said, and put his hand on my shoulder. "God*damn*...!" My shirt was soaked. "Goddamn, cocksucker..." He shoved me away, but he was still laughing. "You're a goddamn motherfuckin' mess!"

The wop's boots *crutched* the gravel siding. The nigger's bare feet *shushed* the small stones.

Ahead, Hogg, with one bare foot and one boot, went *shush, crutch, shush, crutch, shush, crutch,* up to the cab door. He climbed in behind Denny, then leaned out and called:

"Hey, you like that, cocksucker? You like that, drinkin' up that last good pint? How you like that, huh? Come on, you goddamn little wet-faced, two-bit skunk turd! Get your ass on up here—all of you. We got work to do!"

As the nigger and the wop stepped around me, I looked back down the road: under the roadlight, over gravel and asphalt, blood glistened like a sunburst.

"HERE YOU GO, BOY." HOGG PICKED ME UP OVER THE hedge and set me down beside him on dark grass.

Ahead, Denny leaned forward to see in the lighted window. His back was to us. In the faint light, his elbow swung.

There was a grunt; dead leaves crashed. Dago had vaulted over.

"God*damn*...!" Nigg whispered. "Will you keep it down, huh?"

The wop steadied himself on the nigger's shoulder. "Okay, okay.... Let's go, huh?"

"We're goin', don't worry," Hogg said.

We walked over the grass toward the house.

There were white curtains inside, but they weren't completely closed. Hogg and me fell a little behind the others. Once he reached down to pat my ass; and got two fingers in the tear Big Chico had put in my trousers. We stopped, just before the window; I pressed back. One finger slipped in to the knuckle. The other was prodding. "Goddamn..." Hogg whispered. But I couldn't tell if he was talking about my ass or what we were looking at.

A heavyish woman sat on the couch. She wore a house dress. Her hair was curly and brown and loose. She had on slippers and she was frowning at a paperback novel. One button had come loose on a small triangle of stomach skin I don't think anybody else in the room saw.

Her husband—I guess he was her husband—sat in a big, green chair by a fireplace which had been converted from gas a long time ago; the gas nozzles had been hammered down. He wore a sleeveless undershirt. His hair was gray; gray hair stuck out from the crease of his armpits. He was very red in the neck. But his arms were pale. He was looking at a newspaper folded small.

A redheaded kid, maybe my age, maybe a year older, sat crosslegged on the tan rug, at a chess board. (The janitor of the building where I used to live had taught me to play chess, which he said I was good at. Before he died.) We could hear the television set: it must have been right below the window—because we couldn't see it.

The kid moved a piece, but didn't take his hand off.

The woman uncrossed her legs.

"Yeah..." Hogg whispered. We were all crouching. Hogg's face moved next to mine. "That's gonna be some pussy." I felt him close to me, his stubble on my cheek. I smelled him, his sweat and his breath. He chuckled and wiggled his finger and I pushed back against it some more. His arm tightened across my back. "Man, Hogg's gonna have some fun gettin' his pecker into *that*!" The wop was in front of us now, Denny and the nigger behind. "I'm gonna stick it in that slop box and split her up. And split her down again." She put down her book, turned, and look directly at us. Everybody moved, just a little. Except Hogg, who went on:

"She lookin' at the evenin' news report now. Don't even see us out the window above the fuckin' TV screen. Don't even know in a few minutes I'm gonna have that big ol' pussy wrapped around my dick like greased velvet, like itchy meat, like hot oysters with teeth—"

It must have been Denny who flung the rock.

It scared me; but the wop was already hitting out the other big pieces with the flat of his hand. He vaulted up and through. Hogg pushed me up next—the television overturned, and I heard more crashing glass (the tube) and crackling. Then Hogg, the nigger, and Denny came in.

The woman stood up, but didn't know what to do next.

The man was about to stand. His eyes went back and forth between us and his wife.

Hogg's boot hit the chessboard; chess pieces rolled between pieces of glass. The kid, holding his hand over his face—I think he'd been cut—scooted backwards across the floor.

"What the—" The man lunged. I guess that's what he thought he was supposed to do.

Hogg hit him in the face.

The man staggered back.

Hogg followed and hit him again—in the stomach.

The man sat down in the easy chair, blinking and gasping.

Something hit Hogg's shoulder and spun off. It was the paperback book. The woman had thrown it hard as she could. Hogg just flinched his arm a little and didn't even look. She was looking, for something else to throw.

"...motherfucker," Hogg grunted. He locked both fists together and brought them up against the man's chin. The head jerked. Both the man's hands bounced on the chair arms. He slumped to the side; a dribble of blood came out his ear and wormed down his jaw across his neck. "Shit." Hogg grunted again. "Can't bust a son of a bitch like that hard enough the first time—" Fists still locked—there was blood on his knuckles—he jerked them up again.

The woman screamed—I turned—and swung the lamp down at the wop's head; she got his shoulder.

The bulb went out; the glass base shattered and the shade rolled on the floor. The wop put his hand up to his face, took his hand away from his cheek. He had blood on his hands too. He smiled. "You cut me, lady...." He licked his bloody palm. "You cut me, lady, and I'm gonna cut you now." His other hand brought the knife out of his pocket. "I'm gonna cut a hole in your belly and fuck it, lady. I'm gonna cut your leg up like a Virginia ham and fry the slices for lunch. I'm gonna hack out a piece of your gut, poke out the shit, and wear it for a ring...."

"...Jesus *Christ*," the woman whispered, and got back behind the sofa. "Oh, my God...." She was still looking.

Suddenly the wop stooped, lifted up the front edge of the couch: the back crashed into her stomach and knocked her against the wall. I didn't think it was that hard. But maybe she was just scared: "Ohhhhh*hhhhhh*hhhhhhh*hhhhhh*hhhhhh...." Her cry went up and down, weakly, and she tried to turn away and pull herself along the wall, palms flat against blue paint.

Hogg took a handful of the man's hair, held up the head, and punched the mouth so hard the head flew to the side. Things inside the mouth broke. "Shit, I *like* that...." He grinned, and picked up the lampcord that had the broken bulb and holder hanging from it. "Here, tie the bastard up, nigger."

The nigger took the man's limp arm and moved around the chair.

Hogg went to the end of the couch and pulled it, growling over the floor, away. The woman fell against him, flailing. He pushed her back. I guess he thought she was going to fall over the arm of the couch, but she didn't. He slapped her, and grinned. "You like that?" He slapped her again, with the other hand, too hard to be playful, but in a playful way. "*You* like that...?" He slapped her again.

"Stop it...!" she shrieked. "Oh, for God's sake, *stop*...!"

Hogg pulled apart his zipper. "Lady, we ain't even started."

She tried to lunge past him, but he caught her and pushed her back, really hard this time. Only he didn't let go of her dress.

She fell back on the couch, and three more buttons broke. She pulled at the cloth once to cover herself, realized she couldn't, and then just pulled her feet back on the couch, watching to see what he was going to do. As her feet went up over the edge, she lost one slipper.

Hogg bent his knees, hooking his thumb behind his dick. It came out, bobbing.

The expression that was on her face dropped off. She started to get another expression.

Hogg chuckled.

That one dropped off too.

Hogg stepped sideways in front of the couch.

"Jesus Christ...!" the wop said, and began to laugh, his fist crossed with the fist holding the knife, against his belly. "Look at that fuckin' bitch! She's so fuckin' scared, she's gonna shit."

"Suck it!" Hogg said.

She was still trying to pull her dress across her breast; it had a big red circle around the nipple that made me think of the inside of a can of tomato soup.

Hogg knocked her hand: she jerked it away much further than the knock would have. "Suck it, sweetheart."

She just blinked. Her hand closed on the edge of the couch cushion, and I thought, at first, she was going to try and throw it.

"Come on, sweetheart." Hogg bent and pushed her torn dress off both shoulders and stood back. "You better suck it, bitch. Or you gonna be sorry you didn't." He thrust his hips forward.

She blinked at the swinging head with its loose hood.

Then piss hit her cheek.

She jerked her face. He smacked her across the mouth. Which cut his stream. But there was still a wet blotch on her shoulder and one sleeve. Tears of piss crossed her cheek; and in the corner of her mouth was a single drop. She pressed her lips together, pulling them back in her mouth. The drop in the corner rolled to her chin.

Grinning, Hogg moved his legs apart a little and shifted his hips like he was gonna piss again.

She made a sound.

He said: "Suck it."

(The nigger put his hands on my shoulder behind me, to watch. I could feel the head of his dick high on one of my buttocks.)

"Open wide. Take it in."

She opened her mouth. A drop ran across her upper lip.

He leaned forward.

(The nigger's hands tightened on my shoulders.)

"Hey, cocksucker," Hogg said, "squeeze my nuts while this bitch is workin' on me. Come on, come on. Squeeze 'em. Hard, motherfucker." I pulled away from the nigger and came forward.

I reached, from the back, between Hogg's legs. The cloth was cold and still wet. I got his balls in my hand; closed my hand.

"Tighter, cocksucker!"

He was rocking backward and forward, so it was hard to help from pulling.

"Goddamn...!" the nigger whispered. Then, he pushed between me and Hogg, grabbing for her—

"Hey, nigger!" Hogg said.

—and yanked her dress the rest of the way down. Hogg pulled free; he was pissing again, his stream spurting around on the couch; but he was laughing.

I heard her dress go. I heard her underpants tear.

She tried to push the nigger away, gasping and crying out and biting off the gasps. She had a lot of black hair on her cunt. The nigger yanked up one leg; you could see the raw pussy hanging through like skirt steak. The wop grabbed her other leg—and even though he still had the knife, she struggled pretty hard. The nigger, his mouth wide, squatted, grabbed her over the other leg, and pushed his face into her. I saw the muscles tighten along the back of his jaw

She screamed, loud, and flung her head back and then down, and beat his head, clawed his ears, her head flopping, around, back, and forth, her mouth still wide and all the breath running out. She roared in more air, and screamed again, beating his back with her heel.

Hogg's dirty fist turned on the head of his dick. Urine welled over his knuckles and dripped. Some ran down his testicles, making a dark, shiny tongue along his right pants leg.

The nigger came up, grinning. And his cock head was out, like a plum pushing out from a black hose. He jammed it into her scream, between her beating hands.

Hogg lunged—I could see the nigger's teeth marks like three semicircles of red ants on the pale skin near her pussy hair—against her, was in her, one knee on the couch, one over the edge, his boot pulling up the rug, his bare foot wedged between cushions.

The wop, half crouched, grinned and took little breaths. His greasy thumb, across the knife hilt, creased on the blade so deep I waited for blood to roll down his finger.

The wop lowered the knife against his crotch—he glanced down—and, hooking his bell-ringer with the blade-point, moved his hard-on side to side with the knife, hilt wedged back in his groin.

On the couch, Hogg, the nigger, and the woman grunted.

There was grunting behind me, too. I turned.

The man, tied to the chair with the extension cord, was moving his head. But he wasn't really conscious.

Denny had the little redhead across his father's knees, pants down around his shins, fucking him. The kid was holding on best he could. He'd gripped his father's pants leg in his teeth, and grimaced every time Denny pushed. Spit darkened the cloth around his mouth the same way piss had darkened Hogg's pants: though not as big a stain.

I went over to watch as Denny finished. He stood up, panting.

The boy lay there. Once he tightened his buttocks, moaned, relaxed them again and felt his own ass.

"Come on," Denny said to me.

He ran his fist up his thick cock—it was still hard. There was a ring of wet brown around the rim of his thumb and forefinger when his fist came off. He began to suck it away, turning toward the living room door. He took his thumb out of his mouth. "Come on, I wanna find something…."

His hand, glistening with spit along the skin beside his thumb, went back to his cock, flexing absently. We went down the hall.

In the kitchen, the table was covered with dirty dishes. On a platter, grease had dried around what was left of the meat. A crack in the waxy gray went down to gravy.

Denny opened one drawer and looked at the silverware. "Hey… I used to know this guy once who would slam a drawer closed on his nuts. For the fun of it. He'd bet people he could do it; at parties." Denny opened another drawer, full of paper bags. "He'd do it three or four times, sometimes. Fuckin' hard, too." The drawer under it slid out: it had nails and string and a hammer and two screwdrivers and a spool of tape. Denny opened a fourth one, which had a carving set and a potato masher; but went back to the hardware drawer. The head of his cock was resting on the paint-chipped rim as he pawed inside. He took out a pliers and put it on the counter, brushed his hair off his forehead—his sleeve was torn at the arm-hole—and poked again: he took out a six-inch finishing nail, the kind with almost no head, turned from the drawer and closed it with his hip. His cock bounced in the air. "You're gonna have to help me do this, cocksucker." He slid one palm gingerly under his dick, and turned the nail between the nubby thumb and grimy forefinger of his other hand.

In the living room somebody shouted; which turned into a scream. Then Hogg and the wop laughed.

"Okay, now—" Denny pushed the nail point into his piss-hole. He slid it in maybe half an inch; then turned the nail to the side, hard, thrusting it into the wall of his urethra—"Jesus… Oh… shit…" And shoved it in *another* half inch. And kept pushing.

He was standing on one leg, the other bent like he couldn't put his weight on it.

And pushed. Blood ran down the nail, got on his fingers. "Shit…" he whispered. He leaned back against the closed drawers, gasping. "Come on, cocksucker. You push it…push it for me…till it comes on out, huh…?"

I took the nail in one hand and his cock in the other. It had gone half soft. He bobbed his chin down and back, and made a strangling sound. Then he opened his mouth and started panting. "Push it, cocksucker…!"

The nail was slippery with blood. It was like shoving it through a wet wad of cloth. He had one hand flat on his thigh. Once he kicked the counter with his sneaker heel. The foreskin was forward on his glans; first, the nail point raised a little dimple in it. "Go on, let's…let's see it come out…." The dimple turned into a tent. Blood ran down the shriveled scrotal sack between straw-colored hairs. "Come *on*…!" He took his cock himself now and wedged the nail point through the foreskin—the point came through shiny. But blood dribbled from under the loose lip. Denny pushed the nail further—his whole dick was pretty smeared with blood by now till almost two inches of metal were free. He took his stained fingers away. The other end of the nail angled out from his piss-slit, bunching the flesh back on one side. "Oh, shit…" He caught his breath. "Good, huh? Yeah…that feels real…real good… First time I ain't had a fuckin' hard-on in goddamn I don't know how…" He rubbed his thighs and looked at me. He still favored one leg. "I couldn't get rid of that fuckin' hard-on no way, cocksucker. I couldn't. Not any goddamn way…." He looked around the counter and picked up the pliers. "Now we gotta make it into a ring. Like Dago's. I think that ring he got in his dick is so fuckin' cool…."

The wop's ring was just a piece of brass wire; Denny had put in a whole damn nail.

"Come on, gimme a hand with the fucker...." He tried to twist the nail with the pliers, holding one side. But I guess it was a little hard for him. "Here, you take 'em. Come on, you do it." I did the best I could; it still didn't come out very round—more squarish. He made me twist the ends together. While I did it, every once and a while he'd wipe his hand hard against his mouth. I cut off the nail head and the nail point with the part of the pliers back in the jaw. When each piece flipped off, he grunted.

The twist hanging off the end was pretty vicious, and shone.

He had his back against the sink counter, holding the edge with both hands. "Okay...now you gotta turn it through. So the twisted part is inside my cock, see?" He sucked in his lower lip and bit, like he was contemplating if he really wanted me to go ahead. "So it'll look all one piece, see? Like Dago's." His hands were stained brown. There were brown stains around his mouth. Some of it was blood. "Well, go *on*, cocksucker! Turn it through. Go on..."

I started to turn the clumsy ring.

"Oh, yeah...! Oh, Jesus Christ, yeah...! That's...that's fuckin'...! Yeah..."

I had to squeeze the head of his dick to open the slit so I could get the twist inside. It tore the hole up some, going in, but he didn't do anything particular when I finally worked it inside. But after I'd worked it around another quarter of an inch, it got a lot tougher, and he began to bleed more.

Once he lifted his foot up off the ground, swallowing.

His eyes were closed.

"...a little more!"

I worked it around some more.

"...okay!" he whispered.

The blood down his pants leg was like the piss, like the spit. I sucked my fingers. The blood was saltier than piss. I liked it.

Denny still panted; but he had this funny grin. The nail looked pretty odd, stained and angled through the head of his cock on one side; you couldn't help wondering about how it was held together, even if you knew. After a while, Denny blinked: "Now I gotta see if I can walk...!" He took a breath, and two steps forward. "Christ!" He limped on the right leg a lot. He stood, hands cupped under his crotch. "Jesus, that feels like...like somethin' else, cocksucker!" He took another breath. "Come over here and let me lean on you, man. Come on." He put one hand on my shoulder and we walked around the littered kitchen table. "I'll be all right, yeah... Oh, *fuck*!" which made me think he was going to cry. Except he was grinning. And he'd pushed his works back inside his fly by the time we got to the end of the hall.

They were still on the couch. But another table was turned over and the rug was all wrinkled across the room, which made me guess they'd been off the couch and were back on it.

Dad was still tied up in the chair.

I didn't see the kid.

Somebody had stepped on one of the chess pieces—the wooden rook was split, and there was the pattern of a boot sole on the board.

Hogg pushed himself up off the woman. He was sweating, his shirt was open, his belt flapped down his sides, and his dick was hard and shiny. "Hey, wop!" He grinned. "You wanna fuck her, you goddamn dago?" He turned right, left, swinging his hammy arms. "You wanna fuck her, come on." In one fist, Hogg gripped the wop's knife. "Come on, wop!" Suddenly he jabbed the blade straight down.

She shrieked.

Blood fountained around Hogg's knuckles.

Hogg twisted, and ripped.

The blade came up out of her thigh, with stuff on it.

She was hollering and choking at the same time, and kicking and crying and screaming some more.

"Fuck on *that*!" Hogg shouted.

Hogg staggered back, and the wop was over her so fast I wasn't sure what he was doing.

"Get your dick in that, motherfucker! You been talkin' about it all night. Go on, stick your dick in that hole I cut; go on and fuck it." Hogg reeled away from the couch. His own face was pretty scratched up on one side. I guess he'd had a real workout.

The wop—there was a tear across the waist of his jumpsuit and I could see his scar in all that hair, moving between the edges—was *trying* to get it in. I couldn't tell if he'd done it; if not, he was rubbing himself off on her leg like a dog, one hand clutching at her tit while she screamed. Maybe he did it.

The nigger was back on her head. But with her screaming like that, he couldn't really do anything, except bust her one every once in awhile; when he did it, he laughed.

Hogg tossed the wop's knife onto the rug and turned, wiping bloody fingers on his crotch. "Hey, cocksucker, I got something for—" Then I guess he noticed Denny's bloody pants leg. He began to laugh. "Get on over here. What you two been doing?"

"Hey, Hogg…" Denny was still breathing hard; and he was still grinning. "You really been workin' out, huh?"

"What'd he do?" Hogg asked me as we came over. "Cut his nuts off? —Or did he make *you* do it?"

My hands had blood on them too.

With Denny leaning and limping, and once tripping on a fold of the rug (and gasping hard then), we came over.

"Lemme see." Hogg stuck his hand between Denny's legs.

Denny squeezed my shoulder so tight I winced and tried to pull away. The back of Denny's hand on my shoulder was wet. So was his neck; the side of it wrinkled where he dropped his chin to stare down. He panted like a puppy.

Hogg put his hand inside Denny's fly and lifted out his swollen, bloody genitals. "Jesus fucking Christ…." Suddenly Hogg closed his fist on them, so tight his own lips thinned. "You like that?"

Denny jerked one foot up off the floor again and staggered against me. He nodded his head, fast. His mouth was open. He nodded again.

"Jesus fuckin' Christ," Hogg repeated. And let go.

Denny put his foot on the ground, gingerly. And began to breathe: short gasps, with a long time between them.

Hogg turned to the couch. "Hey, you bastards!"

Blood stained the whole of one cushion and half another. Below that, it made an irregular semicircle down the front of the upholstery, almost two feet across. "Drop your loads or get your asses out of here."

Denny said: "It's all right, huh, Hogg? Hogg...? I mean, it's all right now, isn't it?" He pushed himself away from my shoulder. His other hand was down at his dick—which was sloping away from his pants again—not full hard yet, but about half. Denny dug out his bloody testicles. "It don't matter, now. Anything. Anything's all right. That's what you said. It's all right. It don't matter." He moved his fist down the shaft, opening his fingers suddenly just before the pierced head. And then again. He was staring around at the floor.

"Come on, cocksucker," Hogg said. He pulled me away from Denny into the circle of his arm. The wrinkled flank of his shirt was wet with sweat.

The wop stood up and said, "Where's my fuckin' switchblade?" He took a breath and wiped his forearm across his mouth. "Where's my knife?" He turned around. "Huh?"

The sides of his jumpsuit were black and glistening.

Crotch and belly, up to his chest and down to his balls, were matted dark crimson. "I see it." He walked over, bent down, and picked it up.

"Goddamn," the nigger said, backing from the couch and shoving his cock back in. "She's a fuckin' mess! Goddamn, Hogg, you made her one fuckin' mess."

She said:

"Unnnnnnnnnnn*nnnnnnnnnn*nnnnnnnnnnnn...*nnnnnnnnn*-nnnn... Ak-k-k...nnnnnn*nnnnn*nnnnnn... *Hhhhh*... Unnnnn... nnnnnnnnnn*nnnnnnnnnn*nnnnnnnnnn... K-k-k-k...nnnnnnnn-*nnnnnnnnnnnnnnn*nnnnnnnnnn...nnnnnnnn nnnnnnnn*nnnnnn*...

Ch-ch-ch...nnnnnnnnnnn*nnnnnnnn*nnnnnnnnnnnnnnn*nnnnnnnn*—
nnnnnnnnnnnnnnnnnn..." and on and on and on.

The wop looked at himself, took the head of his dick between thumb and forefinger and pinched down at the ring so
that when he pulled his pinching fingers away, brass showed in
the blood.

"Come on, come on," Hogg said. "Let's get out of here.
Where's the fuckin' kid...? Let's get out of here before he brings
somebody around or something."

The wop pressed his switchblade button, and the blade swung
back up into the handle.

Denny still stood in the middle of the rug, swaying.

The wop and the nigger hadn't noticed what he'd done.

They walked right past him.

"Shit," the wop said. "This is gonna be a sticky night."

"We done finished with work," the nigger said. "Ain't we,
Hogg? We don't got nothin' more to do? I'm fuckin' tired." He
rubbed the corner of his mouth with the scar.

"Get on outside into the truck," Hogg said. "You too, Denny.
Move your ass." He gave Denny a shove and the boy started
walking. He wasn't limping quite as bad.

"Hey, what the— Oh, shit, nigger! Will you look at—"

"Goddamn! What the fuck did he...?"

That was the nigger and the wop noticing.

Denny was climbing up into the cab, and the street lamp
had dropped its light through the window across his lap.

"It's all right," Denny said. "Everything's all right. It doesn't
matter. It doesn't matter, anything. Everything's all—"

"Hey—!" Hogg said loudly.

Denny shut up.

Sliding under the wheel, Hogg looked out his window.

"It's all..." Denny began again, then stopped.

Hogg opened his door, wide.

I looked across him.

The kid stood in front of the hedge. Joined hands dangled before his lap.

"Hey," Hogg said roughly. "What you starin' at?"

The light that came on in the cab when the door opened let you see how red his hair was. His belt was unbuckled; his shirt was out of his pants and only buttoned one place. His mouth was open and I saw his tongue-tip, shiny as a sardine head, moving.

Hogg laughed, suddenly.

The boy's hands closed on the lap of his pants.

"Boy," Hogg said, "you look like you want something."

The boy blinked.

Thrusting his big hand between his legs, Hogg turned around in the seat to face him. "Come on and get it, if you want it."

He opened his fly and pulled out his cock.

Behind me the wop laughed.

The boy let go his pants—which sagged down his belly—and walked hesitantly forward. Once he closed his mouth and swallowed.

Hogg slid his feet apart on the sill of the cab.

The boy stopped, looked around to see how to climb up.

Hogg rubbed himself. "Come on, boy. It's got your momma's pussy juice all over it; it's waitin' for you."

The boy reached up over Hogg's left knee, put his foot on the foot bar on the cab's side.

"The little bastards go crazy for it," Hogg said back over his shoulder. "All the fuckin' time, they want it."

With one hand, the boy held onto the door edge and, with his other over Hogg's leg, lowered his mouth toward the half-hard cock curving out from Hogg's fist.

"Suck it, son!" Hogg said: then, three seconds later, he kicked. Hard.

Enough to make Hogg sway way back against me; and the kid hurled backwards, maybe six feet through the air, and rolled, clutching his crotch, and just gagging.

Hogg laughed, turned back under the wheel and slammed the door.

"Oh, shit!" Nigg, grinning, tried to lean over Hogg to look out the window. "Oh, shit, look at the little bastard out there—"

"Come on, come on," Hogg said, "sit down, nigger."

Hogg started the truck.

"Goddamn," Nigg said, dropping his hand on Dago's shoulder and turning to him, "you see how that little cocksucker curled up when Hogg kicked him? Wow!"

"You think he wanted to bite your pecker off?" Dago asked. "For what we done to his Momma and Daddy?"

"Shit," Hogg said. "That little cocksucker wanted to suck some dick. Hey, boy, hunker down and get my load. Got another fuckin' one pushin' to get out. It's all filled and waitin' to spill."

I got down and pushed under Hogg's elbow. The fleshy pole slid into my mouth. Hogg wriggled around on the seat and farted twice, getting comfortable. I took it all the way down, working slowly.

The truck went around a corner; everyone sagged over.

"Oh, man," the nigger said. "I bet he was one surprised little bastard when he gone flying through the air like that!" He laughed again.

"I got me a good cocksucker," Hogg said and changed gears. "Don't need two of'em: I only got one dick." He took a breath. "And it sure had a workout tonight."

"Jesus," the nigger said, "I liked the way you did that, Hogg! I liked the way you did that, kickin' the cocksucker right *in* the balls!"

"It's all right," Denny said. "It's all right, man. Everything…it's all right."

My mouth was full of Hogg's dick. So I couldn't see what Denny was doing; but his voice sounded funny.

"Oh, man…" the nigger said, laughing again. It had really tickled him. "I really liked that. Wish I'd done it."

Hogg reached down and rubbed the back of my head, ran his hand down under my face to adjust his balls, then back up to rub.

"Goddamn," the wop said; I heard him stretching. "You know what would really make my night, is to watch you guys work out on my old lady. Nothin' rough; just nice and calm, nice and cool... Bet she's waitin' for me back at the bar now."

"Fuck off," Hogg said. "We ain't gonna turn your old lady out. At least not tonight. I'm fuckin' tired. The cocksucker here is gonna get my last load tonight."

"Shit." The wop turned around in his seat. "Then I'm gonna climb up in the sleeper and get me some shut-eye. Man, I had me a night."

The nigger chuckled.

"Wake me when we get someplace." I heard the curtain chatter on its runners.

"Watch it, *watch* it..." the nigger said.

"Okay," the wop said. "Sorry, Nigg.... Don't lemme sleep past my pay check." His voice was right above and behind me.

"Fuck..." Hogg muttered.

His leg tensed on the brake.

Everything sagged again.

"Get up, cocksucker." I got off him.

The sky showed the first blue dawn behind the trees as we rolled to the shoulder.

By the door, Denny, asleep, leaned against the window. Spikes of his hair tickled the dirty glass as Hogg slowed, and stopped— as Hogg stopped.

The nigger swung both fists apart and up, stretching his mouth wide and his head back. "...yeah—!" He dropped his ass back on the seat. "I'm tired as a motherfucker." He looked around. "If everybody's goin' to sleep, guess I'll take the fuckin' floor." He got down in front of the seat—I lifted my feet; Hogg didn't move his and stretched out, turning and turning to get comfortable.

Denny's grubby fingers, gnawed knuckles ridged brown with blood, lay in a loose claw on his groin. The top button of his pants had come open under the twine and one side of his fly had fallen back. Above the hair his skin was wrinkled where his leg bent. The nail twisted through his cock stuck from under his wrist. It was so puffy no veins showed. It was translucent as lard around the red, spongy outrage. Blood had clotted the piss-hole and the punctured foreskin.

The wop hadn't pulled the sleeper curtain. His back curved toward us above the seat. Each breath pulled the slash in his jumpsuit over the finger length of scar tissue, back and forth, back and forth, back and forth.

"Move over, cocksucker." Hogg stretched out, pushing himself up along the seat until his head wedged against Denny's hip. Denny moaned, in sleep. (The claw flexed. But he didn't wake.) "Come on, you better use me for a mattress. 'Cause if I get on top of *you*, you'll squash."

I was standing with my sneaker toes under the nigger's side and leaning on the seat back, the dashboard up against my ass. Hogg put his arm around me and pulled me down on him. I crawled around to get straight. Big, firm, his belly spread under mine. His thick arm, relaxing, spread on my back. I nosed the cloth, dry now, in his armpit. Dried sweat smelled half sour, half sweet. He shifted, tried to get his face under mine: his breath was like the inside of a full icebox that's had the plug pulled for a month and then you open the door. "Here…" He pushed a hand around. "Suck it." The bald end of his thumb jabbed my mouth. "And move your knee. I'm gonna jerk off." I moved my knee. One arm slid down my back. His thumb slid in my mouth.

I lay, hugged to the mound of him, sucking his thumb, both fists up by my shoulders. When I felt him start to shake to his own beating, I began to rub off on his belly. The head of my dick was pushing up over the edge of my pants, rubbing on the belly hair between his open shirt flaps. He moved his thumb in my mouth, hairy-jointed and tasting like salty shit; the bald crown butted my tongue's base.

"You know what I am?" he whispered in my ear, grinning. There was a scratch across his cheek; it looked like it was from the last paint tin the girl in the wheelchair had thrown; but I wasn't sure.

"I'm shit, cocksucker. Hogg is all shit, won't ever be nothin' but shit; I'm shit all through and proud to be shit. You like that, don't you, boy? You like this Hogg shit? Sure you do; you lick shit, you suck shit, you eat shit, Hogg shit…yeah," which was because I shot diagonally up his heaving belly. "You're gonna suck shit out of my mouth, my ass, take my shit and shove it up your own…." His thumb's ham wedged between my teeth. "Yeah…!" which was because he shot.

He took one thumb out my mouth and put the other, dripping with scum, in. Then he reached down—I turned and looked down his hairy belly at his groin beyond the bulge of his gut—and with his fingers pulled up the gray drops from his stomach fur, so that the little volcanoes, as his fingers left them, curled their heads down. He pushed his scummy nubs in my mouth, and I sucked them. Like that, he picked up globs of come, his and mine, and fed them to me.

Finally he rubbed the rest of it around on his hair—catching a drop of mine that rolled down his side with his thumb and eating that himself—then lay with his hand over his face, licking his fingers. His red tongue bulged and moved between his knuckles. Then he clapped his wet hand on my face (I looked out between his thickened, callused joints), took a very deep breath—my chest lifted. And when he let it out again, he was snoring.

HOGG CAME BACK DOWN THE GRAVEL.

The sun was very bright.

Behind him, Mr. Jonas scowled, then stepped inside and closed the door.

Hogg had the money in his hand, folded in a sheaf. "Here you go...." He slowed, counting.

The wop, leaning on the fender, stood up and stepped forward, uncrossing his arms. His jumpsuit (the blood had dried stiff and black) was zipped all the way up. His hair was awry. He squinted, not really awake. Two days unshaven, his face was puffy.

"Hey, there," the nigger said. "Hey, there, boy—" He was teasing Denny: he would bop around, making jive talk, hands swinging; when he'd pass Denny, he'd swing his hand against Denny's fly. "You like that? Hey, you like that...? Oh, man! How's that one feel?"

Denny would wince, stagger a little—only the wince would have a grin both sides of it. Denny's hands would jerk out from his sides, and he would turn, unsteadily, for the next blow.

"Hey," Hogg said to Denny, "how you feelin'?"

The nigger stopped jiving.

"It's all right." Denny pushed his hand across the front of his pants, caught his breath. "It's…yeah; all right. Only…I think the fucker's got infected, you know? I got a…fever, I think. But it's…all right…"

"You like it, huh?" The nigger grinned and reached around to slap Denny's pants.

Denny grunted, turned to him. "Yeah, I like it, you black… Go on, Nigg; yeah…"

Nigg swung again and bopped away, chuckling.

"Here's your money." Hogg held it out.

Denny, swaying, reached for it. "Hey, Dago?" His voice sounded dry. "Dago, when you…you got that ring you have, did your dick get infected?"

"God*damn*," the wop said. "Mine is just a piece of brass wire—this guy I know put it in for me; it was sterilized and…you know, everything. He soldered it closed and all, but he used anesthetic and…well, he'd done it for a lot of guys before and he knew what he was doin'…" Dago looked worried.

"I mean it's all right," Denny said. A bill fell from the clutch of bills he held. "It's all right." He shoved the rest into the shirt pocket that wasn't torn; he looked at the bill that had fallen to the gravel, but he didn't pick it up.

The wop did. "Here you go."

"Thanks…." Denny pushed the last bill in after the others. He looked pretty unsteady.

"Hey, boy…" the nigger said, and swung.

Denny winced again, with his funny smile.

"This is yours." Hogg handed the wop his money. "Cock-sucker, I'm gonna keep yours, 'cause a kid your age wouldn't know what to do with this kind of bread—" He didn't even look at me or grin when he said that. "Hey, nigger…?"

The nigger nodded, took his pay, and started to count. In the middle, he suddenly dropped his hand to get in a swing. "You like that…?"

Denny laughed, with short, shallow breaths.

Nigg's bare feet were wide on the gravel. He held the money up near his chin and finished counting. "I guess it's all—yeah—here." With two fingers, he jabbed the bills into his shirt. The money bulged bigger than a cigarette pack. Nigg swung his hand again: "Hey, how about that one…?"

Denny staggered.

"Goddamn, nigger," the wop said. "Let him alone, will you?"

"He likes it," the nigger said. "Look at the motherfucker grin. He likes it."

"I *know* he likes it," the wop said, pushing his hand back through his hair. "Now leave him alone."

"It's all right," Denny repeated. "Everything…it's all right."

"Get on up in the truck," Hogg said. "I'll run you guys back to the bar."

"Man," the nigger said, "now I can get drunk on my *own* bread. They may even be happy to see me!"

"Wonder if my old lady gonna be waitin'?" the wop said. He rubbed the blackened front of his jumpsuit, squeezed it; it squeezed more like stiff paper than cloth.

"Come on," Hogg said, "get on up. Stop standin' around playin' with yourselves," which nobody, not even Denny, was doing.

We climbed back in.

Hogg and the nigger were pretty cheerful.

Denny and the wop looked sort of down.

"Want us to fuck your old lady?" Hogg demanded as he drove. "It'll cost you twenty bucks apiece, Dago! That's goddamn fuckin' cut-rate. Just for you: How you like that?" He let go the wheel, reached over, and pushed the wop's shoulder.

The nigger laughed. "Twenty bucks?" the nigger demanded. "Maybe for you and me, and the cocksucker, twenty bucks. But you gotta pay Denny at *least* twenty-five, 'cause he gonna be sore as hell if he do any fuckin' at *all* today!" He really laughed at that one.

Denny sat by the door, pretty far forward on the seat, sort of carefully, and with a careful sort of smile.

"Fuck," the wop said, wedging over beside me. "That's what guys pay *me* to let them fuck *her*. I wouldn't pay you bastards shit!"

"Hey, Nigg," Hogg called, "reach over and make sure that door's closed. And don't catch ol' Denny's peter," which wasn't even out. But Hogg and the nigger laughed anyway. "Say, you know how I found that bar?" Hogg said, then he looked at me, because I guess he'd told the others before: "You know how I found that fuckin' bar? My brother, Piper, used to go there—I told you about Piper? Now Piper was a funny bastard, a real funny motherfucker. By the time he got there, everybody used to call him Dirty Pip. He would make these bets with the guys there that he'd eat any piece of crap they brought him, but only if they'd buy him a drink with it. Bastards would bring him dead rats and dog turds and beer cans full of piss and old newspapers they'd wiped their asses on and their old ladies' used tampax— and he'd sit there and eat it: one piece of shit after another. And get drunker'n hell. 'Cause he was what they used to call a 'geek' in the old carnival shows. And give you a blow job for another ten bucks—he worked in a couple of them things. I'd started goin' there to see how he was doin'; and, you know, since he was my brother, I'd be tellin' him about what I'd been doin', all the pussy I'd been tearin' up, and—it would never fail—that used to turn him on somethin' terrible, and he'd start beggin' to suck on my dick. Man, I used to call him all kinds of low shit, which just made him whine for it more, and lickin' around his mouth and slobberin', and the guys would stand around and laugh. And when I got drunk enough, I'd say, 'What the fuck…' and let him have it, right there at the fuckin' bar. Man, Piper could give some *fine* head. Then he'd get up off his knees, try to climb back on his bar stool, swearin' all along my dick was the dirtiest thing he ever did eat." Hogg laughed loudly, but came out of it with a frown. "Ain't seen too much of Pip, lately. Maybe, you know, he sucked on my dick once too often and it gave him permanent indigestion. Get your fuckin' hands off my pants, cocksucker! Give it a rest. I'll let you have it later."

In the rough cloth, though, I'd felt his dick stiffen.

As we pulled around a corner of the industrial section, Nigg leaned over Denny to look out the window. "Hey, looks like the old place got some visitors."

Through the windshield, I could see motorcycles, front wheels touching, handles overlapped, back wheels apart and leaning left, in two arcs along the curb, a dozen each, one inside the other. One tall seatback flew a red Nazi flag that looked like it had been used for a grease cloth. We slowed beside them: One had what I thought was a coon tail hanging from the high bar, but, when we pulled up and it went by the windowsill, I saw it was a dead cat, paws curled in, mouth and eyes dribbling, behind spinning galaxies of flies.

The sign over the door (we came up to the front entrance this time) had the letters P and E and A and a K that I could make out.

The cab door, opening, ticked the top of a chrome handlebar; we climbed down, edged between the bikes (the cat stunk!) to the sidewalk. The nigger pushed open the door.

I waited for Hogg, stepped in just after him—

A bottle shattered over the counter.

A girl screeched and ran at us.

The wop caught her, swung her, laughing: "Hey, honey, what's 'a matter?"

Waving the ragged neck above the bikers clustered at the bar, Ape Townley turned left, then right ("Hey, man, it's okay—" "Come on. Come on, man—!" "All right, man. Hey, all right—!"), and finally flung it against the plastic tabby stalking the sign above the mirror. PIEWACKET, it said, which must have been the bar's whole name.

Near us, the bartender scratched his gray crew cut and, shaking his head, watched beer dribble the mirror, like clear snakes belly to belly.

Ape, laughing, broke away from the Monk and nearly fell. Big Chico caught him by one arm. Rat was at his other side, his shrill laugh cutting through the general shouting. Now Hawk got up to the bar and malleted the counter with his fist: "*I* want a fucking beer, too." His other hand clawed between the denim flaps, blackrimmed nails and greasy knuckles furrowing dark belly hair, wet from the splash.

"I just gave him one," the bartender said. "And he went and broke it."

The other bikers laughed.

"You just gim*me* one!" Hawk shouted. "Gimme a fucking beer!"

"Yeah!" Ape called. "You heard him!" The Monk followed behind his gangling brother, grinning.

The bartender slid another bottle across.

Hawk grabbed it, raised it over his head.

"Hey, come *on*..." the bartender said, stepping back.

"Shit," Hawk said, "I think I'll *drink* this one." He lowered the bottle.

Everybody laughed.

"Hey, nigger," the wop was saying; the woman was tucked tight under his arm (she had very blonde hair, wire-framed glasses, and a very short, long-sleeved dress: purple. And purple nail polish), "I want you to meet my old lady!" The wop had his other hand on the nigger's shoulder.

"Are these your friends?" she asked. "Oh, wow!" which was slow and surprised. "Oh, wow, these are the friends you were telling me about...?"

Hawk, hair all down his forehead and leading with his bottle, grabbed the nigger's shoulder and swayed, grinning at the wop: "Am I your fuckin' friend? This is your old lady, huh? Well, I wanna be your fuckin' friend too!"

"Oh, wow," the blonde repeated. She looked very mysterious; or very stoned.

At the bar, the bartender slid three bottles across to Hogg, who came back with them; he gave one to Denny. "Here you go, boy. Why don't you go stand by the wall where you can lean on something." Hogg handed a bottle down to me.

It was Coca-Cola.

I held the cold glass and watched Hogg put the neck of the third bottle in his mouth, up-end it, then lift it from his lips so that you could see the beer waterfall. Some foamed over his cheek and dribbled down his jaw (the foam dying); but he kept swallowing; then he dropped the neck, closed his mouth around it, and swung the bottle down. Beer spurted as he took the neck out his mouth, and ran down his hand. But he grinned and wiped his face on his forearm.

I drank some Coca-Cola.

"Get on over there," Hogg told Denny. "'Cause somebody's gonna knock into you and you gonna pus up all over your pants."

"Yeah," Denny said. "Yeah, it's all right."

With his bottle down against his groin (maybe the cold glass made it feel better) Denny turned, unsteadily, and walked—unsteadily—away.

Hogg took another swallow, then put his hand on my shoulder. "Go over and watch out for him, cocksucker. Don't let him hurt himself again. Too much. You know?"

I followed Denny down the bar around carousing bikers. Ape had gotten two more beers and was looking around for somebody to give one to. Denny stopped by the bright jukebox and wedged himself beside it and the wall. The colored lights rioting in the plastic panels reflected in the sweating bottle he still held against his groin. Every once in awhile he lifted his right foot up, as though it was still hard to stand full on it. I stood next to him, but he didn't look at me.

So I drank some more Coke.

Finally I squatted, leaned my back on the wall, and looked over at Denny's bottle. He hadn't drunk any beer.

The wop's old lady squealed. (I looked over and saw that Denny wasn't looking.) With ten hands on her, and her own pressing the shoulders around her, she was being lifted up to the bar, where, looking bewildered, she got her footing, frowned down, and ran her hand through her pale hair; she kept looking around sharply and brushing at it, as if she was calculating hard but couldn't come up with the right sum.

"Okay! Okay, now," the wop hollered. "Who wants to gimme five bucks for a crack at my old lady, huh?"

"I'll give you six," I heard Hogg shout. But I think he was just trying to egg things on. It worked.

"I got ten right here—!"

"Don't give her to that motherfucker for ten, man!"

"Fifteen! Fifteen, right here!"

"For a piece like that—?"

"For a piece like that, twenty, goddamn it!"

Her calculations began to fall apart; she frowned, once tried to smile, but just looked stoned. And her hand had come down from her hair to the shoulder of her purple dress and rubbed there.

"You know what I think, Ray—?" That was Hogg again. Him and the bartender were ambling around the crowding bikers. "I think I ain't never met a normal, I mean *normal*, man who wasn't crazy! Loon crazy, take 'em off and put 'em away crazy, which is what they would do if there wasn't so many of them. Every normal man—I mean sexually normal man, now—I ever met figures the whole thing runs between two points: What he wants, and what he thinks should be. Every thought in his head is directed to fixing a rulestraight line between them, and he calls that line: What *Is*."

"Come on, now..." the bartender said.

"Naw, Ray. I mean it." Hogg swung his hands around, huge and grubby, to make his point. "I mean it, now: I think about things like that. And thinkin' about it, I think I got it figured out. That's what a normal man thinks is reality. On the other hand, every faggot or panty-sucker, or whip jockey, or SM freak, or baby-fucker, or even a motherfucker like me, we *know*—" and his hands came down like he was pushing something away: "We *know*, man, that there is what we want, there is what should be, and there is what is: and don't none of them got anything to do with each other unless—"

The bartender was shaking his head.

"—unless we make it," Hogg went on anyway. "And the only way you can get from one to the other is to know that, don't you see? Ray? And they don't know that, so that makes 'em crazy—"

"You talkin' about normal men," Ray said. "What about normal women, say?" He nodded toward the counter.

Somebody yelled:

"I'll give you thirty, man. Right now, thirty—"

And somebody else:

"Naw, man! Naw, the bitch ain't worth no thirty bucks—"

While somebody else:

"I'll give you thirty-five. Sure, I'll—"

Hogg hooked his thumb in his pocket. "Ain't no such thing. There can't be, Ray. Not in the place we live at. And if there was, that'd be the most abnormal thing there was."

"Look," Ray said, as he and Hogg passed. "I'm normal! And I ain't crazy. Now you, Hogg, you're funny but you're a nice guy. Still, you shouldn't be thinkin' things like that, 'cause it just ain't real."

Bikers shouted and jeered, hooted and cackled, pressed to the bar and pounded one another's shoulders. Guys were jumping up on the shoulders of guys in front to see.

From the crowd, Big Chico staggered out. Rat, behind him, both hands on Big Chico's arms, followed, laughing: "Oh, man!" Rat shouted. "You see how Ape was doin'? Fuckin' her right there on the goddamn counter!"

Big Chico's laugh got louder, cutting under Rat's shrill chitter. "Sure was fuckin' her right there! And Hawk, up by her head, just givin' it to her in the mouth like that!" Big Chico shook his head. Dark hair swung across his brass earring. "Ape and Hawk, they're too much—both at the same time, right on the goddamn counter!" (One of Rat's filthy-nailed claws fell off Big Chico's shoulder; Big Chico stopped to scrub at his mouth with the heel of a tattooed hand.) "*That's* gonna give the Monk somethin' to think about nights!" Chico guffawed again, lurched on, pulling from Rat's other hand, the tip of his boot-sheath swiping the floor.

Rat staggered after him.

They went in the same direction as Hogg and the bartender.

I watched them.

None of them had seen me.

I looked up at Denny.

He was finishing a swallow from his beer. As the neck came from his lips, I saw beer run down his chin. His mouth, wet, hung half open. Blue light slid on his overlapping teeth. He looked more stoned than the wop's old lady had. The cool bottle went back to his groin; he turned it a little, back and forth. Once, he caught his breath.

I moved my shoulders against the wall, pressed my lips together, ran my tongue-tip along the crease.

Denny moved his sneakers—or, rather, moved his feet around inside them. His right heel was off the ground.

I tried to figure out which side of the bottle his dick was hanging on. His pants were pretty baggy. The blood—in two long streaks and a short one—had dried black-brown.

I touched the cloth of his pants leg.

He didn't look.

I put my palm against the bony side of his near knee. His leg moved. He still didn't look. But his heel had gone down flat. I moved my hand up his thigh. He quivered, like a wire inside had been plucked. And raised his beer for another swallow. This time he put the bottle on top of the jukebox, and left his hand up there, sort of holding on.

I hooked one finger in the bottom of his fly—I felt his cockhead, hot and dry, against my fingertip; then the twisted nail.

He turned a little toward me, limping. His hand was still on the jukebox top. He was looking straight ahead. I opened one of the two buttons he had closed.

Somebody walked right past.

I opened the other button. I guess it was pretty dark. I took his cock in my hand: it was half again as thick as it had been, and leathery. Even though it hung straight down, it felt full. Gently as I could, I pulled it out his fly.

It looked funny.

The flesh clamped the nail so it couldn't move at all. Even in the shadow, with nothing but the jukebox's pastel lights, I could see it was the wrong color.

I stuck out my tongue, touched it against the place where flesh, warm, touched metal, also warm. Denny gasped and swayed. One hand swung out and flapped by his thigh. And the jukebox shook. I got my mouth real wet—spit ran down my chin—and slid it around his bloated flesh. He didn't make any other real response; just swayed a little, so it slipped in and out. The nail, in the back of my mouth, felt funny. Once I bit a little.

"Yeah..." he whispered and kept pulling and pushing.

I let it slip more. You couldn't tell if it was hard or soft because the skin had become so stiff. I mashed it between my teeth, this time when the head was up near the front of my mouth. From the corner of my eye I saw his hand jerk—and fall back.

Something squirted, out the piss-hole and out the side. It was a lot thicker than cum and tasted bad. I swallowed. And Denny kept swaying.

"Jesus Christ," a familiar voice said behind me. "Little cocksucker don't never stop!"

Somebody else laughed: that was Nigg. "Take it out and get it ready for 'im. Go ahead, I know the cocksucker...."

"Shit, nigger," the familiar voice said. "I been fuckin' that kid's face all summer. He used to be over in Pedro's cellar—"

"Well, *hey*, Hawk? *You* used to go over there, too?"

"Sure." The familiar voice was Hawk's. "Me and the boys used to be there practically every goddamn night."

"Well, Jesus Christ!" the nigger said. "Goddamn motherfucker. Jesus Christ...."

I was really getting into Denny's cock, even with the taste. I went down to the hilt, and came back with my teeth narrowed and nipping. Denny's hand came up, hesitant and jerky, rested on my head; every once in a while I could feel his thumb twitch in my hair.

"The kid gives a fuckin' good blowjob," Hawk said, "don't he?"

"It's..." Denny whispered above me in the oddest voice I'd ever heard, "it's all right."

The nigger chuckled, like he knew something.

I pushed my mouth into Denny's rough hair (his cock and the nail wedged way down); lots of it was stuck together, and some of what stuck it had dried sharp. I went back for the tip and got my tongue through the nail. I thought about the twist working inside the head, worrying the infected flesh, tearing the rigid sponge. I went down to the hilt again. And you could tell he was stiff now. My hands were on his thighs; one of his thighs kept shaking. And sometimes his arm.

Whenever I mashed him between my teeth, near the head, more of that stuff leaked.

"You wanna make some money, Hawk?" Nigg asked.

Hawk said: "Huh?"

On my head, Denny's fingers twitched; his leg shook under my hand. And Hawk and Nigg went on like he wasn't even there:

"Yeah," the nigger said. "Really. I know where we can get ourselves some bread, man. If you wanna go in on it with me, see?"

"How?" Hawk asked; it was the kind of question where the voice, disbelieving, goes down at the end, not up.

I kept on sucking Denny, like they weren't there.

"You know at the dock, man? Where all the niggers got the fishin' boats?"

"Over on Frontwater Pier—"

"Naw, man. Naw… I mean down at Crawhole, where the nigger boats are."

"You mean down on the *other* side of the spit—"

"Yeah! Yeah, that's it. I know some niggers down there, man, who'd love to fuck this little blond-headed cocksucker's face. Bet we could get forty-five, fifty dollars for him."

"Yeah? A white kid?" Then I heard Hawk frown. "He's white, ain't he?"

"Sure he is," the nigger said. "You got your bike; you could run us over there; and I could set up something. I'd split it with you, man. It would be real easy."

"You wanna sell the little cocksucker down on the nigger boats?"

"Sure," the nigger said. "Just take 'im down there, get our money, and leave 'im."

"Shit," Hawk said. "They'd really buy 'im?"

"Sure they would," the nigger said. "They like cocksuckers like him—white ones."

I sucked harder. Denny's hand slipped down to the side of my face. About every ten seconds he'd take a little gasp. For the rest he just held his breath. He'd begun to pump, too. I was beginning to dribble cum in my pants.

"I don't want Hogg to see us take 'im," the nigger went on. "He's taken a shine to the little bastard, and he might just not like us runnin' off with him right now, you know?"

"Hogg?" Hawk asked. "You mean that big motherfucker back there? Shit, I've gotten drunk with him a couple of times in here. He don't care about nothin'—all he'd want would be a cut of the damn money."

The nigger laughed. "*That's* for goddamn sure!"

"What about this guy here he's suckin' on?" Hawk asked.

"Shit," the nigger said. "Just look at'im. Denny's so out of it, he won't be able to remember nothin'...will you there, boy?"

"...all right," Denny said again, softly, and strangely.

"Jesus," Hawk said. "What's the matter with him?"

"He crazy," the nigger said. And chuckled.

I think Denny's "all right" had been to me. It felt like he was about to come.

"Well, let's go, then," Hawk said. "Come on and get him out of here."

Someone grabbed my shoulder, yanked.

I fell back against someone's knees

"Come on, cocksucker!"

—and tried to stand up against the hands pulling at my arms.

Denny said: "*Uhhhhhhh*...!" One hand flapped at, but didn't quite touch, his cock, bobbing and discolored and pierced with metal. His other hand still held the jukebox edge.

"Come on, come on!" Hawk hissed. As I got my feet under me, they pulled me back.

In jukebox light, Denny's face was streaked with red and blue tears. His eyes were unfocused and had that white stuff in the inner and outer corners. His hand jerked forward on the jukebox. The beer bottle overturned, fell to the floor.

Islands of foam slid across the boards.

"Come *on*...!" Hawk's boots and the nigger's bare feet splashed.

They dragged me through the back door. The sky opened up outside, darker blue than the jukebox light.

Through the open door, I heard Hogg shouting: "Hey, wop—! Come on and get another one of these cocksuckers up here for your bitch. Come on!" A lot of bikers were yelling and shouting over him.

But through the laughter, I heard: "Okay, okay..." That was the wop. "Which of you motherfuckers is gonna be next? Come on—look at her, she's crazy for it! She's so hot, she's gonna bust. Come on! She's my old lady, and I know how hot that pussy can get. Who's gonna be the one…yeah, you? Well, you're a lucky motherfucker! Let's see your money, boy!"

Hawk in front of me and the nigger behind, we pushed among the motorcycles.

I stopped at the one with the dead cat.

"Move!" The nigger pushed me from the back.

Hawk's was another one—the one with the flag.

Hawk's hands—red knuckles, black-lined cuticles, crescents of black at the front—seized the black rubber handles. The bike wobbled back on its kickstand, clunked and settled like a black-and-chrome lion.

"Can we all fit on there?" the nigger asked. Hawk smacked the seat with one hand and grinned back over his frayed denim shoulder—it had come apart since I'd seen him last at Pedro's, and he'd laced the frayed cloth up with rawhide, still bright orange and new-looking. "The cocksucker's just a little shit. Squeeze 'im in between us." Then he frowned. "You gonna have to watch out for your bare feet, nigger. You hit the muffler, and you gonna burn your damn toes off—"

"Man," the nigger said, "I rid the fuckers before—"

"I mean you should really have some boots. 'Cause even sneakers'll melt if they get down on the—"

"Come *on*, motherfucker!"

"Sure thing." Hawk swung his leg over the seat. "If you say so." He twisted the throttle. Muscle rolled under the dragon and the swastika.

"Get on," the nigger told me.

I did.

The nigger climbed on behind.

The nigger's belly slid against my back; my belly flattened against Hawk's denim. I put my arms around Hawk to hold on. One hand was on denim, the other on his hairy side. I could feel the skin stretch when he breathed.

The nigger put one hand around on Hawk's other side; with the other he held onto me, settling in behind.

At the bar door, Denny staggered out.

He looked like he was drunk. But I knew he hadn't drunk very much. His head moved around like a blind man's, sniffing for smoke. Only his eyes, a crazy, bright blue, were wide. His hands sort of jerked and fell and jerked again at his sides.

Hawk rose up in front of me, bounced down, stamping the kickstart—

I thought we were going to fall.

But the engine slugged over and roared.

"Y'on tight?" Hawk called.

"Move your damn ass!" the nigger said. "That crazy bastard's comin' out here. I don't want him seein' which way we go."

"Shit," Hawk drawled. We jerked forward. "That kid, the shape he's in, he couldn't see a fuckin' fist comin' at his goddamn jaw!" We leaned away to the left, spun around, *ka-klammed*! off the sidewalk, and came around again.

We practically ran over Denny's sneakers.

His fly was still open. His cock was still out. He was limping. And he didn't look like he saw us at all. His face was all wet. And when I looked back, he was staggering toward Hogg's truck. The last I saw, he'd gotten the door open, and it looked like he was trying to reach in and feel around for something under the seat.

I could still taste that funny stuff.

I wish I'd made him come.

With Denny it never did take that long.

"**S**HIT!" HAWK STOOD ON THE GRAVEL SHOULDER, scowling and knuckling his crotch with one thumb. "Goddamn motherfuckin' *shit*!"

"Cocksucker," the policeman said. He wasn't talking to me. It was halfway into evening. "Do I ever have *your* ass! Three people on the bike. None of you got helmets. The black boy's riding barefoot—I don't know, but that's *got* to be illegal. And then that—" With a sick grin he pointed to the limousine, on its roof, wheels to the sky and still turning. One headlight fanned off into the trees. "Do I *ever* have your ass, cocksucker!"

"He was the one who tried to run *me* off the road!" Hawk shook his head. He was really angry. But he was scared too. "The motherfucker came screaming up behind us—he jumped the damn divider, man—and went rollin' wheels over headlights down the goddamn highway! I mean, look at him...." Hawk gestured with a greasy fist.

The policeman was looking at Hawk. "You guys who like to run around wavin' your armpits in the batman costumes, or whatever you call that get-up: I get a kick when I get a chance to put one of you fuckers in your place." He gave the same sick grin to Hawk he had to the wreck. "I really do."

"Aw, fuck off!" Hawk said, and looked around.

The nigger was standing quiet by the back of the bike, his arms crossed, one foot across the other and digging at a twig or something with his toe, pretty much staring at the ground.

I walked away from the 'cycle toward the car.

"Hey…" the policeman said. "Where the fuck is the kid going?"

"Same place *I* was," Hawk said. "Same place *you* ought to be. Suppose somebody's left *alive* in that thing!"

"Hey, you!" the policeman hollered. "You can't go messin' with wrecks like that. Sometimes they explode! Or just catch fire or something. You can get hurt. Hey!"

Gas was running from under the hood. The green gum of oil snaked through, gleaming in the evening. It was a big, black limousine, with curtains in the back windows, like a hearse. It slanted off the road, head first, tilted down. The car radio was playing an old Mamas and Papas song, "This is Dedicated."

The driver looked like he'd been trying to climb out the window, but, held back by the seatbelt I guess, his head had been thrown out sideways though the glass. They couldn't see him from the road, but he was pretty cut up. His head and his shoulder and one arm, upside down, hung out.

His head moved. He'd been slashed across the eyes. Even so, I recognized him.

It was Mr. Jonas.

"Hey, kid!" the policeman yelled. "Get the fuck away from there! It might go up any minute!"

Inside the car, the music halted.

"This is Edward Sawyers, interrupting our program, to bring you a special bulletin. Minutes ago—not long ago, a bloody and terrifying massacre occurred at the Piewacket Bar and Grill in the Lower Frontwater area. The bartender, Raymond W. Arnold, identified the assailant as seventeen-year-old Dennis Harkner. Mr. Arnold made this statement from his stretcher while being carried to the ambulance: 'We all knew Denny. He used to come into the...' What? Excuse me? Oh...yes: Raymond W. Arnold was dead on arrival...huh?...dead on arrival at Frontwater District Memorial Hospital of shotgun wounds in the chest, neck, hip, and groin. I'm sorry; back to Mr. Arnold's statement, before...he died, I guess. Yes... 'We all knew Denny. He used to come into the bar all the time, for about the last three months, even though we knew he was under age. He didn't drink anything. He would just stand around and listen by the jukebox. Sometimes, maybe, somebody bought him a Coke. A few times I let him sweep up. But he was a nice boy and didn't drink anything at all.' According to the first reports here—and I have the second report to read you right afterwards—allegedly young Harkner left the bar shortly after quarter past five, removed a shotgun from the cab of a truck belonging to one Franklin Hargus and, returning to the bar, fired into a crowd at the counter, killing one Alvin Riley, a member of the Phantoms Motorcycle Club, which had stopped there for beer. Harkner fired again, fatally wounding one Jerome Townley, president of the club. When two other members tried to get the gun away from him, he managed to club George Townley, Jerome Townley's younger brother, to death. 'By this time,' states Alice Danatto, wife of Anthony Danatto, also in the bar at the time of the shootings, 'We were all just terrified. Oh, wow! And he wouldn't let us leave. We watched him, standing beside one of the guys he'd just shot, astraddle the one he'd just clubbed, reload and shoot Ray, point blank—that's the bartender, Ray.' Dennis Harkner, seventeen-years-old, has been identified as a runaway from Womack County in Southern Pennsylvania."

I heard a siren behind me on the road.

"Before Harkner left the Piewacket, he smeared in blood the words 'All Right' across the floor with the toe of his sneaker, while holding a gun on the rest of the terrified customers. And when he was gone, there were four corpses on the bloody floorboards, and three more people seriously injured—one of those, the bartender Raymond W. Arnold, as I said, has just died. Franklin Hargus, whose shotgun was used, drove the Danattos home. They were unhurt. But we have been unable to reach them for comment beyond Mrs. Danatto's first statement...."

"Come on, goddamn it!" the policeman shouted over.

Mr. Jonas raised his head, fell back. A piece of glass broke under his cheek.

I turned around and walked back toward the motorcycle.

A second police car was pulling up by the first.

The nigger half-sat against the back of the bike, arms folded across his unbuttoned shirt, one foot by the kickstand, one foot rubbing his ankle.

A breeze shook out Hawk's curly hair, tugged at the nigger's torn shirttails and frayed pants cuffs.

"Aw shit, man!" Hawk knuckled at his belly. His denim vest flapped. "I wasn't doin' nothin' to *him*! Look at the goddamn *tread* marks! The bastard jumped all the way across the fuckin' divider!"

"Hey, Bill?" Another policeman stuck his head out the second car window. "Come on, Bill. Whatcha doin'?"

"Monty?" The first policeman turned, his grin getting a little less funny. "I got one of these hotshot bikey cocksuckers. And I got his ass, man, too! Run a fuckin' limousine off the road and probably killed everybody in it—"

"Man, look!" Hawk protested. "I'm tellin' you, *he* run *me*—"

"You better let the ambulance mop it up, Bill," Monty said. "You an' me got to get to work...didn't you get the call? This is something big."

"What call?" Bill pushed up his visor with his forefinger. "What you talkin' about, Monty?"

"You sayin' you didn't get no call 'bout that Harkner shit?"

"What shit?"

"It just come down a few minutes ago. There's this fuckin' seventeen-year-old kid gone berserk, runnin' around murderin' people! Chief wants everyone from here to Fairhaven to get their navy-blue ass back down to Frontwater."

"Huh? Some kid—?"

"He shot up the Piewacket Bar in Lower Frontwater, got away from there—I don't remember *how* many people he killed. Then he got into a gas station about three blocks away—while the boys was all holdin' their peckers and lookin' stupid at the mess all over the barroom floor—and strangled some old guy who ran the place, with a jumper cable. Beat his wife to death with a big old pair of wire clippers, got another gun from the drawer—a pistol this time—walked out calm as you please and shot a guy and two girls in a car who was pulling up for gas: right through the damn windshield—bip, bip, bip: just like that!"

"And they ain't *caught* him?"

"No!" Monty exclaimed. "We can't fuck around with—"

Somebody turned on a vacuum cleaner with the hose right at my ear. At least that's what it sounded like.

Hawk hissed, "Jesus...!" and squinted.

Both cops turned.

The flames from that wrecked car must have spired thirty feet.

Inside the *Whoooooooosh*, things crackled, snapped, and popped.

Hawk took a step back and wiped his wrist across his mouth, making another smudge. His face had gone flickering bronze.

"You comin', Bill...?"

"Man, I gotta wait for the ambulance to see if anybody—"

"You must be kiddin'," Monty said. Still sitting in the car, he took off his cap, wiped his hair back, then put the cap on again. The light made his face very pink. He looked at the raging car. "Ain't nothin' you can do there. Send the clowns on their way and let's get goin' after the real action!"

"Oh, man," Bill said. "I really got this cocksucker's *ass*! Three on a bike, no helmets, runnin' the car there off the road—"

Wind snaked the flames toward us. Under the roaring there was a smell like when you leave bacon in a frying pan and it starts to burn.

"God*damn* it!" Hawk said. "I *didn't* run him off the road! He come bouncing over the damn divider and nearly run *us* down!"

"He says he didn't do it," Monty said. "Let 'em go. If you don't show up, the chief's gonna have *your* ass."

"Shit!" Bill said.

In a television show once, I saw a cop throw his cap on the ground and stamp it. That's what I thought Bill was going to do. But he didn't.

Bill jerked the door to his police car open and threw himself in, bumping ass over the seat. The door slammed. Monty's car had already started. Bill frowned out the window at us, at the flames. For a moment I thought he was going to get back out. Then his car started.

The nigger looked up with his tongue in his cheek, unfolded his arms, and began chuckling.

I looked from the receding police cars back to the fire.

Hawk ambled to the edge of the asphalt where the shoulder broke away to dirt and grass and, with a bowlegged slouch, pulled his zipper down, then paused with two fingers in his fly to look at the flaming wreck.

Another gust, and I could feel the heat.

Hawk's face twisted. Dirty fingers worked his crotch; he shook his head, pulled out his cock—I'd forgotten how far down it the hair grew. Piss splattered the ground.

Suddenly Hawk grimaced, bent his knees a little, and cut his stream. "Hey, cocksucker." Three drops fell, bright with firelight, one after another from the wrinkled collar. "Come over here." He squeezed so that the black creases in his red knuckle smoothed. He moved the club of his thumb, with its black-crested nail, over the hairy haft and thick veins worming to the bulge the glans made.

I came over.

"Take it, boy."

I squatted in front of him—his jeans button had pulled down below his buckle, so there was a little triangle of hairy skin right in front of my eye—and took his cock up to his fist.

"I know how you like it, cocksucker. There's the rest."

My mouth bloated with brine. I held onto his hips. He still didn't let go: he pushed his thumb in my mouth and began to fuck my face with his half hard dick (pissing like a trooper) and his thumb, at the same time. I swallowed as much as I could. I heard the nigger, after awhile, coming over:

"What the fuck you doin'?"

The gasoline and charred meat smell was awfully strong.

And Hawk's dick was full hard.

"Figured if we was gonna sell 'im," Hawk said, "I ought to check out the merchandise one last time." He swayed back, then pushed in, pulling my head forward so my forehead hit his buckle. "God*damn*, that pig made me mad!"

Three cars went by; I saw their headlights on Hawk's hip.

I think.

It was hard to tell their sound from the sound of the fire.

"Man," the nigger said. "You had him just about believing you. What got into you, anyway? Runnin' that bastard into the divider, then off the other side like that! I'm surprised he didn't just plow into you. He could've creamed us."

"I don't know," Hawk said. "Just felt like it. I guess he could've rammed us. But he was chickenshit, man. I mean he was just scared and runnin'. Them big guys is always scared and runnin'. Don't matter who they are. I didn't know he was gonna turn over like that, though—'specially when that goddamn pig was comin' by. Boy, that pig pissed me off!"

The nigger laughed again. "Shit, I gotta take a leak."

Urine was running down my chin, back down my neck and under my collar.

"Put it right here," Hawk said. "I wanna see the cocksucker's mouth get a little more—how you call it? Lubrication."

"Huh?" the nigger said.

"Piss on my fuckin' dick, nigger! Is that so goddamn strange?"

"It'll get your pants wet," the nigger said.

"Aw, man—"

"All right, all right," the nigger said.

"I been pissed on before," Hawk said. "You know how we initiate a guy in the Phantoms, man?—right here, that's it." His knuckle prodded my mouth, stretched with his cock and thumb. The nigger's knee was right next to my elbow.

It hit the side of my nose first, then my cheek.

"On his mouth, nigger—yeah! We get a guy in his new jeans and his new jacket, and first he's gotta take his bike apart, change the oil in the crank case, empty the front and back forks, do a complete overhaul so we know—"

"Man, why don't you fuck the kid's face and cut this—"

"You just keep pissin', nigger. And lemme do my thing?"

"Okay," the nigger said. "All right. See, I'm pissin'!"

I had to bend to the side to get a breath. Hawk pulled me back, and I was bubbling through my nose. His belt was wet. I could see flames glitter in the brass: "—a complete overhaul now, so we'll know he knows the bike. We got this big hanger out in Rye Hill that's the clubhouse. And after he gets his bike apart, all the pieces all out over the drop cloth—and them jeans don't look all that new no more—we all have a drink. And then the guy starts puttin' his chopper back together. Only then we make him take another drink, see. And maybe a couple more. And him still down there workin' and tryin' to get his pins in place and his gaskets aligned. Good guys'd get it about two-thirds done before they realized what was happening, you know? And then they'd look around the drop, man, and see about three hundred little screws and nuts and cover plates and body-rings and ratchet-pins; then they'd realize how drunk they was—'Get it fixed, motherfucker, before you pass out! And have another drink!' Then we'd really go to town. Oh man, watchin' a drunk, dirty biker tryin' to put in the last fifty nuts and bolts can about get me off without even touchin' myself, you know? Just standin' around and watchin'."

"Don't you do nothin' more'n that?" the nigger asked.

"Well, once they pass out," Hawk said, and slowed his stroke (I felt him soften a little), "then it's home-free for the shit freaks. Once he's lyin' down dead drunk—he may still be movin' some— the motherfuckers turn him into the club toilet bowl. You have to take a piss, you piss on 'im. And there's always some loose-assed motherfucker droppin' his pants and squattin' down to lay out that soft stuff you get when you been drinkin' hard. Drink too much, and you chuck your cookies on 'im. But that don't get to me none though they did it to me and I done it to them. We got it in the rules that they can't wash the clothes, never again: they just have to live it off, you know. And they don't take a shower till after the next meeting. But what gets me is those last screws and bolts, man, goin' *in*...." He stiffened all over again. "Goin' in, nigger—and wobblin'!" He shot. "Jesus...!"

The nigger had finished pissing anyway.

Hawk pulled out. "What's the matter? You think that's strange?" He pushed himself back into his wet jeans.

"Naw." The nigger shook himself, then put himself back inside his fly. "I can get off behind just about anything anybody else can. Come on, cocksucker. Get up."

The flames were half as high as before.

The nigger had been about a quarter hard when he put himself in. So I wasn't surprised when he said, while Hawk was getting on the bike: "Guess I could fuck 'im while we actually ridin'." He looked at me with his scarred grin. "You're a good fuck, ain't you, cocksucker. And he all wet down and ready. You still got that good juice in your mouth?"

I hadn't swallowed Hawk's cum; but I'd sloshed it back and forth between my teeth some, and it had foamed up a lot.

"You just slick up my pecker and sit right here—" He was digging in his fly again—"and I'll throw you a good one; just wedge on down between Hawk and me."

"Goddamn," Hawk said. "You really gonna tear his ass up now...well, the little freak'll probably dig it. Come on, let's get it on." The motor roared.

The nigger's black cock jutted in the evening air. I wedged my head between Hawk's back and the nigger's front as they sat on the roaring bike and drooled Hawk's cum over it. Then I pulled the seam in the seat of my pants open. Hawk leaned forward; the nigger leaned back. Dots of firelight circled in the studs on Hawk's belt; flakes of it slid down the dark veins on Nigg's glistening shaft. A couple more cars poured their headlights around us as they passed. I climbed on; his cock slipped in me, catching once and stinging, then going all the way. Hawk sat up, the nigger sat forward, sandwiching me. I lay my cheek against Hawk's denim-covered shoulder.

"Man, that's *fine!*" the nigger said. His chest expanded against my back.

We took off.

"...paint-rag sopped in blood, wrote across the back wall of the Martinez's grocery store, 'All Right' in eighteen-inch letters. Of the owner and his wife and the five customers in the store at the time, only Carmen Martinez remains alive. She is on the critical list at Frontwater District Memorial with bullet wounds in the chest and stomach. 'What I want to know,' said Police Inspector Haley to reporters, 'is how he got from one side of town to the other so fast.' Your commentator, Edward Sawyers, would like to suggest the 13-A bus, with a transfer at Twenty-third."

The music started again: "A Very Special Love." But nobody was listening except me.

The radio was on the windowsill.

Behind it, in the light from the boardwalk lamp, the dim dock moved up and down.

Outside, the water slapped and splashed as another tug puttered off through the night. Our rocking stilled.

Inside, an iron skillet hung on a nail above the galley's aluminum sink.

Nigg slapped his hand down on the plank table like a charred chuck steak. "Hey, Big Sambo! What do you say?"

Big Sambo just grunted. "Gotta get this fucker workin'." He meant the boat. "If she don't bring no money in, she just pulls it out. And I keep too much time on my hands, nothin' to do but fuck around." The other tug was too far to hear now. "Course—" He grinned at Nigg and Hawk—"if the fuckin's good enough, don't see why I should rush to be over with it." He reared back in his chair. His heavy boots squeaked on the galley floorboards. "He cute. Maybe give Honey-Pie a rest. But I don't want him if he don't eat ass."

Hawk held his coffee cup under his chin and leaned against the sink.

A little barefoot nigger girl stood behind Big Sambo's chair, in a dirty green dress. She was maybe twelve.

"Eat ass?" Nigg said. He started bopping around the table again, gesturing and pointing, mostly at me. "Why, eatin' ass—? Nigger, that little blond cocksucker'll eat *any*thing. He'll suck it. He'll sit on it. He'll wriggle like a stuck puppy under it. He'll make you happy, nigger! He'll make you glad to be alive!"

Big Sambo put his black arm—the sleeves were torn off his blue workshirt like the sleeves off Hawk's denim jacket—around the little girl's waist and pulled her up to him. "Well, Honey-Pie here is probably about gettin' tired of her pappy's big ol' pecker shoved up her pussy all the time." His hand went under her dress. His knuckles made humps in the cloth at her lap. Honey-Pie spread her brown feet a little apart and looked serious. A drop of something rolled down her leg; it stopped at her knee.

Hawk sipped his coffee.

"He cute," Big Sambo repeated. "Ain't he, sweetheart?" He glanced at Honey-Pie.

She just blinked.

"That your little girl?" Hawk asked.

"Sure is." Big Sambo thumped one boot up on the table top and reared back again. "I run her momma out of here about eight or nine years back when I couldn't put up with the old lady's complainin' at me all the time about me wantin' to fool around with the little girl here." Big Sambo grinned. "Been pretty happy since then, ain't we, baby? Prettiest little pussy you ever seen, huh?" His knuckles kept working.

Honey-Pie blinked, scratched her ear.

"What about the boy?" Nigg said.

"I sure would enjoy him, now—if he eat ass. But I don't like to force a kid."

"Nigger!—" Nigg made a real funny face—"you just *pull* down your pants, bend over, and spread it open…!"

They both fell to laughing over that.

"Hey," Big Sambo called to Hawk. "You like eatin' pussy? They always sayin' how you biker-boys like eatin' pussy." He pulled his hand from under Honey-Pie's dress. Three of his fingers were wet. "This here—" He ran the middle one into his mouth and pulled it out real slow, turning out his big lips even further—"is some of the best eatin' nigger pussy you'll ever get your face in, boy."

Hawk grinned into his coffee cup and reached down to pull at his pants.

"Honey-Pie," Big Sambo said, letting the front chair legs hit the floor, "you just go on over there and give that white boy a lick. So he'll know him what a really good pussy tastes like. Just a lick, now…"

Holding one thumb real tight in her fist (her other hand scratched the place where the neck of her dress hung down about her chest; even though she looked about a year older than me, she didn't have no more tits on her than I did), she walked around the table and up to Hawk. Her hair was short, but stuck out in little tufts like somebody had been plucking at it. I thought she was pretty.

Hawk gulped his coffee and put the cup down on the metal sink counter. A fork rattled.

Honey-Pie put her fists on her lap—I couldn't see her expression—and pulled her dress up a couple of inches.

"Go on, go on," Big Sambo said. "Get her up there on the sink edge where you can get at it, boy. 'Less you wanna kneel down on the floor—I like it that way too, sometimes."

Hawk glanced at me, then at Honey-Pie. Then he grinned again, put his hands under her arms, and lifted her up to the edge of the sink. Still with her serious expression, she wriggled herself back and spread her brown knees.

"Well, go on, lift her dress up," Big Sambo said.

Hawk did. She didn't have no underpants on. She still looked serious.

"I guess—" Big Sambo took his boot down off the table, scraped his chair back, and spread his own legs—"I'll give the little bastard a chance." He dug his thumb into his fly and hooked loose one brass button. I figured he must have sewed them on himself because they were brass military buttons, not the regular flat, blue jeans kind. "Course, what I really like a little bastard like that for is to lick out my asshole when I'm bunchin' and hunchin' up on some bitch. You know, that and lick my balls."

"Well, he sure like to do that." Nigg, looking at Hawk and Honey-Pie, pushed his tongue-tip out the corner of his mouth, like rare meat squeezing through a crack in a charbroiled burger. He sat on the table corner, banging his bare heel on the table leg. "Yeah, sure. Just try him out."

Big Sambo's boots moved on the floor. He lifted his ass off the chair, hefted his crotch, settled, and pulled loose another brass button. The fork of his pants legs was threadbare. I could see part of an oversized black testicle pushing through. "I mean," Big Sambo explained, "I like to get my dick sucked as well as the next nigger. But I really like it when a nice little pink tongue is pushin' around in my ass."

Hawk had hunkered down between Honey-Pie's knees. Now he lifted her leg back over his shoulder. Honey-Pie was holding onto his hair with one hand and trying to pick something out between two teeth with the thumbnail of the other. She swayed as Hawk's head moved, and looked curiously down at the top of it—like she saw a flea or something crawling in his hair.

Which, with Hawk, was possible.

Big Sambo motioned Nigg to move back on the table so he could see.

Honey-Pie took her thumb out of her mouth, moved something around inside with her tongue, then went back to picking.

"Pretty good, ain't it?" Big Sambo said. Inside his pants, his hand made a fist. "That's real good stuff."

"Try him," Nigg insisted. "Go on, Sambo. Try the cocksucker out, now."

Sambo's fist, with his dick in it, came out his fly. "Come on over here, boy."

I had to squeeze my ass between the table and his knee. Nigg patted my butt and grinned at me as I slipped by.

Sambo moved his boots a little wider. I squatted. The head of Sambo's cock was brown. The foreskin was black as crepe. I could smell recent fucking. I put his dick in my mouth: it was probably Honey-Pie. When I dug in to pull out his balls, he grunted and moved his knees apart even wider. I guess he liked it. I got one hand inside his fly and scratched the tight hair above his cock. Niggers like that when you suck them. "Now, hey..." Sambo said. Then, a little louder: "Move around a little, so I can see you eat on that sweet chocolate, white boy. Ain't that taste good?"

"Don't he suck nice?" I heard Nigg say.

Big Sambo chuckled. "Which one? Both these white boys suck pretty good it looks like to me. How you say, Honey-Pie?" Big Sambo laughed.

Honey-Pie didn't say anything.

"Lick up those pan-fried drippin's. Here, don't let her leg go down. I wanna watch—that's it. That's it, hey. That's it, lick it real nice... nice...."

Without even moving much, or touching me, Big Sambo shot. "About twenty dollars you want for him?" The heel of his hand against my forehead, he pushed me off. "That's about what he looks worth to me." His cock, lowering in little jerks that must have been his heart beating, sagged, sagged again. "Course, I still don't know if he'll eat ass." At about half-hard it stayed and just bobbed. "Like I say, that's all I'm really interested in him for—Hey, boy." Big Sambo gestured over my head at Hawk. "Get your face out of that pussy. I done shot my wad, and I can't have you gettin' the little bitch all worked up again."

On my knees, I glanced back across the tabletop.

Hawk said, "*Huh...?*" and stood up. He looked confused, and when he turned around, the lower part of his face was all wet and you could see his cock slanting across under his jeans. "What—?"

"Come on," Nigg said. "Sambo'll give us twenty dollars for the cocksucker here."

"Shit." Hawk pushed at his cock through his pants, and bent one knee to get himself more comfortable. "*That* ain't very much."

Big Sambo grinned. "I'd give you twenty-five if he was pure white. But you can see there, he got a touch of the tar-brush. Right around his nose."

"Aw, nigger, what you talkin' about?" But Nigg was grinning some too, looking funny with that scar. "He been suckin' so much dick, he just got it a little squashed there, hittin' it up against some fella's crotch bone."

"Naw," Big Sambo said. "I got me a first cousin, look as just as white as he do—if you can believe that, black as my goddamn ass is. Bet he don't got no moons on his fingernails, either, 'ceptin' on his thumb. That be another way you can tell."

Honey-Pie put her knees together and pushed her dress down. She looked at her daddy and blinked. She didn't look too worked up to me.

"Hey—" Hawk looked back at Nigg—"I thought you said we could get fifty or sixty dollars for him..."

Big Sambo stood up, pushed the chair back, and reached in his pocket. "Lemme see, here." Digging around in it made his cock, still hanging out his fly, wobble. "Now what do I got here to give you...?" He came out with two crumpled bills. "I'll give you this here fifteen for him."

"Hey, man." Nigg kicked the table leg again. "You just said twenty-five a minute ago."

"Well, I only *got* fifteen," Big Sambo said. "Why am I gonna pay twenty dollars for some nigger kid?" He rubbed the two bills together between thick thumb and stocky forefinger. "See here, one of these is a *five*. I *thought* I had two tens—but I can't very well give you what I don't got, now, can I?"

"Shit," Hawk said. "I thought you said we could get fifty. Fifteen bucks? That ain't worth the fuckin' trip!"

"Come on," Nigg said. "You take the ten. I'll take the five, okay?" He took the money from Big Sambo, looked at it, then handed one of the bills, still crumpled, to Hawk.

"Shit!" Hawk snatched the bill from Nigg's hand and jammed it into his hip pocket. "I mean, goddamn!"

"Okay," Nigg said. "Now come on, let's get out of here." The bill Nigg had actually kept and was shoving at his pocket—he missed twice as he went for the door—was the ten.

Shaking his head, Hawk followed him out and pulled the handle to. Pretty loud.

Big Sambo stood up. "Come here, girl."

Honey-Pie got down from the counter. Her dress caught on a splinter under the metal lip of the counter front. She turned to unfasten it, her hem tight across the back of her legs. Her toes curled on the gritty boards with concentration. Then the hem fell back.

With one hand, Big Sambo fingered his belt free of its buckle and, with the other, he grabbed up my hand. "Look a' there!" Big Sambo's fingers were thick and rough. "See...? He got them half moons. They didn't even see those. But I did, soon as they brought him in here. On two of his fingers, you can see 'em, just peekin'

174

out from under the skin. God damn. He may look like a nigger, but this cocksucker's *white*—least, just about. Either way, I got me a deal." He let my hand go and turned back to Honey-Pie. (She didn't look much older than me, by more than a year or so.) "The cocksucker here took my last one, quick and nasty. I got a long slow one for you now, little girl. Come on and bring it to your daddy...."

When she came, with that same serious expression, Big Sambo lifted her up to the table. One of the table legs was loose on the metal brace it was attached to the floor with. A coffee cup rattled.

"If your momma could see us now—" Big Sambo chuckled as his jeans slid down his ass—"Shit, that dick-hungry bitch would just want it—" He glanced down; Honey-Pie had taken her daddy's dick in her hands and was tugging—"all for her own damn self." He hunched his back to drop his mouth on hers. Her cheeks hollowed, and her eyes blinked fast, half an inch from his closed ones. He pushed her back on the table—her elbow hit the cup, and it almost overturned.

Her bare feet swung up, wrinkling her dress and his shirt.

Boots braced wide on the floor, Big Sambo clamped his buttocks. Over the crease below them, his jeans slid further down. His skin was dark as raw oil. He pushed it in her. The table leg tapped.

I got behind him, squatted, and, hands against his hips, pushed my face between his buttocks.

"Eat it out, cocksucker," he grunted.

The skin around his actual asshole was even darker.

I stuck my tongue in it. As I prodded, I felt it loosen; I licked harder. The puckered flesh turned out around my tongue. Sambo farted, which felt funny but smelled good.

"You like that, cocksucker?" He chuckled. "Eat out my black ass! Yeah, we got us a white boy."

In about a minute, it was so soft and wet I could've fucked him. He was moving very slow in Honey-Pie, like he didn't want to dislodge me. I reached between his legs and hefted his jog-gling balls—

"Yeah?"

—and slid two fingers in a peace sign around the wet haft of his cock. My knuckles kept getting pressed between his wiry groin and the hairless hill of Honey-Pie's cunt.

"Okay..." he grunted. "I'm shittin' and shootin'..." His asshole, loose as it was, opened further around my tongue. Something nudged my tongue-tip. I held a buttock with one hand, his balls with the other, and tried to scoop.

Shit stinks. But it don't taste like anything.

That nigger shit a horse turd too!

I bit. It mashed out against the corner of my mouth. I chewed. It was like sour starch paste. And grainy. And, when he shot—I felt the under-tube on his cock thicken across the skin between my fingers—my face was pushed back by his clamping butt. When I could go forward, my cheeks slipped on what coated his. I licked some more.

Sambo lay still, panting. "Yeah..." Again his ass loosened. He let his knees bend. Honey-Pie was still under him. I listened for her breathing under his; and wasn't sure I heard it.

I took my face away and wiped my chin. My palm smeared brown. I spit out about half of what I still had in my mouth into my hand. I looked at it a few seconds. Then, kneeling back on the floor, I put it inside my open fly and rubbed it around on my cock and nuts. It felt good; but it only got me half hard.

While I was rubbing, I happened to look out the window.

On the dock under the street lamp, a policeman stood, scratch-ing the back of his head. One thumb was hooked over his bullet belt. For a moment I thought it was Bill or Monty. But it wasn't. Because of the way his cap was over on the side of his head, I could see that he had real curly blond hair—curly as a nigger's almost; though I think he was white. (Even though my hair's curly, because it's yellow and soft a lot of people *call* me white.)

He was looking vaguely in our direction. But I couldn't tell if he could see inside the cabin or not. The windows were pretty dirty.

"Come on," Big Sambo said.

I looked back at his ass.

"Clean it out." He farted again. It looked funny: his buttocks pulled apart, his hips tilted up, and the puckered bud suddenly blew me a kiss. I stuck my face in it once more, with my tongue out. Once I heard him yawn.

Honey-Pie swung her legs down now—she kicked me on the shoulder, but I don't think on purpose. I moved away because I felt funny about touching her.

And kept licking.

When Big Sambo began to snore, I kneeled back and stood up. The policeman was gone.

I looked at the table. Her chin just over the ragged shoulder of Big Sambo's shirt, Honey-Pie had closed her eyes. Her lids quivered, though, so I don't think she was asleep. He must have been awfully heavy on top of her; but sometimes, I know, it's easier to sleep that way.

By the coffee cup, Big Sambo's hand hung off the side of the table. His pants were all wrinkled down around his sagging knees. His boots rested on their sides, the toes in.

I watched him awhile.

Then I squatted again and pushed my face back between his buttocks. He grunted once, shifted a little, snored again.

While I licked I thought about Hogg.

I pretended Big Sambo's ass was Hogg's, and licked harder. For all Hogg's talk, I'd eaten more nigger shit than Hogg shit. Big Sambo shifted again, grunted again: then he reached back and rubbed my head. "Hey, boy," he said. "That was real fine. But you give it a rest now, you hear?" Even though I couldn't pretend anymore, Big Sambo's rubbing my head made me feel better. I'd been about to cry.

When I stood up, Big Sambo was snoring again.

From the radio on the windowsill, the Hillsiders finished furnishing the world with love:

"Good evening, ladies and gentleman. This is Edward Sawyers here. Of course the only thing anybody is interested in, in tonight's news, is Dennis Harkner. Young Harkner, as of this broadcast still on the loose, has been on an afternoon and evening-long rampage—*allegedly* been on an afternoon and evening-long rampage of mayhem and slaughter, that threatens to outdo Starkweather, Speck, and Manson together—if not present a serious challenge to Gacy. Seven dead in a Frontwater bar; five in a gas station three blocks away; six in a grocery store on the other side of town. And the latest tragedy? Shortly after seven this evening, at the edge of the Fairhaven district, Mrs. Violet Sims, passing the window of a friend's house, saw a strange young man she did not recognize through the glass. Her screams brought out concerned neighbors, including two men with rifles. The young man inside the house turned out to be a visitor from Heartsdale; but, in the confusion, one of the rifles went off, fatally injuring thirty-two-year-old Michael Rhomer, who was among the spectators gathered outside the house with some friends to watch. Five streets away, perhaps at the very moment this incident was occurring, Dennis Harkner—someone alleged to be Dennis Harkner—let himself into an open garage on Treemont Street minutes before Fred Stevens and his cousin Jim Hicks returned home from a camping trip at Arrowhead Ponds, in Fred Stevens's secondhand Volvo. Once the car was in the garage, as the two boys were getting out, young Harkner, as far as the police have been able to determine, leapt from his hiding place under the garage workbench onto nineteen-year-old Fred Stevens and stabbed him with a screwdriver nine times in the back and side and belly. When the stabbing began, Jim Hicks, eighteen, apparently tried to start the car again but crashed into the edge of the garage door. Harkner then dragged Hicks from under the wheel and, with the same screwdriver, stabbed him twice, once through the eye and once in the throat. With Fred Stevens's keys,

Harkner then let himself into the stairway that led from the garage into the three-story house whose living room and kitchen were above the garage itself. The sound of the car crash, meanwhile, had brought Mr. George Stevens, Fred Stevens's father, and George Stevens's fourteen-year-old stepdaughter Phyllis—the only member of the family to survive the debacle, incidentally—out the front door of the house and down the porch steps to the garage—much of this, ladies and gentlemen, was reported to us by fourteen-year-old Phyllis Stevens not forty minutes ago. Upstairs, still in the house, were Mrs. Alicia Stevens—Fred and Phyllis's mother—Frank Stevens—George Stevens's brother—and Mrs. Mary Stevens—George and Frank's mother and the children's grandmother, who lived with her son and daughter-in-law in a room on the third floor—and also Ted Hicks, John Hicks's father. Phyllis and her father had to break in the garage door. The lock had been jammed by the crash. It took perhaps a minute and a half to open. 'Actually,' Phyllis Stevens told reporters, 'the lock had been sprung, but we didn't know that...until it just fell open while Dad was fooling with it.' Phyllis and her father burst in on the sight of the wreck and the two dead youths. 'Just then,' Phyllis went on, 'while we were standing around and trying to figure out what had happened, we heard two shots, and then a third, upstairs. Daddy just turned around and ran back out the garage to go up through the front door. But I was so frightened—I think that's when I saw the inside door from the garage was open a little bit. I don't know what I was thinking something like, whoever it was wouldn't come back the same way they went up. Which is crazy. But when I heard the fourth shot, and Uncle Frank started to scream, I ran to the door—I think I stepped on Freddy's hand—and started up, trying to be quiet.' The cellar stairway of the Stevens's house emerges into the kitchen. Pressed back behind the kitchen door, staring with one eye through the crack under the hinge, Phyllis saw a young man whose description fits that of Dennis Harkner: '...thin, blond, with acne—he was about sixteen or seventeen. He had on very dirty clothing with all these brown stains that I guess were blood....' He was holding a gun. Mrs. Alicia Stevens and Frank Stevens lay on the living room floor, shot to death. Phyllis's father and grandmother and Mr. Hicks stood by the couch with their hands raised. While Phyllis watched from her hiding place, the young man shot her grandmother in the stomach. 'He shot her twice after she fell,' Phyllis recounts. 'I guess that was when Dad realized they were all going to be shot anyway. He jumped for the boy, and knocked him back into the fireplace. And the boy dropped the gun. When the boy hit his head against the mantle, I thought Dad would get him then—but he didn't hit it very hard. The boy snatched up a poker and hit Dad across the ear with it. The poker broke—it was just an ornamental one; and the fireplace isn't real either—and Dad went down on his knees. Then the boy began to stab Dad with the broken end of the poker—he held it in both hands—in the back and the shoulders and all over and in the chest, too; and Dad fell over. It was all so fast. From the time we heard the car crash to the time Dad was dead was maybe two, three minutes.' Ted Hicks, apparently in something of a state of shock, was still standing with his hands raised and, according to Phyllis, with his eyes closed when, after finishing with George Stevens, the young man picked up the gun, went over to Mr. Hicks and shot him through the head. 'I crouched behind the door, waiting for him to come in and get me,' Phyllis explained. 'I was sure he'd seen me a dozen times, every time he turned around. Once he shot Ted, I just closed my eyes and crouched there.' And that was how the police found little Phyllis Stevens, fifteen minutes later, when they arrived after being alerted by concerned neighbors who had called them after hearing the gunfire. Harkner had apparently stayed only long enough to write, 'THAT'S ALL RIGHT,' in blood on the mirror above the mantle—the young killer's motto. With a total of twenty-four murder victims, not counting Michael Rhomer, Dennis Harkner, at this report, has still not been apprehended. Police Inspector Haley says: 'We will catch this psychotic monster before midnight! We have to. We've got every man on the force combing the Fairhaven area, from Harrison Avenue all the way to the upper edge of Frontwater.' Good luck, Inspector! We are all in a state of shock at the horrors of this day. Decent people are afraid to walk the streets! We here at the station are waiting with you, the listeners, for the moment we can announce that this killer has been apprehended and the nightmare is at an end. Phyllis Stevens has been taken for observation to the Frontwater District Hospital, where she will be picked up by relatives in Ellensville."

Carly Simon began to sing "Move in Together."

I went to the green door, sort of loose on its black metal hinges (with a piece of plyboard tacked over the broken round pane), pushed it open, and stepped over the sill to the deck.

It was a warm night.

I looked across the other boats. The Crawhole docklights picked out an oily chain here, wet deckboards farther down.

I thought about Hogg. And about Denny.

Once I heard a siren.

Big Sambo still didn't come out after me. Finally I decided to walk up the dock for a ways. I went to the gangplank. Underneath the ribbed board, water slapped and sloshed.

Alongside the docks, concrete alternated with planked stretches. There were small warehouses here and there; mostly, though, heavy brush grew right up to the walk. Insects spun and crawled and fluttered at the high dock lights, like flies around the glistening eyes of cats.

Walking by the boats, I thought about Big Sambo, too.

Two niggers sat on a boat railing, laughing at one another. Their bare feet were on the dock boards. When the boat rocked, their feet got lifted to their toes; when it went down, their frayed knees bent. The one with no shirt looked at me and then said something to the other one and laughed more. As I passed, their feet were lifted completely off, and the one with the leather wristband wheeled his arms and almost fell. They thought that was pretty funny too.

Behind the bushes, a pickup truck rolled in over gravel, stopped; its lights went dark in the foliage. The door opened, slammed, and I heard someone clomp a half a dozen steps into the brush: urine chattered against leaves.

I stood still and tried to see into the bushes—till a dark trickle leaked out across the dirt.

More brush got clomped and this big nigger came out of the bushes, adjusting his greens. He wore one of those navy, woolen shirts, the sleeves rolled up around his forearms, and an old cap. He glanced at me, then walked across the docks to one of the boats.

I squatted and put my palm flat in the trickle, lifted it, and licked. It was piss; and dirt too. Still squatting, I turned to look at the boat.

The nigger had stopped, one boot on the dock, one on the deck. Swaying as the boat swayed, he watched me. After a few moments, he put his hand between his legs, closed his fingers on what was inside his pants, lifted it a little, rubbed some, lifted it again.

I stood up and walked on.

When I looked back, though, he was going down inside the cabin, shaking his head.

In the lighted screen window of the next cabin, I saw some people moving.

On the deck after that, someone was playing the harmonica.

Across the water, clouds pulled from a yellow moon close to the horizon and big as an ashcan cover.

The harmonica player sat on an overturned zinc washtub, shoulders hunched, knees askew and bare feet sole to sole. As the boat rocked, his bullet head was silhouetted now against moonlit clouds, now against ivory-shot water. As I passed, he paused, swatted the harp against his palm twice, once against his knee, and played again.

A few boats down, a bare bulb above a door threw fangs of shadow from the tattered tarpaper over the barge's cabin wall. A big white man stood on the littered deck. His mustache went into dark stubble on his cheeks and chin. Where his shirt hung open, I could see part of a big white-headed bird tattooed on his chest, its blue wings wide. His black hair was stringy and brushed his shoulders, but he was starting to go bald. He scratched his stomach and looked around. On the back of his hand was a tattooed snake.

"Hey," he called—not to me.

"What?" a woman inside the cabin answered.

"Come out here!"

"Why?" —but she stepped out behind him. She was barefoot.

Torn, her dress hem hung down one scarred calf. She was a big nigger woman with sweat drops across her forehead up under her rough hair, which was dark mustard-colored like it was dyed; but some niggers got hair that color naturally. She had a baby on her shoulder, darker than him, lighter than her. Its head lay against her neck. Its hands were curled up near its chin. It was asleep. Its hair was short, brown, and curly. I couldn't tell if it was a boy or a girl. "What you want?"

"Pretty night."

"Yeah...." She looked around; suddenly she frowned. "Go on with you! *That* what you call me for?"

"Yep." He put his arm around her shoulder and grinned.

"Shit." But she grinned too.

"You think he looks like me?" He reached across her with his other hand and rubbed the baby's ear with his foreknuckle. "You think he looks like his daddy?"

"Who in hell else he gonna look like?" she asked. "Shit...." Then she laughed again.

His hand went down to the belly of her blue print. "Wonder what *this* one is gonna look like."

She laughed with her head back and her shoulders shaking. "For a man what gets it on as regular as you do, once in the mornin' and once at night, you seem pretty worried about who your kids gonna look like. You keep it up, I'm gonna think you like the idea of them lookin' like somebody else. Don't you suppose they look a little like me too?" And she laughed again. "You don't give me *time* to have 'em look like nobody *but* you, Harry—"

"Nice night," somebody said from the next barge.

He came down across the mounds and piles, dislodging things that rattled and clattered around his workshoes, another big nigger in a green tanktop, which had a couple of grease stains, a couple of holes. He put the heel of one big shoe on the barge edge and leaned on his thigh. Around his ashy knee the jeans made a frayed circle.

The white man said, "Sure is a nice night."

The nigger woman said, "'Specially since the wind's goin' down-dock. Rufus, when are you and Red gonna take that garbage scow of yours out of here? When the wind change and come up-dock, Harry and me, we just about can't *stand* it."

Rufus laughed: "You get used to it, after a bit. You folks been listening to the radio?"

"You mean all that stuff about that kid going around and killin' everybody?" Harry said. "That's just terrible. Mona was listenin' to it before and gettin' all upset; I made her turn it off. That's just terrible stuff to put on the radio."

Mona said: "You just don't wanna think about people doin' stuff like that; and around here, too. I mean right up in town and all. That poor little girl, who watched her whole family get killed—what was it? He stabbed her daddy to death with a broken fire poker...." She shuddered a little.

Harry glanced down, pulled her a little closer. "I made Mona turn it off," he repeated.

Mona's hand moved on the baby's back. "I just feel so terrible sorry for them all. The one that's doin' it too. It all just sound so terrible."

Rufus snorted; it might have been half a laugh. "Disc jockey didn't get to play two whole records before they had another report after that one." He had a real boomy voice, the kind that even when he was talking soft, you could hear twice as far off as anybody else's. "Seems next he was in a—"

"I don't want to hear it," Harry said.

"—in a damn supermarket," Rufus said. "That was already closed up, too. Somebody seen him writin' his thing on the inside of the big front window, you know, with a wadded up piece of newspaper, like he do—" Rufus began to sweep big letters into the air, and said, like a kid puzzling a hard word in a first-year reader: "*ALL—*"

"I don't wanna hear it now," Harry said.

"—*RIGHT*...right across the front window, there, between the three-cans-of-soup-for-thirty-nine-cents and the forty-nine-cents-a-pound-for-chicken signs. Just this skinny, dirty kid. The guy who saw it, he run for the police, and when they got in there, Harkner was gone, of course, and they found, in the storeroom in the back, he done killed—"

"Rufus, now, I *said*—"

"—four people; and a fifth one that's probably gonna die in the hospital, it sounds like: the manager, two girls and a guy who work the cash registers, and a stock boy. He shot three of them, stabbed one; the stock boy he tried to choke to death with a piece of wire, but I guess he didn't quite manage—"

"That's just terrible!" Mona shook her head, nuzzled the baby, and really did look like it might be upsetting her more than she was letting on.

"Hey!" With his ragged shirt all the way open, a real tall white man came over the biggest mound on the barge. "You all talkin' about the Harkner business?" He slid halfway down the near side, arms out for balance.

"No, Red!" Mona said sharply. "We ain't!"

"Oh...." Looking around, the tall man hooked both thumbs in his belt and pulled it up over his hairy belly. He came up beside the nigger, put his bare foot on the barge edge beside the nigger's workshoe. (They were about the same size.) In the light from the unfrosted bulb over Mona and Harry's cabin, on his chest and his arms and his head the hair was the color of shavings off a copper bushing street-workmen drop from a pipe-threading machine. Hanging across his knee, his hand was big as something hacked off a beef side.

Rufus, I guess, had decided it was time to change the subject. "Mona and Harry here was just complainin' about the stink—"

"Rufus!" Mona said. "Now we wasn't really complainin'!"

"Shit," Red said. "Every few days we take her out and dump her." He dug around in his nose with his finger, got something out, and looked at it like it surprised him. "So you get a few mornin's when it ain't too bad." He dropped his hand to his hip and laughed. "Course, I guess when it's just sittin' here, fillin' up, there ain't nothing to do but hold your breath. Man—" Red turned to Rufus beside him—"that stuff we was listenin' to back on the cabin radio—!" He nodded toward the cabin I could just see over the garbage that piled their scow—"that's really pretty unbelievable, ain't it, Rufus?"

Rufus didn't say anything.

Mona said: "I just don't even like to think about it."

"I guess—" Red looked around at the others—"I don't really like to think about it either." Down by his hip Red was rolling his nosepickings into a ball. One leg of his pants was so torn up at his shin that it hung around his ankle like a collapsed chimney.

"Naw," Harry said after a moment. "We ain't exactly complainin', but when the wind comes up-dock, Christ, does it get powerful!"

Red and Rufus laughed.

"Now don't take it personal," Mona said, "'cause you two are good people, and it's a pleasure to have you as neighbors, but I swear, when you take her out, it's a blessed relief to be shut of you!"

She and Harry laughed too.

I stood there listening, still thinking about Hogg.

"Who's the kid over there?" Harry nodded towards me.

"No kid ain't suppose to be out on the docks this hour." Mona moved the baby up her shoulder.

They all glanced a moment. Red used the opportunity to put his pickings in his mouth, sucking at his thumb and forefinger. "Maybe that's the kid I heard Big Sambo got over with him on his old, broke down tug. You don't see too many little white kids runnin' 'round here this time of the evening. I guess he must be. What is he—ten? Eleven? He don't look like he's even twelve." From the oval of dirt around each, I could tell he bit his nails too—about as bad as Hogg.

"Yeah?" Harry frowned at me. Then he looked back at Red and Rufus. "Say...that nigger don't do all them things the guys is always sayin' he does, does he?"

"*What* things?" Mona asked.

"Well—" Rufus had one hand in his pocket. He looked like he even could have been playing with himself—or at least scratching.

Red rubbed his nose, then put his hand on Rufus's black shoulder, crossed by the grimy green tanktop strap. Red's big hand was all covered with freckles and hair. So was the rest of him.

"I guess he don't do too much," Rufus went on. "Big Sambo's a pretty good nigger."

"What things?" Mona repeated. "I hear these niggers all up and down the dock talkin' about Big Sambo this and Big Sambo that, and I come walkin' by, and they shut up right away they see me."

Rufus glanced back at Red; Red patted Rufus's shoulder; the two garbage men chuckled.

"Shit, woman," Harry said. "Why you got to know so much? It's like the radio: you don't like it when you *do* find out."

"I'm *askin*'," Mona said and shifted the baby back. Its hand clutched at the shoulder of her dress; the brown face screwed up, whined a little. She began to shake it and make mumblings down at it. The hand let go, the face relaxed. The small fingers curled around the neck of her print.

"I mean," Harry was saying, "you two guys spend time with him on his tug. But I don't really know him. He still owe Mona money from that six weeks last winter when they had me up in jail over that goddamn dockin' fine."

Rufus laughed. "Big Sambo owe everybody money all up and down Crawhole. He's a good nigger."

"But I was just wondering," Harry said, "about what they say."

"Well, I'll tell you," Red said.

Rufus stood up.

Red's hand slid forward on the nigger's shoulder so that he was leaning there with his forearm now. "That nigger ain't done nothin' with no kid I wouldn't do. He just likes to look out for 'em—and take care of 'em when they don't got nobody else."

"Well, you see there," Harry said. "You see, it was all just talk. That's just what I thought it was, too."

"I don't know." Mona hefted the baby a little higher. "Some of the stuff I heard about you, Red Conroy: he may not do nothin' you wouldn't do, but I don't know if that's all that high a recommendation."

"Aw, come on, Mona—" Harry said.

But Mona and Red and Rufus were laughing.

"Big Sambo?" Rufus put both hands on his torn knee, shook his head. "That nigger's all right. He may not be too smart and talk a little too much big talk—he owe Red and me money too. But what he do is all right."

I couldn't help thinking that though maybe Big Sambo had more weight on him than Rufus, Red, or Harry—or Mona for that matter, because she was pretty big—Rufus and Red, at any rate, were a good bit taller.

"You see?" Harry said again. "All we know, that boy maybe wouldn't have no place to sleep if Big Sambo hadn't took him in."

"Yeah," Red echoed Rufus, and he almost sounded a little drunk, leaning there on Rufus's shoulder, "Big Sambo's a good nigger."

"Better nigger'n I am." Rufus nodded.

"Well, Rufus Finks, I don't know if *that's* saying too much either." But Mona was laughing again.

The harmonica cried, whined, and, over breathy *choo-choo* chords, dragged long, hot notes across the night. Harry cocked his head. "Andy can sure make that harpoon wail." He grinned, looking over the boats.

"Sure can play," Rufus agreed. "Used to wish't I could play me a harmonica like that." His hand was still working in his pocket.

"Harry still does," Mona said. "He's always talkin' about how he'd like to play on a mouth organ like Andy do, every time the sun goes down and Andy starts in."

"Whyn't you ask him to teach you?" Red said.

Harry rubbed the side of his thumb on his chin and frowned, "Now I never thought of that. You think he would?"

"Why wouldn't he?" Mona asked. "Andy's a nice old boy. I betcha he'd try."

"Well, I sure would like to learn," Harry said. Suddenly he dropped his hand from Mona's shoulder and slapped his thigh. "I'm gonna ask him! First thing tomorrow, I'm gonna go down there and get that black son of a bitch to teach me—I ain't gonna be much good at first, now; but I bet I can learn!"

"*Lord*-y...!" Mona cried, the first part high and long, the last just laughter. "That's gonna be something. Well, I put up with the rest of your shit, I guess I can put up with you tootlin' and tweetlin' around the scow too."

"All I got to do is practice," Harry said. "You tell me what else it takes to learn how to play some music? Go on, tell me what else."

Mona was joggling the baby again, turning in a circle. "Lordy!" she exclaimed once more. "How I got myself hitched up with such a nigger-lovin' white man, *I'll* never know! Harry's as bad as you, Red. He want to be a nigger *so* bad—" and stopped her turn, shoulder against Harry.

Harry settled his arm around her broad back. "I don't wanna be no nigger—"

"You *was*," Rufus said, "and *she* wouldn't have nothin' to do with you, you can be *damned* sure—"

"Rufus, you get on!" Mona said.

Red and Rufus chuckled again.

Mona laughed out over it.

"I don't," Harry repeated with a shake of his bristly chin, "want to be no nigger. I just wanna learn how to play me a little nigger music on the harp. Then we wouldn't have to run the goddamn radio all the goddamn time. And listen to shit like that Harkner stuff!"

"Rufus?" Red dropped his forearm; Rufus looked over. "Didn't you pull a harmonica out of the scrapin's about two months ago? You had it on the windowsill for a while, but I think it fell down behind the bedstead in the cabin. I betcha it's still there. *You* don't use it, nigger. Whyn't you let Harry have it?"

Rufus shrugged. "Sure. If he want it. The lowest note is a little squeaky, but the rest play fine, a-puffin' and a-suckin'."

Which made Mona giggle and cracked Harry up.

"You pull it out of the garbage?" Harry asked, rubbing his belly from laughing. "Out of the garbage, man? Hell, I'll probably come down with cancer or pee-neumonia!"

"It play fine," Rufus said, "'cept the lowest note."

Andy's music threaded the docks, blowing sad and silvery on the warm night.

We all listened.

"I'll come over and take a look at your mouth harp tomorrow morning," Harry said at last. "Then I'll go down and talk to Andy."

"Sure," Rufus said. "I betcha Andy'd like teachin' somebody. Most of the guys around here think Andy's a little funny in the head and don't spend too much time with him. But Andy's a good ol' boy. He might like that just a whole lot."

The music drew down, low and growly, then reared up, all high and pained and drawn out sharp against the moon and clouds.

I started walking again, up the dock.

Passing Red and Rufus's scow, I looked at the dark shack on the back. Garbage was piled all the way up one side to the roof; and there wasn't hardly a clear space on the deck at all. Once I got on the other side, the smell did get strong.

What was still going through my mind was Hogg; and all those speeches he used to make that sounded like he'd said them to other people before. Thinking about the people I'd just been overhearing, I wondered how much of what they said were things they repeated and repeated among the four of them, night after night, months running; and how much was new. It was pretty easy to figure, actually. Which made me think about Hogg again.

I missed him.

The harmonica drifted down and along.

A few boat decks on, another nigger fisherman and a policeman were talking low and drinking from a flat bottle one passed to the other, then back. The policeman was the one with the kinky blond hair I'd seen through the tug window.

They looked at me—the policeman had the palest eyes I'd *ever* seen. In just the light from the bug-swirled dock lamp, they looked like floodlit ice. The fisherman took the bottle, lifted his head for another swallow, and looked away. He handed it to the policeman, who took it—but was still watching.

I walked on.

There was only one more boat after that, and nobody was on it. But empty docks went on a ways. So I kept walking. The brush and weeds and trees between the docks and the old warehouses were higher here.

About twenty-five, thirty yards on, in the gravel behind me I heard steps.

I didn't turn, but when I slowed, the steps slowed. When I stopped, they *shushed* off into the bushes. I didn't look back, but I was pretty sure it was the nigger who'd hoisted his meat at me when I'd tasted his pee down by the first boats, come up after me now, here beyond the end.

Well back in the brush, two, five, three at a time, with pauses in between, the steps came closer.

I turned and pushed into the brush too.

Leaves slapped at my face. Twigs caught on my shirt. Then, three or four yards in, I found a clearing where the stuff wasn't even up to my knees. The steps came on, slowed—perhaps he wasn't sure I'd come in, though I couldn't believe he hadn't heard me. Some more steps came closer. Then I realized: it was more than one person. It was two people, together.

I turned and started away again. One time, about a year ago, on Federal Street over by the University, two guys together caught me and took me to some burned-out building. (The young one, I think, was from the college.) Most of the things they did with me I didn't like at all. And it took me three days before I got away. The brush here was so loud, there wasn't any hiding. But I moved toward where it got thicker and higher, going beside the docks, in the direction I'd been going before.

My steps quickened. Their steps quickened.

So I stopped and turned around, ready to run off. Outside and over some warehouse door, a bulb in a wire cage was burning, its light all splintered through the leaves and branches. Really, you couldn't see much by it.

They stopped, first one, then the other—right next to him.

"Hey. That's you, ain't it, white boy?" It was a nigger's voice, calling softly; but familiar. "You out here lookin' for somethin'?"

"We got somethin' for you, if you want it." That was a white man's, also quiet, also familiar. "You like black cheese? I got a whole handful of *just* what you want."

The nigger laughed, low and rough.

I took a couple of steps forward.

From the warehouse bulb behind the leaves, a sliver of light glistened on a dead black shoulder the way it never would on a white guy's. Someone shifted—and beside it I saw freckles in the copper snarl.

I took a couple steps more.

Then I smelled them.

"You just come on over here, boy," Red drawled. "Yeah, you'll like this, cocksucker. If you Big Sambo's boy, I *know* you gonna like this."

Like something happening in an underground cave, Rufus chuckled.

"Right in my hand here I got a *big* piece of funky nigger meat," Red went on. "Here it is, right here. Got this big black nigger bastard partner of mine's big old black dick right in my fist. You see what's in my other one—workin' on old red-capped leaky? Both of 'em big, both of 'em juicy. But I guess you can see that from where you are already." (Through the brush I couldn't see *too* much of anything.) "Which one you want? You like cheesy nigger meat? You like smoked salmon? You can have 'em, one at a time or both together, in whichever hole you want—anyway you want 'em, cocksucker!"

"Come on, boy." Rufus's voice came, just as smooth, from out his chuckle. "I wanna see my partner Red here feed my dick into your little honky blond motherfuckin' face!"

I took another couple of steps forward. Only four or five feet in front of me, I could make out Red and Rufus, standing next to each other. A little light picked out where Red's sleeve was rolled up on his forearm; his arm slanted down across Rufus's belly. And it was moving. I could see the strap of Rufus's tanktop over his big shoulder, moving when he breathed. But there wasn't enough light to see any of Red's freckles—or, really, to guess Rufus wasn't white if you didn't already know it.

One of them took a step. The other came with him. And Red's hand, shifting on a big, sideways-curved dick, slipped into some glow that got through the brush. (I felt a lot better, 'cause they weren't like the guys on Federal Street at all.) Red had some big hands on him, too! But even pulling on it like he was doing, he didn't come near to covering Rufus's cock.

Rufus asked, serious and deep-voiced: "You think that's big enough for him to see it, now?"

Red chuckled this time.

"Come on, you hungry little son of a bitch." Rufus said. "Let my man here feed you some nasty black dick. I wanna see you lappin' an' a-lickin' on it, white boy!"

I stepped up and squatted in the leaves.

Red left off Rufus's cock—which bobbed half an inch higher, with its funny side curve. He put his palm on my face; it was horny and rough. Red slid his thick fingers into my hair and pulled me forward. The blunt, night-black shaft butted my cheek and left a wet spot.

"Go on." Red tugged me forward. "Suck it."

I did.

"Yeah…" the nigger whispered. He pushed forward. It was real salty. And his lap heated up my whole face when I went into it, with the smell of grimy cloth and nigger crotch.

Red turned loose my head, took hold of Rufus's cock again. He slid his hand along the part I didn't have in my mouth yet. A few times, his walnut of a knuckle beat my face.

"Get on his ass," Rufus said. "Go on, Red. Get his ass up and fuck 'im."

When Red took his hand away, I went down on the nigger till one side of his zipper and, on the other, stiff hair tore at my mouth.

Red got behind me, stooped, got one hand in the back of my pants, and yanked me up. He was still jerking his own cock with the other—I could feel his rhythm in the fingers splayed on my butt. He had to yank me a couple of times—my pants waist pulling and pulling under my belly. Without losing Rufus's cock, I held onto the nigger's pockets. One was ripped; and each time Red yanked me, it ripped more. As I got my feet under me, Red found Big Chico's tear—"Oh, shit!"—and got his other hand in through that. He dug two fingers between my buttocks.

Like I said, his fingers were big.

"Go *on*, fuck his ass!" Rufus hissed. "I wanna see ya'! Go on!" He shoved his cock deep in my face, grabbing my head and leaning forward. (Though I didn't know how he could see anything.) "Go on. Fuck 'im!"

Red held my hips now, positioning them—and shoved in. "Oh, *shit*!" I heard him catch his breath—and heard the grin in it, too. "The kid's got one of them assholes that wets up like a pussy, Rufus! When Big Sambo gets 'em, he gets 'em good." Red moved his hands up the small of my back, rocking and leaning. "Nigger, this is a fine fuck...." He went in again. "A *fine* fuck, nigger!"

"I wanna see ya' in his face, Red." With a few tight-curled hairs on it, Rufus's ball sack hung warm against my chin, his nuts swinging under. "Come on, Red. You gonna have to dick this white boy's face. He take it all the way down in his fuckin' belly!"

"From either end, too!" One of Red's hands moved up my back, over my shoulder, around to my cheek. He fingered Rufus's wet cock slipping in and out of my mouth.

I remembered how Hogg liked his fingers sucked. So, alongside the nigger's dick, I sucked two of Red's. They were sandpaper hard, hammer-haft thick, and tasted of machine oil, with salt under it. Red seemed to like it, too.

"Come on," Rufus was saying. "Come on! Turn him around!"

Red's fingers in my mouth hooked up my head. Rufus's cock slipped loose. Red's dick slid out my ass. I stumbled in the long grass but they both held me up. Red laughed while they turned me.

The nigger was panting. "Let's do him this way awhile," Rufus said. "We'll do him this way, then we'll do him back the other."

Though I had my nose full of its stink, I couldn't see Red's cock very well: but it looked like the last inch or so bent straight down in an L! I went lipping after it when the length of it slapped my cheek. "Yeah, eat that pig fucker, boy!" The stink was my shit.

And Rufus was pushing at my asshole. When his dick had been in my mouth, I'd felt the curve. But I couldn't feel it at all up my ass.

Red got my head in one hand, pushed his dick in my mouth with the other. It was real fat, with an unholy lot of foreskin off the end. (It wasn't bent, I realized; that was just his goddamned *curtains* hanging down!) Under the shit, it tasted about like his fingers, only a little less oil, a little more salt. He'd been joking about the nigger's cheese, but when I tongued inside Red's long, leathery cuff, I swear, it was like he'd sat down earlier with a half pint of Breakstone and packed a tablespoon of smallcurd in there around the head. The only way I know a guy can raise *that* much dick cheese is from something the super I stayed with showed me a couple of times, back when I was first with Pedro and Maria: he'd only *had* about two-and-a-half inches of cock, even hard. Red had more like nine. But they both were guys with two inches of skin overhang; and sometimes, when he'd beat off, the super would keep the scum inside it, tie his foreskin in a knot, and let the stuff stay in there five or six hours, with a little piss. (If you only had as much skin as the wop or Denny, say, I guess you'd have to use a rubber band to hold it to cover the cum.) Inside, it would ferment. After half a day, it was as thick and curdy as you could want. He'd untie the skin and make me suck him off that way—till he realized I liked it. Then he wouldn't do it for me no more. I think he wanted to eat it himself—'cause I caught him doing that, once, too. But that's the only way I knew Red could get up that much of the stuff. Even if you *never* washed it, it just couldn't get that way without *some* help. Or he took half the nigger's and put it in with his own— once I knew some guys who did that, too. I tongued out Red's crusted sleeve, the soft stuff and the harder stuff under it, went down to the hilt, came back, turned his curtains just about inside out and shoved hard with my tongue, on one side, on the other, then around the top, getting off what was stuck there, peeling it loose, holding the haft in my teeth. (Cheese tastes *awful* good!)

I went down again, then came back to clean the last curds from either side the skin, holding his foreskin to the underside of his dickhead. "Nigger," Red said, and I could hear his grin was even bigger, "this cocksucker *likes* me!"

Behind me, Rufus went in, and Red grunted; like he could feel it all the way up in my face. Red went in too, and I put my arms around his hips. I held my wrists around under his ass so that he pulled at them each time he went back.

Rufus grunted out, and shoved: "His little honky ass—" and shoved—"sure seems happy with—" and shoved—"my big black dick!"

Red chuckled. Grunting, Rufus held my hips, leaning harder, pumping faster.

When Red went in this time, he halted, laid a fart—and laughed again. At least at first I *thought* it was a fart: something like ten inches of broom handle fell down into the seat of his pants, over my wrists.

"What'd you do?" Rufus asked, without letting up on my hole.

"Shit in my fuckin' pants!" Red laughed out. He started humping my face again. "Oh, Jesus…!" I heard him shit again—and felt another six-incher fall. When he went out this time, he tried to wiggle his ass as though he wanted it smeared around. I spread my hands, moved them up the gritty cloth and mashed. Inside, I felt the turd squash against his hard buttocks. "Oh, fuck, yeah…." His pants seat, first under one wrist, then under my fingers, then my palms, wet through.

"Goddamn, Red," Rufus got out between humps. "You never smelled exactly what I'd call sweet. But—oh, *man*."

I took one hand away from Red's ass—the cloth of his seat was all stuck to him—reached around the front and into his fly, back under his balls. With his hip movements, his nuts drew back and dragged, real sweaty, beside my wrist. "Huh…? What you…?" When Red opened his legs wider, zipper teeth scraped my forearm. "Hey…!" His cock came out of my mouth, but his hips were still going. The thick head kept butting my cheek, the wrinkled hose again hanging off the end. His work-hardened palms still clamped my ears.

The hair of Red's legs was very long. I felt around between, got to his ass where it was all pasted with shit, and scraped as much as I could from his matted buttocks and out from the seat of his pants. Red even squatted a little so I could get some more. "Nigger, you can tell he been down there with Big Sambo. You know what he likes…"

Rufus chuckled now.

With one hand, I held Red's belt. The other loaded with crap, I came out of Red's fly and grabbed his cock. Red drawled: "Oh, *yeah*…!" I rubbed and rubbed it, back into his hair and up over the loose, long nozzle, and back down on his balls, and up again. Then I got his belt in both hands; and started licking at his dick like I was going after the drippings on a sausage. "Oh, man," Red said. "Goddamn, cocksucker, you're too fuckin' much!" He got the head in. And went home. This time he locked his hands behind my head and held me close while he humped. "Nigger, he got a mouth *full* of my shit! An' I'm fuckin' it, you black bastard! I'm fuckin' it!" I slid my hands around to his wet backside again. My mouth filled up with crap every time he drew out. Red went in, and got it all mashed around. "Rufus, you got to *try* this—"

"He Big Sambo's boy," Rufus said, "an' you *know* he like shit!" He worked the small of my back with his broad, rough fingers. My ass turned up like a cat's pussy. One spot about five inches up my asshole, each time when his dick rubbed over it, all I could do was squirm and drip. "Yeah, that sounds fine, Red. Maybe it's gettin' 'bout time to turn him around again and see what fuckin' a mouth full of *your* shit feels like—"

"Well, you got a shitty dick, nigger. And shit is sure what this cocksucker goes for." Red laughed down at me, and pressed my face—like we had a secret between us. Maybe it was all his cheese. "I ain't never seen a cocksucker this young who went after shit as much as—"

Then the flashlight beam hit.

Red staggered. Rufus stopped.

"Now what the fuck you bastards think you're doing!"

Rufus's hands tightened on my back. Red's belly moved against my forehead. I could hear them both breathing.

"Hey, stop workin' your face on that dick! And keep your ass still, I say!"

Which was hard, because Red and Rufus were too—even though they'd stopped moving.

"Come on, cocksucker! Calm your ass down, now, and let Rufus go. Red, get your fuckin' dick out of his face—*now*!" Footsteps came through the brush.

"That you, Whitey...?" You could tell Rufus was squinting in the flashlight glare.

"I'll let him go," Red ventured, "but it sure looks like he's still hungry...."

I felt Rufus shift inside my hole.

Then somebody yanked me up by the hair. Red's cock slipped free. I staggered. Rufus's dick came loose—and that time I did feel the curve. It kind of hurt.

"What kinds of sons of bitches are you, both fuckin' the little bastard at the same time?" Even with just the flash, the ice-colored eyes going back and forth between Red and Rufus looked like they had bulbs on inside. The way he held me, my arm was rubbing against his cartridge belt. "Shit!" With the jerk, his blue cap had gone crooked on all the nigger-tight, ash-pale hair. He looked awful angry. "You are two *low* motherfuckers!"

I opened my mouth wide and let my tongue slop back and forth over my lower lip. Spit and shit ran down my chin.

The policeman looked down at me, frowned, and said, "Jesus Christ...!"

"I tell you, Whitey," Red said, a little warily, "I think the cocksucker's still hungry."

Suddenly the policeman shoved me. I fell back into the brush. "What'd you do to him?" The policeman raised his flashlight to move it back and forth between the two garbagemen. "What kind of little freak is this?"

Bits of light slid on the leaves beside my face, caught on the side of Red's torn pants—I could see a stretch of hairy, freckled shin as the light shifted—and I could see the shadow each hair made. I looked up at Rufus; the flashlight turned the torn, greasy tanktop, which had been green out under the dock lights, gray. His shoulder gleamed with sweat. So did Red's grinning, spotted jaw.

Then the light swung down, so that for a moment, with it in my eyes, I couldn't see.

On my back, I lifted my legs up in the air, reached between them, opened up Chico's tear, and dug into my asshole with my fingers. There was still a lot of shit on my other hand, so I put it in my mouth and started to eat.

"Jesus," the policeman said. "Is the little fucker *crazy*?"

Rufus's low, rumbling chuckle grew and fell. "That boy just need his pussy pumped a little more, Whitey. You see how he tryin' to do himself like that?"

I stuck my tongue out between my fingers. I rocked harder and tried to get my hand up far enough to reach that spot the nigger's cock had made feel so good.

The light stayed on me.

The policeman said: "He's fuckin' crazy…!"

"But he got a sweet ass," Rufus said.

"Shut up, nigger," the policeman said.

Still sucking, still digging, I raised my head.

Behind the flashlight, I could see the policeman's other hand hooked to the bullet belt by his thumb. He dropped it to scratch himself between the legs. His hand sort of stayed there a little too long, started to raise again, then went back. He had on a wedding ring, I remember. And his hands were very short and wide.

I had my thumb and three fingers up to the knuckles in my ass. My forearm rubbed my balls. I kept grunting and pushing harder.

Suddenly the light swung away. "Shit—!" the policeman hissed. He just dropped the light in the brush; I heard the batteries clunk together.

His zipper rasped. His shoes crashed up in the leaves. He grabbed me by one leg and squatted. I heard him spit on his hand.

"You don't need no spit for that pussy," Rufus said. He squatted beside me.

Still standing, Red put his hands in his pockets, shifted his weight, and cocked his head.

The policeman jerked my hand out, set his cock in my asshole, shoved, and nearly fell on me.

Where the flashlight was laying on the ground, it caught Red's dirty ankle under the frayed cuff. Red squatted.

My face was almost under the policeman's shoulder. Rufus squatwalked around to get closer to Red. Red just sort of slid his hand into his fly to play with himself. Rufus had his out already and was shucking, his thumb on the top, fingertips underneath, like he liked the feel of his nails—which were pretty workworn and short; they were dirty, but he didn't bite them, it looked like. I wondered if his foreskin was long enough to make the same kind of cheese Red's could. His dick was as long as Hogg's, I couldn't help thinking; and thicker.

The policeman's bullet belt ground my belly, and his gun holder wedged under my hip. He was panting and humping with his forearms on the ground.

With my face mashed on its side, I could just see Red's pants, moving with his hand inside.

Rufus let go his dick, reached down under the policeman's shoulder and stuck three fingers in my mouth. I started to suck them, but he was scraping around—his hands were horny as wood—to get some soft shit. He pulled them out and rubbed them over, then under, then over his dick again, finally going back to shucking.

"Hey…" the policeman grunted. He was really humping me

hard. "You smelly motherfuckers get out of here.... Come on, you two stink like a shithole out of lime...." I heard the policeman's hands close on dry leaves, open again. "Nigger, get your dick out of my face.... I don't want to sniff at your black pecker. I wanna *fuck* this ass!"

Coming up like wind in leaves far away, or the sea, Rufus chuckled again.

I held onto the policeman's shoulders. His jacket was pretty thick. I tried to wrap my legs up around him like Maria used to do when the guys fucked on her. But I could only get one up. His gun got in the way of the other.

I lay there, getting fucked, and watching Red's hand working inside his pants. I kept on hoping he would pull it out and shuck on it like Rufus was doing; I wanted to see if he had freckles on his cock too.

"Come on, Red," the policeman said again, still grunting, still humping, but a little whiny. "You and Rufus get away from me, now. I just wanna get my rocks off in this kid's—"

A woman screamed.

It was out on the docks, but I couldn't tell how far down.

The scream ended up funny, twisted off like a piece of metal.

"Jesus!" The policeman stopped humping.

A man shouted; only the shout was cut off by a shot. Then two more shots, right after.

The woman screamed again—well, it wasn't a scream, now: just a sound that was loud enough to hear this far in.

"Holy shit!" The policeman's dick came out of my ass as he pushed back to his knees.

My ass stung.

"What the fuck—!" He stood up, almost falling, pushing at his cock, half hard and still shitty, but thick and white under it as a parsnip. The flashlight in the leaves leaned so that you could see it, clear back into his fly. "What's goin' on out there—"

Rufus, still squatting, looked up. "Ain't you gonna finish him off, Whitey?"

Red, looking down, said, "That's an awful sweet hole to let hang around empty."

Whitey's zipper stuck the first time he tried to pull it up— "Fuck—!" Then it came free. He swiped up the flashlight, took about three steps, then looked back: the light swept across us. "Look, you two better leave that—" Then I guess he changed his mind. He just shook his head, and crashed on off through the brush. In the leaves the light flittered away.

Rufus's chuckle swelled up again in the dark, and this time broke out to full laughter.

"Goddamn," Red said, laughing too. "Goddamn, nigger! Ain't that Whitey a bitch!"

I heard Rufus stand up. "What you suppose that shootin' was?"

"I don't know," Red said.

I thought Red was going to stand up too, so I rolled over and put my hand on his foot. Red said: "I guess we could finish up on the little cocksucker, then go take a look."

"Hell." Rufus took a couple of steps off; looking up, I could see him trying to see out over the bushes. "He done got a taste of what we can give 'im. He want some more, he get tired of Big Sambo, he can always come on down to the scow and get him some good stuff. He know where we anchored."

I pushed myself up on one hand, reached in for Red's cock. He took his own hand away so I could get it. "I guess he do," Red said. But he didn't get up. It was too dark to see about the freckles. So I put his cock in my mouth. It still had some shit on it. Red's hands came together in my hair, while I sucked. "I guess so," Red said again after a moment. "But I think I'll work out here a little more anyway. I sort of like the little bastard's style, you know, Rufus—hey, come on, cocksucker. Get up on your knees. I can't shoot all squatted down here like this."

So I got up on my knees and Red stood.

He held both my hands in his—they could have wrapped around mine twice—and began to pump again. "You go on, if you want, Rufus. I'll be out in a second...!"

In his big black workboots, Rufus came back over, though. "Yeah, he is a good little cocksucker, now, ain't he. I wouldn't mind gettin' him down on the scow for a couple of days, you know, Red? I wouldn't mind swipin' 'im from Big Sambo, maybe for just a while. A week or two, now. Hey, boy: you could have shit-pie with nigger-piss three times a day if you wanted—didn't I pull out an old dog leash and a collar from the dumpings, Red? We could chain the little bastard up to the bedpost in the cabin so's he wouldn't get out and folks'd see him. Shit, Big Sambo'd never know he was there...."

Red had got his feet apart—the toes of one foot were propped on my knee—and holding my hands tight against his thighs, was scooping his hips into my face. For a while I tried to stay pretty far back and get into his foreskin again, but he wanted to put it in deep; finally he let go my hands and grabbed my hair, hard. I reached between his legs and felt the seat of his pants; his pasted-up buttocks swung back and clamped forward again. He shot. It was a strong, long spurt; and he went out once and came back in again in the middle of it too.

Rufus was standing so close to us his knee brushed my arm.

Red took a breath, let go my hair, and said, "Nigger, *what* are you doin'?"

Rufus chuckled once more. "Pissin' on yo' knee." I came off Red and grabbed for Rufus, got one ear full of pee; the other was still a-rumble with the nigger's soft, bass laugh. "Come on...easy, boy. Now, easy..." His big hands clamped my head while I tried to get it in my mouth. "Easy, boy..."

I had piss all over my face.

"...that's right. Easy..."

Red was still breathing hard. And still standing close, too. His hand came around the back of my head, now. I held the warm, hard pipe and sucked. "Go on, Red," Rufus said. "Play around with my nuts and stuff; you know I like to feel you feelin' around my dick when I'm peein' in a cocksucker's face. Still got a mouth full of shit, too."

Red's hand came around to the cock in my mouth—he was still panting, and with his other arm he was leaning on Rufus's shoulder. And he was grinning too; you could just hear it in the sound of his breath.

"Yeah," Rufus said, "sometime in the next couple of days—maybe when Big Sambo's gettin' tired of him—we gotta get this little cocksucker down on the barge, where we can really put 'im through his paces, you know? And you know something else, Red? I don't think he gonna mind comin' along. Not a bit." Brine streamed hot from the head. "I'd be a good nigger for ya', boy," Rufus said. "You could take it out, nurse on that big, black fucker anytime, day, night, if I'm sleepin', wakin', workin'—no matter what I'm doin'. I wouldn't care—long as we were someplace where we wouldn't get in a whole *lot* of trouble. And a little trouble now, that ain't so bad—Red'll tell ya'. Somebody sees me doin' somethin' nasty, an' it just makes me feel all good and warm inside."

"A *little* trouble?" Red said. Now that he'd come, he was pulling himself together and stepping around, probably trying to get the seat of his pants loose from his ass. "That nigger plays with himself all goddamn day long! He'll flip it out and beat on it anywhere, I swear. I never seen him with his fuckin' fly closed more'n an hour at a time. Two years ago, they put him in the hoosegow for jerkin' off somewhere uptown—"

"It was just in a movie," Rufus said. "When I do it in the street or in the parkin' lots, I'm always a lot more careful. But it was in a movie an' it was dark; an' I was sitting by myself—there wasn't many people sittin' around me, 'cept'n some faggots, what was gettin' off on it. But Red's right—I *don't* mind showin' what I got!"

"It wasn't even a *dirty* movie, either," Red said. "One of the ushers called in a policeman. After they took him to jail, they put him in the hospital."

"Once they caught me," Rufus explained in that vibrating basso he had, "I figured there wasn't no reason to stop then. It was better them thinkin' I was some kinda crazy, than just a pervert or a criminal or something. So every time they turned around, I'd pull it out and start to beatin' again. If they *hadn't* of put me in the hospital, Red, you wouldn't of seen *my* black ass no more!"

"I had to go and get him out and sign a paper sayin' I'd be his guardian. Nigger, how many times Harry or Mona caught you on the back of the barge, sittin' there with it out and you beatin' off?"

"Harry thinks it's funny," Rufus said. "And Mona, she just pretends like she don't see it. And goes away. So I pretend like I don't see her either. Though I like her peekin' at me."

"Jesus!" Red laughed. But he seemed to think it was funny too. "You bad as Big Sambo, nigger—you two black bastard's just alike!"

"The hell I am," Rufus said. "That nigger ain't nothin' but a damned child molester! You don't do a little girl like that, even if she is your own—less'n she wants it bad as this little fucker here do. I know she like it but I don't know if she like it like him." Rufus moved his feet in the loud leaves. "Somebody watchin' you get a blowjob, now," Rufus said, "or pissin' on some cocksucker—or him eatin' your shit, that's better than just flippin' it out and wavin' it in the sunlight. We gonna have this cocksucker on a dog collar, we gotta take him out for a walk, now and then, don't we Red? Don't we? But you could have dick—black or white—whenever you wanted, boy. You think you'd like that?"

I was going to nod, but as Rufus's urine ran out he began to hump my face.

So I wrapped my arms around his leg and began to dog-off on his shin, while I sucked. Rufus was going side to side, too, as well as in and out. Red had slid a couple of fingers in there by now. Rufus's cockhead was really stirrin' around in my gullet. "…Little sucker's bad…" Rufus grunted, "…as I am. He pissin' all over…my leg…." Which was true. But it got him off. And me too. He came, half a minute later, like a black Mack backfiring!

So did I—right in the middle of pissing in my pants, and I didn't hardly stop shooting hot water.

I clung to his leg while he panted: "Aw, shit, Red...ain't he gonna be a *nice* neighbor...to have here down on the docks!"

"You wanna take 'im with us now?" Red said, dragging his big hand back and rubbing my face. "I'm for it if you are, nigger." Maybe he was getting worked up again.

"Come on, cocksucker." Rufus laughed like a big engine turning over and pushed my head away. "Get up off it."

I kneeled back in the leaves. I was breathing pretty hard too.

"Like I said, Red. Just take it easy. The cocksucker know where we are. It's funny now," Rufus said, "Red bein' my guardian an' all. This carrot-headed honky's crazy, boy. He's a good ol' white boy, but he's crazy. I got to beat his hairy red ass from time to time—figuratively speakin', that is—'cause I'm the only one of us who got any sense. But we make good partners. Look, Red, he wants it, he knows where to come lookin' for it. Ain't no need to get Big Sambo all upset on the first night the little bastard's around." Rufus pulled at his pants, kicked his leg a little—where I'd wet it down from the knee—and stepped up, pulling at his fly. "Can you walk, boy?" Rufus reached a hand under my arm and hauled me upright. Piss had collected in the knees of my pants and ran down my leg and ankle. You could hear it spill out on the brush, and over Rufus's shoe. I was a little unsteady. But I felt good.

"Guess you right, Rufus," Red said. He ran his big hand through my hair, frowned, shook the piss off it, then did it a couple more times. The last time he wiped his hand on his pants. Then he said, "Guess that'll have to do you for tonight, boy. But I'll tell you, I'm sort of lookin' forward to seein' you again."

On the docks a siren sawed the silence.

"Come on," Rufus said. "We go see what all the commotion is out there."

Red stood up, took a breath.

Rufus started walking. Red started after him.

Rufus looked back. "Come on, boy." I caught up; the nigger put his hand on my shoulder. "You be okay. Puke if you want. All that piss in your belly, you go on an' puke."

"He ain't gonna puke," Red said. "He likes it."

I felt a little funny. But not like I was going to throw up. Just lightheaded.

We came out the bushes onto the docks.

Somewhere in the bushes, Red had shucked out of his shirt. He was barechested now, and, under the dock lights, looked like a big red bear.

"Jesus," he said. "What you suppose...?"

Fifty yards down, a scarlet police-light flickered across the heads of some dozen people. Another truck was just pulling up among the loose crowd. As we walked, some older black kids ran by us.

"Oh, shit!" Rufus took his hand off my shoulder. "That's down by *our* scow, Red!"

"What you think it is, Rufus?"

Another siren whined across the dark.

The van rolling up now was an ambulance. The spot turning on the roof of the police car, already parked, bled over its white sides.

"Nigger, maybe we better go check this out!"

"Think you're right, Red!"

Booted and barefoot, the two garbagemen lumbered off along the planks. There was a sudden, clear smell of seawater. It surprised me—till then, Red and Rufus's smell had just about covered all the warm night.

I watched them hurry ahead.

I was still half-sopped in nigger piss—that what wasn't my own. I wiped my hands on my pants, wiped my mouth, and wiped my hands again. I had piss in both sneakers. Trickles ran out my hair and down my neck, even though Red had wiped it for me. I pulled my shirt loose off my chest and let it fall back. Then I licked my salty fingers.

It would have been okay if it was Hogg piss.

I tried to remember what he smelled like.

A breeze came up the dock, loaded with the stink of oil and the stuff that floats around dock pilings.

Hogg smelled something like Red and Rufus. Only different. But I couldn't say exactly how.

As I walked toward the crowd, I could hear people muttering, whispering; I even heard two people laugh.

More than half were boatmen. When I got closer, I saw some white cops shooing people back from the edge of the water. I came up beside the ambulance. An orderly—this young nigger with his head shaved clean bald and wearing wire-framed glasses—in a short-sleeved white uniform, leaned against the ambulance's turned-back door. Another, this one white, with blond hair back in a rubber band—he had glasses too, but black-framed ones—came up through the crowd.

"You find out what the fuck is going on?" the nigger asked. He sounded disgusted. He didn't uncross his arms or stand up or even move.

The white one—he wore tennis sneakers that had a flag design on them and red socks—made fists in his white hip pockets and hunched his shoulders. "I don't know. After all that hurry up and rush but would you wait awhile before you start—"

"It's more of this Harkner shit?"

"That's what I heard. But when I asked a cop down there, he just told me to mind my fuckin' business."

"If it's Harkner," the nigger said, "there ain't no use to rush. Everybody's gonna be dead."

"Yeah," the white one said. "Not as many people dead, but it's supposed to be a bigger mess than the Stevens's place."

The nigger looked off through the loose crowd. "I hope it's Harkner. 'Cause if there're *two* of them crazy maniacs runnin' around, I don't even want to *know* about it."

I looked through the crowd too.

All the activity was around the barge beside Red and Rufus's scow. Searchlights had already been set up to shine over the water. Others shone on the barge cabin. A couple of cops came out the cabin door. On the peeling tarpaper, in wide, brown-red swatches—some of it was still wet and redder—were the big letters:

ALL RIGH

—followed by a smear, like whoever'd written them had been interrupted. There were dribbles from both L's and the G.

One cop turned another spotlight on the wall: all the little tongues of shadow from the tarpaper tatters swung up, then went away. Flashbulbs popped.

Parts of the letters, still wet, glistened. Parts had dried a dull rust.

"Shit," the nigger orderly said. "That's Harkner. Might as well get ready for another leisurely trip to the morgue."

"Naw, man: we gotta rush." The white orderly gave a grin like a cup of cold coffee. "I mean, you never know when we gonna have to make the *next* one!" I guess he didn't like his own joke, because he scowled and shook his head. "When I went up close, I could see part of the woman through the door, when one of the cops came out. Man, she looked like a fuckin' watermelon somebody's taken an ice-pick to—for about an hour!" He took his hands out of his pockets, opened them, closed them, put them back. "Jesus!"

"Whyn't they just scrape 'em into a couple of baggies and let us haul 'em in, huh?" The nigger still hadn't really moved. "You know? Instead of makin' us stand around like this?"

"They got measurements and pictures to take and stuff." The white one put all his weight on one hip, shook his head again, then put it all on the other. "Besides, they're looking for a baby."

"A baby?" The nigger uncrossed his arms and let them drop. "Aw, man, a *baby*?" His dark hands hung against his white pants. Behind his round, rimless lenses, his eyes got all scrunched up.

"There was supposed to be a baby on the barge, but nobody can find it now. We're supposed to wait around in case they got to get it to the hospital fast or something—"

"Jesus God," the nigger said softly. He took a breath, crossed his arms again, again looked off through the crowd.

I walked on, trying to get a better look.

Police were on the garbage scow too.

Rufus stood on the deck, one wide black thumb hooked under his tanktop strap. One leg of his pants—a searchlight swung across his face and made him turn aside—was wet.

Arms out for balance, Red was climbing to the top of the highest garbage pile. He turned around to watch, back pretty much to me. There was a dark stain all down his ass.

Two cops with shovels came over to talk to Rufus. I couldn't hear what they said. But finally Rufus shrugged, then gestured back with his chin. The cops, lifting their shoes pretty gingerly, went to the heap bottom, and started shoveling.

On top, Red shifted his weight, glanced down; his bare foot loosed a can that clanked toward the diggers.

The can bounced right in front of one of them—it startled him, and he danced to the side, looked up, shook his head, then went back to digging.

On the other barge, a man in a rumpled brown suit, with a loose, knitted tie, came from the cabin. A chain of sweatdrops crossed his forehead under his gray hair. He squinted among the searchlights, saw the two shoveling on the scow and hollered: "Hey! What the hell do you guys think *you're* doing?"

The cop who'd been surprised by the can stood up. "Well you said to look all over for it."

"Come *on*," the man in the rumpled suit shouted. "He wouldn't have had *time* to bury it. That would have taken him at least five or ten minutes. He didn't *have* no five or ten minutes. We figured out he couldn't a' been on here no more'n—"

The first cop called: "Maybe he didn't bury it very *deep*!" The second cop had stopped shoveling too.

"Look! You two jackoffs start *lookin'*! And I mean lookin' someplace sensible!"

With their shovels, the cops walked to the edge of the scow. The first cop used his like a cane. The other just swung his alongside of him.

The man in the rumpled suit took out a handkerchief that, even from here, I could tell he'd been using for at least a couple of weeks. He wiped his forehead, then turned to talk to one of the guys on the floodlights. They must have been pretty hot, because already the letters on the tattered tarpaper only had a few palm-sized spots of clear red left. One, nearest the light, I could actually see drying.

A van, bigger than the ambulance, rolled into the crowd—the back doors were already open and three guys and a woman all wearing earphones jumped down—and stopped. The woman was smoking a cigarette.

Inside the truck, another man was handing down coils of cable to the guys. "You want to take this stuff, Mary? It's pretty dusty—"

"Come *on*. Come *on*. Gimme." Her cigarette bobbed as she gestured for the powerlines. Carrying them around to the side of the van, she left them with the others against the front wheel and came back for another load. On the third trip back, she picked up a clipboard from where it lay on the van floor, stopped a second to speak into the mike on the wire curving from her earphone. The cigarette bumped plastic and lost its ash. When she finished talking, the other men with the earphones began moving much faster.

She took one of the ballpoints out of her blouse pocket—she had at least half a dozen pens and pencils in there in one of those plastic pen-cases that have a lip that goes over the pocket edge—made a mark on the clipboard, and put it back. She must have smudged the paper, because she looked at her hand, rubbed her fingers together, frowning, then wiped her hand on her gray skirt.

Through the van doors I saw banks of tape recorders and electrical equipment. There was an old bridge table in front. Inside, a guy was rearing back in a folding chair, reading a *Fantastic Four* comic and sipping from a Styrofoam coffee cup.

When I looked back, the woman was walking towards me. A man in a sports jacket, also with headphones (all the other guys were in shirt sleeves), wearing a string tie like a line of blood down his blue shirt, came with her. I heard her say: "…on in four minutes."

The man said: "This on-the-spot ought to keep the ghouls out there in Radio Land happy."

The woman said: "Too bad it isn't TV. Then we could go inside and show them the mess." She frowned at the barge. "Have *you* been in?"

The man shook his head. "And I don't want to. I've got one of the cops lined up to describe it." He shook his head again. "He gave me a little sample. Mary, this Harkner kid is a real monster!"

"*Alleged* monster," the woman said. "You've been doing fine up till now. But if the station gets into a lawsuit because you leave out an adjective, Martin will have your left testicle for breakfast, my dear, on a gold toothpick."

"A real, alleged monster," the man said. "Okay?"

But she was running her finger down the clipboard. "Let me see…. Oh, here. Lend me your pen a minute—oh, never mind." She took one out of her pocket, a yellow one, this time, with a blue cap. She made a note and put it back. "You've got somebody looking out for all your interviewees so they don't run off?"

"Yeah—if they haven't run off anyway. Don't worry. It'll go."

She turned up two pages, took out another pen, made another note. "Teddy's giving you a thirty-second delay."

"Why not just five?"

"People get excited at these things." She let go of the pages, stabbed at her pocket a couple of times before she got it in. One, then the other, the pages flipped back down. "If somebody says something they shouldn't, it's likely to be more than the usual 'shit,' 'God,' or 'fuck.' Teddy's a good tape jockey. I brought him along because he can edit on the run. Just don't let anybody make any mistakes over ten seconds long." She took her cigarette out her mouth, looked at it—it still had an inch to go—and put it back. "I've directed some strange radio shows before but, really, this has *got* to be it!"

A man came up. "Here's your mike, Mr. Sawyers. You want to leave the wind-ball on it, Mary?"

She frowned at the sky. "It's pretty calm, but I think I felt a breeze a minute ago. Besides, it'll cut some of the crowd rhubarb. We'll keep the ball."

"Okay."

The man in the red string tie took the mike.

The other man fell behind him, dragging lots of cable and spreading it out in big S's.

"At least he only got two this time," the man in the string tie said, not into the microphone. "I suppose that's something to be thankful for."

"You mean they *found* the baby?" the woman asked, looking up from her clipboard.

"Well, I guess it is three, counting the baby. No, they haven't found it. *I* just hope they don't trip over it when we're on the air!"

"Oh, I don't know." The director leered around her cigarette. "I doubt Martin feels that way. It'd probably make his week."

"You know, I really think Martin's getting a charge out of all this. The on-the-spot was his idea."

"Not only do you have the sweetest voice on the A.M.—" The cigarette bobbed again—"you're even beginning to get some smarts. Go on. I'm calling One Minute."

"On my way, Starshine." The man in the string tie touched the microphone's gray plastic ball to his forehead in salute, grinned, and started forward.

The producer, holding her mike in one hand, spoke down into it. Once she stopped to move her cigarette from the center of her mouth to the side, but noticed it was all ash and dropped it, ground it under the brown leather toe of a low flat, and went on whispering.

I followed the man in the string tie.

Once he adjusted his earphone and said, softly, into his mike: "Sure, Mary...ready when you are."

The light on the police car was still turning, but as I came up beside the open windows I saw no one was inside. Someone had left the radio going. "American Pie" was playing, though not very loudly. About ten feet away, the man in the string tie began.

"THIS IS EDWARD SAWYERS, IT'S JUNE 27TH, 1969, AND I'm at the Crawhole waterfront tonight, walking through a crowd of people who have gathered behind a loose police line to watch the investigation of this nightmare day's latest—and we all pray the last—act of mindless slaughter. There are searchlights set up on the barges around the docks. There's an ambulance here—it arrived only seconds before me. But, from what police have already told me, there isn't much need for one—except to take the bodies to the morgue. Thankfully, there are only two known victims this time—Harry Bunim, twenty-nine, and his common-law wife, Mona Casey, thirty-four. Right now the police are searching for a missing year-old child, the Bunims' little son, Chuck. And we are all hoping here, as I know you are all hoping out there, that he has not been..."

Through the police car window, "American Pie" finished, and over the sound of Mr. Sawyers in front of me, I heard from the police car's radio speaker: "This is Edward Sawyers, it's June

27th, 1969, and I'm at the Crawhole waterfront tonight, walking through a crowd of..."

I listened about half a minute, then looked back. Sawyers was beckoning to one of the shirt-sleeved men. The assistant led over a fisherman from the ring of spectators—a barefooted, bullet-headed nigger. Up in front of his plaid shirt, he clutched a harmonica.

Sawyers was gesturing with one outstretched hand and saying: "...that's right, over here: You want to tell us what it's been like down here today?" He held out the mike to the fisherman.

Beside me, the radio was saying: "Thankfully, there are only two known victims this time—Harry Bunim..."

Still clutching his harmonica, the fisherman leaned over Sawyers' microphone: "This is a pretty peaceful place, like, mostly. After a little fightin' and a little fuckin', there ain't really—"

"Come on, now." Sawyers pulled the microphone back sharply. "Let's watch the language. We're on the air. Teddy, cut! Okay, pick it up...from: Why don't you tell us something about what it's like down here?"

"Eh...well," the fisherman said, much more slowly. He'd lowered his harmonica about to his belt. "People fight some. Sometimes they...you know, mess around. But usually it's pretty peaceful."

"Until tonight?"

"Well, this here tonight is just terrible."

"And can you tell us where you were when the screaming started?"

"Down on my boat, playin' on my mouth harp." He gestured with the instrument, caged in ten dark fingers. "And I heard Miss Mona scream. And then the shootin'."

"What did you do?"

"I was scared as a—" He looked at the microphone. "Well, I was real scared. You know, you don't hear nothin' like that around here much."

Beside me, the car radio said: "...are hoping out there, that he has not been hurt. We're going to talk now with Mr. Andy

Prescott, who works on a boat not far from the barge on which the most recent multiple slaughter took place. Mr. Prescott told me earlier that he comes from Mitchuan, Kansas, but that he's been a fisherman out of Crawhole for the past seven years. We're going to be talking to Andy in just a moment now. Come right on, yes, that's right, over here: You want to tell us what it's been like down here today?" Somewhere in there was a click, but it went by pretty soft.

"Eh...well. People fight some. Sometimes they...you know, mess around. But usually it's pretty peaceful."

"Until tonight?"

"Well, this here tonight is just..."

But the assistant was leading Andy from the man with the microphone, while another was escorting up a black policeman. Sawyers was saying: "...you, very much. We're going to talk now with Officer Horace Pelham, who was the first police officer at the scene of the crime; who was, indeed, the first person to enter the barge cabin: Without getting too gory, Horace, can you tell us what you saw when you went in?"

"I wasn't the first one in," the cop said. He looked pretty sober. "It was another guy, one of the dock cops—one of the guys who works Crawhole regular. I told him that."

The man with the microphone grimaced at the assistant. Behind the cop's shoulder, the assistant shrugged.

The cop started to glance back, and Sawyers practically followed him around with the microphone. "Well, you were *one* of the first ones in, then—"

"I was the second," the cop said, turning back. He pushed his cap up and scratched his forehead. "I don't think I *can* describe it without gettin' gory. The woman had been all hacked up. First we thought the man was just shot, but when we turned him over, it looked like he got hacked up too. It's just a *mess* in there! I mean, I've seen killings before, but this is about the worst one I *ever*..."

The fisherman with the harmonica, and the first assistant, had come over to watch from near the police car. They stopped about three feet from me. After a few more moments, the fisherman said: "I thought he was gonna let me play my mouth harp. You said before, I was maybe gonna get a chance to play my mouth harp on the radio." He turned the instrument around in his horny black hands, frowning. "That's what you said." Suddenly he lifted it to his mouth and blew a clutch of bending blues notes, loud and twisting—they ended squawking: the assistant had grabbed the harp away and was making *Shushing* motions.

Sawyers, the policeman, and the second assistant glanced over. But they went on talking.

And from the radio, Andy's voice: "...because Harry always liked my music, you know. I'd see him, sometimes when he'd come by, just stop and listen. Miss Mona, too. It's just terrible. An' she gonna have another baby—"

And, from the radio, Sawyers': "Thank you, Andy. Thank you, very much. We're going to talk now with Officer Horace Pelham..."

I looked back into the center of the circle of spectators. Officer Pelham was saying: "...no, but I was at the Webster's gas station. I didn't have anything to do with the Stevens' place, so I don't know what it was like there. But I tell you, I just never seen anything like that inside, here. We're just hopin' now that the baby is all right, or maybe just hurt a little. What everybody is afraid of, of course, is that he's been killed, or that the Harkner kid—"

"The alleged Harkner kid," the man with the string tie said, then frowned when that didn't sound right. "Allegedly it might be Dennis Harkner..." He frowned at that too.

"Yeah," the policeman said. "Anyway—we're just hoping that he didn't go and kidnap the baby. That's a pretty terrible thought. I mean, you don't even know which one would be worse, the kid being killed, or being carried off with someone like that. We're lookin' all around, hopin' that we can find it while it's still—"

From the car radio came a blast of harmonica music.

The man with the string tie glanced over again.

The assistant beside Andy gave an immense shrug, then pointed into the open car window.

"...um, alive," Officer Pelham finished.

"Yes," said the man with the string tie. "Of course. And we're all, all of us, the listeners and all of us here on the mobile unit, praying with you that little Chuck will be found in time, before..."

Andy looked down at the mouth harp in his hands. He had a vague smile. He glanced in the car window, then back to his harmonica.

From the car radio, Officer Pelham's voice came on: "...because it gets all thick—the blood. You bleed that much and it don't run no more. It makes like a jelly, you know? And it gets—but you said not to get too gory, huh? Describin' things like that, that's pretty hard."

Sawyers' voice: "And you were at the Stevens' house, earlier?"

And Pelham's: "Oh, no. I didn't have anything to do with that—no, but I was at Webster's gas station..."

I wandered away from the car and Andy and the assistant, and made my way out of the circle of fishermen and police who had come up to hear and watch the man with the string tie. I went down to the water a little ways along the dock.

A big, split beam was set into the gravel. Below, sludge, thick and dull, slopped the rocks. I walked along the beam, looking down.

It was floating near a piling. A muddied island, with four small islands around it, its back bobbed in the oil, wood chips, and algae. The head must have been hanging straight down—if it still had one.

It bumped the pile, floated a few inches away, was carried in, and bumped again. I watched it awhile. Then I looked back at the crowd.

Four policemen were circling the gathering.

One was Whitey.

He glanced at me, saw I was watching him—suddenly he left the others, with a gesture to keep on going, and came over. "Hey, boy." He nodded, put his hand on my shoulder and said, real quiet: "Look, I don't got time to mess with you now. But after they finish up with this thing, if they don't put me on no special detail—" His pale eyes flicked back to the other policemen, then swiveled, like small lights, to me—"I'll meet you right there where we was foolin' around before, okay? Then I'll really throw some dick into you and you can have you a—"

While he was talking, I looked down at the water.

Whitey glanced too—and his eyes got bigger, and brighter; suddenly, they got real small. Then they opened up again. "Jesus—!" He dropped his hand. Three times as loud, he said: "Oh my God...!" Then he whirled, calling: "I found it! Hey, I found it, right here!"

People in the crowd turned.

About six of them hesitated, then—one was the nigger orderly with the shaved head and the round glasses—started over.

From the barge, the gray-haired man in the rumpled suit called: "What you got?"

"I found the goddamn baby!"

The whole crowd started for us. Other cops were coming too. People reached us, pushed around us. In the crowd, the director was making large semaphore gestures at the assistants, who were trying to keep the cables from underfoot. The man with the string tie was coming forward too, talking into his mike the while. But you couldn't hear him because other people were shouting too much. A lot of niggers got in my way and somebody else—it was the white orderly; I looked down and saw his red socks flash below his jean cuffs—pushed me back.

And while I was trying to keep from falling, another person grabbed my shoulder and spun me around, hard: I stared up into the face of an angry black, in a blue workshirt with the sleeves torn off. I didn't even recognize him till he bellowed: "Where the hell you run off to, you motherfuckin' little son of a bitch?"

It was Big Sambo.

"You *get* your yeller nigger ass back down to the tug there with Honey-Pie, or I'm gonna bust your yellow-headed self all to *hell*!" He raised his hand to hit me. I cowered back. "An' if I *don't* find you there when I come, you better not *never* let me see you again, or it's gonna be me and you! You hear me?"

His fist fell—caught me on the shoulder, because I ducked. I dodged through the two fishermen pushing up behind me, and ran. I ran until I got to the tugs.

Then I stopped.

I looked back at the crowd. I looked at the squat, rust-hulled tug at its dock. I looked over the roadway that Nigg and Hawk had brought me down on the motorcycle.

I looked at the tug again.

I walked out on the dock, crossed the sagging plank, went to the cabin door, pulled it open, and went inside.

At the galley table, Honey-Pie sat on a chair with her bare feet wrapped behind the rungs and her fists in the lap of her dress. She looked at me, blinking.

On the windowsill, the radio was still going: "...have been other mass murderers—indeed, man has committed atrocities against man, even in this decade, that render the terror here insignificant; yet the concentration of all this violence into a single day, in a single town, coupled with the alleged youth of the assassin—" Sawyers' voice was interrupted by another, further away: "Oh my God!" Then, louder: "I found it! Hey, I found it, right here!" There were murmurs, whispers, shouts; then, one shout among them: "What you got?" And Whitey's bawling reply: "I found the—" *Bleep*!—"baby!" Sawyers' voice returned in an intense whisper: "Wait a minute... Wait...! I *think* they've found something. Yes. I think they've got the... Everyone is running toward the water. I'm moving with the crowd. I'm moving.

Fishermen, policemen, and those who are simply curious on-lookers are clustered at the water's edge, crowding onto the docks to see, staring down into the...! What? No, we're trying to find out for you if he's all right. Hello? Hey...? Is he all...? One of the orderlies has just pushed by me, making for the ambulance. Now he's getting out the stretcher. People are making so much noise, you couldn't hear the sound of a baby crying even if— What's that...? Two of the policemen now, with grapple-hooks, I can see from here, are reaching down into the— Yes...? Oh my God, folks, the poor thing is..."

The cup of coffee sat in front of Honey-Pie. I thought she was going to pick it up and drink it. But when I walked around the table, I saw there was a ring inside it, half an inch above the liquid, on which gray skin quivered and wrinkled. It was maybe two, three days old.

There was a mattress, folded over on itself once and stained over the narrow blue and white stripes. I went to it and sat down.

Honey-Pie watched me as I hunkered back against the wall. I pulled my sneaker heels back against my ass and wrapped my arms around my knees. One knee was coming through. I was breathing hard, and my belly, pressing again and again against my thighs, felt funny. I shook back hair that was tickling my forehead; it fell again, still wet.

Sawyers was saying: "...makes at least thirty-one people dead today: by gunshot, rifle and pistol; by stabbing—knife, screw-driver, broken fire poker; by clubbing, with a rifle butt, with a pair of wireclippers; by strangulation, with jumper cables, bail-ing wire—and now the latest victims include a pregnant mother and her year-old child. That thirty-one does *not* include Michael Rhomer, tragically killed in the street because someone mistook him for the murderer. There are over half a dozen people in severe condition at Frontwater District Memorial Hospital. This city, I think it is safe to say, has never seen a day like this before. And we all hope it never sees one like it again. I'm going to be talking to Police Inspector Haley in a few seconds. Inspector Haley is going to explain what the police will be—Oh, yes. That's right. Yes, this is Inspector Haley. Inspector?"

"Yeah? Well, we're all agreed this has been pretty terrible." It was the voice of the man in the rumpled suit. "Anyway, we're sure he hasn't gotten too far away. He's only had minutes to run, this time. And the place is surrounded with just about everything we have. We got it from a couple of people at the bar where he did the first bunch in—people who knew him there—that the kid don't even know how to drive. We've already done some checkin' on him. We're gonna catch him, soon now."

"Can you tell us why you're so sure the capture is imminent, Inspector?"

"Well, there's that thing he always writes.... Is that all right to talk about? Do they know about that?"

"If they've been listening to their radios, Inspector. Ladies and gentlemen, Harkner—or the killer alleged to be Dennis Harkner—at the scene of each crime has written 'All right,' somewhere on the floor or a wall or a window. This time, it's on the front of the barge cabin where the murder was committed. Would you tell us something about how he writes it, Inspector?"

"Huh?—well, in these big... Eh, with blood... Eh...blood. The murder victims' blood. That's pretty—you know—grim."

"Yes, Inspector. And you were saying?"

"Oh, yeah. Well, he didn't get a chance to finish it this time. He wrote 'All' and the first four letters of 'Right.' Then there's this smear—you can see it over there on the cabin wall of the barge."

"Yes, I do, Inspector. Ladies and gentlemen, the spotlights are illuminating the front wall of the barge's cabin where the victims, Harry and Mona Bunim, with their year-old son, Chuck, worked and lived. Next to the door, across the torn tarpaper, you can read, plainly and clearly, the gruesome words the Inspector has described."

"Well, see," the Inspector repeated, "he didn't have time to finish. So he must not have had time to get too far away." In the background whispers and talk, someone playing a harmonica passed close to the microphone. "Somebody, Inspector, just told me…I just was handed a note that the officer who, minutes ago, discovered the mutilated body of little Chuck, floating in the water, was also the first to hear the gunshots and shouts of the victims and to come running to their aid, apparently scaring Harkner—the alleged killer—away. And that it was he, *not* Officer Pelham, who was first to enter the cabin, to be greeted by the horrendous sight."

"Yeah," the Inspector said. "He's one of our regular Crawhole fellas. Whitey's a good old boy."

"Thank you, Inspector. Ladies and gentlemen, this is Edward Sawyers, and we've been talking to Inspector Haley, here at the Crawhole docks, not thirty feet from the barge on which, perhaps half an hour ago, occurred another in the series of slayings that have branded this day as one of the blackest in the annals of mass murder. The Inspector has assured us that the capture of the killer, alleged to be seventeen-year-old Dennis Harkner, is imminent. A net of police has been set around and throughout Crawhole. From evidence at the scene of the murder, we have been assured that the killer is somewhere in the—"

Then the door crashed back.

Honey-Pie's fists jumped onto the table and she jerked her chair half a foot, without standing.

"Aw, shit," Hogg drawled. Grinning, he lowered his booted foot to the floor, and let go of the jambs. His bare foot was gun-colored with filth, to the frayed cuff. On the sill, his club-like toes, the nails picked back like they were bitten bad as the ones of his dirty, sausage-thick thumbs, flattened. The workboot, crusted with dirt, flexed with the foot inside. He grinned, wide enough for me to see, as well as his big, yellow front teeth, some of the side, rotten ones. His close green eyes were bright in his grimy face. Greasy hair clawed his forehead. Chin, cheek, and upper lip were dark with stubble like sand. He looked around the galley. When his eyes went from me to Honey-Pie and back, his grin got even looser.

Hogg stepped inside, real slow. The slab of his hand slid up to his belly. He furrowed the matted yellow around the creased pit of his navel, between the hanging shirt edges. Then he dropped it, to hook the scuffed belt with his thumb, pulling the brass buckle down his gut. Things inside the hammy, hairy forearm moved. "Cocksucker, you wouldn't believe the shit I just been through, tryin' to find your ass." He barked out one syllable of rough laughter. "You know them two motherfuckin' bastards, Nigg and Hawk, had the nerve to come back to the bar? Well, like I was goin' up to save them a run-in with all the fuckin' pigs what was still hangin' around after all Denny's shit—I mean, I seen 'em hustlin' you out the goddamn door; they must've thought I was asleep or something—anyway, I just took 'em back around in the alley, you see, explainin' to them why all the cops was there and all about what Denny had done and all. Soon as I got 'em out of sight of anybody—well, I began to bang heads. Couldn't bang Nigg's too hard 'cause he works with me too often and probably will again, but I did *in* the white boy! He told me where you were."

From the radio, Sawyers said: "...loading the sheet-covered bodies into the ambulance for that final..." and outside, along the docks, a siren made Hogg glance toward the window; red light swept the bottom corner of the screening. "...while the tiny, towel-covered figure—one of the orderlies nearly dropped his side of the stretcher, but now he catches it up, and they move on to the ambulance's open doors. Yes, the tiny, draped figure is now inside. The orderlies are climbing in. Inspector Haley is over, talking to the driver. One of the orderlies looks out the back door— has he forgotten something? No, he's just taking a last look at the scene here, as we shall be doing shortly, with its floodlights, its police cars, and the dozens of police officers still checking the barge for evidence. Now the door is being locked. The ambulance, starting slowly at first among the crowd of fishermen and other locals who are wandering around it, is beginning to drive off." And from the radio speaker came the sound of the siren— thirty seconds old. "Momentarily, we'll be switching you back to the studio for a final rundown on the search for Dennis Harkner, a wrap-up of the local and national news, and music till midnight with…"

"Hey—!" Hogg jammed a thumb at the windowsill—"how you like that shit, huh? I guess Denny's just about the most famous person we know, hey, cocksucker?" He scratched his belly again and ambled forward, like a huge blond gorilla. "I'd a' thought the goddamn infection would a' laid him too low for that kind of mess. But I guess there's some spunk in the little jack-off yet." He scratched down under his belt. "I guess tomorrow we gonna hear about how twenty or thirty big brave pigs done finally smoked him from some outhouse with mace and what-all and machine-gunned his ass down. But, shit, the cocksucker ain't no more'n seventeen!" Hogg laughed. "I just sort of wish I'd get a chance to see him once more and maybe shake his hand 'fore they kill him. Man, you should've seen him in the bar, there, clubbin' them bikeys and shootin' old Ray in the belly—*Wham!* The wop and his old lady and me was just a-laughin' and applaudin'—dangerous? My syphilitic left nut! Before he cut out of there, he give me a big grin. I gave him one right back. 'Go on, motherfucker,' I told him. 'It's all right. Go on!'" A puzzled look broke, here and there, through Hogg's grin to pull together on top of it. "I don't know why he's doin' it. Don't expect I ever will. But it sure is something, huh?" He pulled his hand out from his belt and reached down to dig at his crotch. Down on his greens where the head of his dick would be was a wet spot the size of a waterglass bottom—from the drip his work got him, I guess.

Thinking about it in there, thick as my wrist and long as a flashlight, with an inch of foreskin swinging off it (I was still breathing hard), I felt my own dick move in my pants.

Hogg turned to close the door—the latch didn't quite catch and it drifted open an inch as he turned back. Once more he looked around the room, at Honey-Pie, at me, at Honey-Pie. "Motherfucker," he said. The grin was back on his face. He moved his feet apart and, at his thighs, flexed his hairy hands. "Well, looks like we got us some nigger meat here." Hogg shook his head a little. "Hey, baby... Ain't nothin' like sweet young nigger meat! Maybe you didn't land yourself in such a bad place after all, cocksucker. Come here, nigger meat."

Honey-Pie stood up so fast the chair overturned. She stepped back, looking serious and blinking.

"Come here...." Hogg stepped forward.

She took another step back.

"Come on, honey. Lemme see some of that chocolate pussy. Go on, pull up that skirt and let me see some sweet, brown, nigger pussy." Mouth wide open, Hogg stuck out his tongue and wobbled it like a wet fish. A drop of gray spit hung from his lower lip. "Hey, cocksucker, you gonna help me fuck this little black bitch...." One hand got into his fly; on the other a single hairy finger bent, beckoning. "Come here, nigger meat. Lemme see some pussy...."

Her next step back, Honey-Pie's heel landed on the mattress. I wasn't sure, from behind her, but it looked like she started to bunch her skirt up.

"Shit..." Hogg whispered, came around the table, pushed her. "Lay down—!"

She grunted when she hit the mattress, rocked back against me; I caught her from hitting her head on the wall.

Hogg's hand did something inside his pants; another fly button hit the floor, rolled under the table, clicked against one of the iron braces, and fell over.

His wormy cock came out, hard as a pipe, dangling its rag of skin. His knees hit the mattress, and I caught his stench. I tried to remember how many times his clothes had been soiled since I'd met him. With his thumb, he jabbed at the fleshy petals of Honey-Pie's cunt. She jerked against me.

I let go and scrambled around to get my face between them. I licked her pussy around where his thumb dug—she didn't have much hair. Then I tried to get at his cock—the rim of his fist beat at my mouth—but he wanted to get it in her. Hogg shoved forward and my head got caught between his fleshy gut, his wrinkled jeans, her bunched-up dress and smooth brown belly. I pulled out. Hogg was already humping her, hard. His knees were on the floor and he was grunting like a pig. She was gasping like one.

I crawled down his legs, and for a while I gnawed on his bare, black, cracked heel.

Then I got up, crawled onto the mattress again, and pulled at the back of his pants. They came down over his heaving ass; coming up, the buttocks opened, shit-stuck either side. They fell, clamping, then rose, the hair pulling apart the half-dried paste. The sphincter, discolored and wrinkled, suddenly puckered, then bubbled. I stuck my tongue in it. His buttocks ground my face. "Yeah," Hogg growled, "you finally eatin' shit, you little bastard." His hand came back and pushed my head further down. With a palm on one cheek, I ate out his asshole. I put my other hand between his legs. Sweat ran down his balls. When I fingered the fat, sliding cock and the rolling edges of Honey-Pie's pussy, he humped harder. I licked and thought about the way, when he finished fucking a woman or a girl, right afterward he would sink his scummy pole into my mouth and loose another load or fill my belly with pee. Thinking about that and eating out his asshole while he fucked Honey-Pie made it better than eating shit out of—

The door crashed back.

—Big Sambo bellowed: "MOTHERFUCKER!"

I heard Big Sambo's boots bang across the floor; the nigger roared, "What the *fuck* you—!"

Hogg came up off Honey-Pie, rising in one movement—I got pushed aside onto the mattress—to turn, crouching, his cock still up and gleaming. He was grinning, all stubbly-jawed and yellow-headed.

Honey-Pie rolled against the wall, terrified. The way she curled up made me think of a brown beetle somebody had stuck with a pin and then just pulled it loose.

"Oh, man," Big Sambo said, beside the table, real low. He was crouched too. "Oh, man, you fuckin' on my *daughter!*" His fists came up like slow cannonballs with corners. "I'm gonna kill you, motherfucker…"

"Aw, shit," Hogg drawled; in the same tone as when he'd come in. He hefted up his trousers, enough to close the top button. His belt still swung. His cock still hung out, glistening. But it was pretty much down. "Try, nigger."

Big Sambo's face snarled up like a prune. One black workboot stamped forward. One of those cannonballs swung by his hip. When it stopped, there was a knife in it; I'm damned if I know where he'd hidden it.

Hogg grabbed the edge of the galley table. It came up, the clamps on three legs yanking loose nests of splinters. The fourth leg just broke. Hogg brought the table back with both hands and heaved.

The cup crashed, splashing tan and splattering pieces.

The table corner hit Big Sambo's chest. The nigger grunted and went back. Both fists hit the wall over his head—he didn't drop the knife, though. The table landed upside down. The nigger came forward, among the upright legs (and one stump), stumbling against the brace across the underside.

Hogg was already at the sink, though. He snatched the ten-inch skillet from its nail—the nail pulled loose, clinked on the stained aluminum drainboard, rolled into the basin—lumbered around, fast, and swung.

It gonged the left side of Big Sambo's head. Clutching his face, Big Sambo staggered right—and right into the pan as Hogg brought it back again. This time the knife fell on the floor.

Three seconds later, so did Big Sambo.

Feet wide—the bare one in spilled coffee—Hogg rubbed at the arm from which the pan dangled. It looked like he'd wrenched it. Then the pan clanked to the floor and wobbled around with a sound like somebody swallowing it. Breathing hard, Hogg looked first at Big Sambo, then back at the mattress.

Honey-Pie sat, her cheek pressed to the wall, one wrist against her mouth, one hand spread on the wood. She was blinking at Big Sambo.

"Come on, cocksucker," Hogg said. "Let's get outta here 'fore somebody comes around to see about the noise."

He wasn't even thinking about Honey-Pie at all, now.

I got up but, as I stepped over the nigger, I looked back at her. She was staring at me… I felt my face trying to mimic hers, as though that would let me know what was going on inside her.

"Come *on!*" Hogg's smack just caught my ear; it stung so hard I almost fell. If he'd caught me full in the head, he might've knocked me out.

I got to the door—scraped my shin against the broken table leg, but not bad—and pushed it open. I looked back at Hogg, who was rubbing his arm again. He wiped his mouth on his shoulder, kneaded his biceps, bent his elbow a couple of times, then kneaded his forearm.

Behind Hogg, taking her hand from the wall now, Honey-Pie was still looking at me.

"Go on, go on," Hogg said.

I crossed the deck. Hogg came on behind me. I heard him laugh. "Shit, cocksucker—" I glanced back. Stuffing his meat back into his pants, immediately he gestured me to keep going—"but I sure like to beat up a nigger. Can't beat on old Nigg too much 'cause we always on jobs together." I heard him buckling his belt. "Beatin' on the bikey was fun. But it ain't like a nigger." At the head of the gangplank, Hogg stopped me with a hand on my shoulder. "Pretty soon I may do some beatin' on you too—just for the fun of it."

From the deck we could see down where the police cars were still parked by the barge. The red light was off now. The van from the radio station was pulling out. Police were all up and down the dock. There was still a crowd. There were still spotlights.

On the barge beyond, a figure, arms out for balance (from here, in just the dock lights, I couldn't tell if it was Red or Rufus) walked to the top of the pile and turned to look. It was joined by a second (Rufus—or Red...). After a few seconds, they went down the other side.

"Come on—!" Hogg started. "No...wait'll they go by."

The radio van was rolling up, very slowly. Some of the assistants, the director, and Sawyers walked beside it. A guy with a roll of cables over one arm came running up and, jogging along, handed them up to somebody in the open back door.

The director looked behind her, saw him, and called, "Hey, hurry it up. You guys were supposed to have that all packed before we took off." She turned back to her clipboard and, still walking, got out a pen and made a mark. "Well, let's just hope we don't have to do anymore of *those* tonight!"

"It went okay," Sawyers said. "It seemed to me like it went okay."

The guy who'd handed up the cables into the van grabbed the van door and tried to vault inside. He didn't make it, and some of the assistants laughed.

"What'd you think about it, Mary?" Sawyers' earphones were around his neck now. The wire looped across the blood-red strings. "You think it went okay?"

The director turned up another paper on the clipboard. "I guess so. Maybe that part where you were getting Pelham to describe the inside of the cabin was a little much."

"Aw," Sawyers said, "this is a liberated age! And Martin'll love it—you know I really thought he was the first cop in there. That's what I *asked* for. That's what I thought I was getting."

The director looked up and saw the guys horsing around at the back of the slowly rolling van. "Hey," she called. "Cut it out, huh? I don't want to have to do an on-the-spot coverage about one of you breaking a leg." She turned back to Sawyers. "Babes, have you got a cigarette? I'm out."

"Sure. Here you go."

She took one from the pack he offered, but made a brushing gesture when he started to pat himself for a lighter. "No, that's okay. I got matches. It's all right...." She put the clipboard under one arm, bent her head; flame flared on her chin and cheeks. She'd stopped about seven feet in front of us. When she looked up, suddenly she frowned. She was looking straight at us, too— no, not straight at us: between us.

Without thinking, I pulled back a little bit. I heard Hogg take a breath; almost as though he was getting out of the direct line of her stare, he stepped back too.

I glanced behind us.

What she was staring at was Honey-Pie, who stood in the cabin doorway, one hand high on the door frame, the other on the doorknob, one foot inside the sill, one foot out. Her dress was all torn. Her head was all low between her shoulders, her mouth was sort of loose, and her eyes were wide. She was watching, not intense enough to call it a stare, back. She didn't look all that much like she was hurt or anything—maybe she looked like she was sick. Or maybe just funny.

I looked back at the director. I could tell, her eyes were flicking back and forth between me and Hogg; and back to Honey-Pie.

I looked at Hogg. He'd just glanced at Honey-Pie too; now his eyes went to fix on nothing in particular in the general direction of the director. He wasn't looking *at* her, I could tell. But his jaw was clamped so hard it almost looked like the muscle was about to shake.

The director lowered the still flaming match. Her frown got deeper. Sawyers was walking on. Again she looked at me, at Hogg, at Honey-Pie. I could see her start to turn away; then I could see her not do it. Her own jaw clamped, loosened. She shook the match suddenly, tossed it away. "Hey," she said. "Little girl? Are you okay...?" Hogg still wasn't looking at her. "Is everything all right?" (There were police all over the place, so I guess there wasn't too much Hogg could do.) "What's the matter?"

Honey-Pie blinked a couple of times at the director. I don't even think she was thinking particularly about me or Hogg. She moved her head a little, blinked again, and in a low voice answered: "Nothin'."

The director, her frown become all questioning disbelief, raised her cigarette slowly. At this point, I don't think she was thinking about Hogg or me either. I thought she was going to march up across the plank.

She didn't.

She turned away, took a couple of steps, looked back, frowned again—even then I thought she might come back—went off half a dozen steps more, glanced back at us again, then turned away.

Hogg let out his breath.

She glanced back a couple times more.

Hogg looked at Honey-Pie. She still stood in the doorway, looking down at the deck now. Once she looked up at us both, then let her eyes drop again.

The director had caught up with the van. She grabbed the side of the door, vaulted up—brushed away one guy who tried to give her a hand—and turned, holding onto the side, and looked back again, her cigarette a red pinprick in the gauze of shadows that pulled across them, van and all.

"Come *on*, cocksucker," Hogg whispered, "let's get *going!*"

He glanced at Honey-Pie once more, then lumbered over the sagging plank. I hurried after him.

We went by two policemen talking to about six fishermen.

None of them even looked at us.

"**A**LL THESE DAMN COPS," HOGG GRUNTED. "IT'S LIKE A fuckin' pig pen!" The muscles in his jaw clamped again. I think the director had made him nervous. "Let's just hope they're *all* here for Denny."

One policeman passed under the street lamp on the other side of the lot. As we reached Hogg's vanless truck, the cop swung around and came toward us. It was Whitey.

The breeze carried the dockside smells across the bushes and through the wire fence strung up behind us. Among the old automobiles, half a dozen pickup trucks were parked on the grass-veined tarmac. Near three police cars, one junked-out and windowless wreck sat on its axles by the brick wall. Talking, a dozen cops lounged together over by the lamp pole. Outside the fence, under another lamp, another clutch of police broke up into pairs and triplets, to saunter off, down and up the street.

"Shit." Hogg's hand worked on my shoulder. The last step, his bare foot landed against my sneaker. I felt his foot move through the damp cloth. "Fuckin' Denny sure has caused a pas-sel of trouble." As Hogg reached for the cab door, the policeman came around the bumper of an old green Chrysler twenty feet away, flashing ice-chip eyes.

Hogg pulled on the door handle, which made door-handle opening noises. "You get on up in there, cocksucker."

I climbed past Hogg into the cab.

And something grabbed my leg—

I looked down: the thin acned face, dirty and stained, hair mussed and clotted, looked up. Crouching down under the dash-board, his eyes wide and blinking (like Honey-Pie's, I thought), he pressed one grubby-knuckled, nail-gnawed finger up across his mouth to *Shhhhh* me.

The door slammed. The face went out.

I looked up again, out the window.

Outside, Hogg let go of the handle, turned around and said, "Hello, Officer."

I could feel each finger separate and hard on my shin. His arm must have been shaking a little. I could feel that too.

"Evenin'." Whitey's luminous glance flicked up at me, dropped back to Hogg.

Hogg's hand slid up the door to the open window. The wide, dirt-ringed wrecks of his nails, the thick, dirt-grooved knuckles slid across the crack with glass glinting down between the felt strips. Thick fingers hooked and hung. "Guess you fellas have been havin' a pretty rough day of it, huh?"

"Shit," Whitey said. "I don't want to ever see another one like this!" He slid his short, wide hands under his cartridge belt. His cap was still tilted pretty far to the side, but I guess that's the way he wore it. "Where you takin' the kid?" He nodded toward me.

Hogg's knuckles shifted an inch along the sill. "Back where he belongs." Hogg's voice shifted, too.

"'Cause I mean," Whitey said, "for most of the day he been hangin' around with the nigger on that broke-down tug up this end of the dock." He nodded toward the road we'd just come up that led back to the water.

"Yeah," Hogg said, "with Big Sambo." I could see the top of Hogg's head. His hair was greasy and strung together like pulled pieces of yellow wax. "Naw, the kid had his fun runnin' around Crawhole all day. But it's late now and it's time for me to get him back home—that's what I come down here for. That's what I'm gonna do."

"Oh." Whitey considered. "Then he's kin of yours?"

"Nope," Hogg said. "But he ain't no kin of that nigger, either. He got folks home waitin' for him, all worried about him bein' out here where all that murderin' and stuff is goin' on. Good God-fearin' white people—they sent me down to get him. I'm fixin' to take him back."

"Oh." Whitey's bright eyes came back up to mine. He pursed his lips a moment, then said to Hogg: "He's a nice kid. Him and me got to be sort of friends, you know, while he was playin' around down here. That was before all this Harkner shit come down." Whitey's head went over to the side a little. "Sort of sorry to see him go."

"What *you* sorry for?" Hogg asked. But then he laughed.

Whitey took his hands out from his cartridge belt and sort of smiled.

Down in the dark, fingers slid up to my knee. A hand caught my other leg. He was moving down there.

"What you haulin'?" Whitey asked.

"Ain't haulin' nothin'," Hogg said. "I'm bob-tail tonight. Can't you see I don't got no van?"

"Oh, yeah. Sure," Whitey said. "I was just wondering what you had in there that stunk so bad." He scratched his ear; his cap joggled on his tight, light hair. "Truck of yours smells about as bad as that goddamn scow moored up next to the Bunim barge— the Bunim barge—" Whitey nodded—"that's where Harkner did in the last ones."

Something tried to wedge between my knees. So I opened

them. I could feel his mouth moving against my jeans, like he was whispering to my leg.

"Jesus—" Whitey shook his head—"that really is some stink in there!"

Hogg laughed again. "Well, I'll tell you how it was, if you really want to know. Last night, see, I did myself a little too much celebratin'. 'Cause I got me a new job. Tied a pretty good one on, you know how you do? I came out the party and made it to the truck—in time to be sick all *over* it!"

Without looking down, I put one hand on the head between my legs. The hair was all stuck together.

"Then I passed out," Hogg explained. "Pissed myself up like a goddamn ten-year-old. Shit all over myself. When I woke up this mornin', I was a mess! Ain't had a chance to really clean nothin' up, either. But I guess if we keep the windows open, once we get rollin', with the breeze comin' through, it won't be so bad."

"Oh." Whitey frowned. "Yeah." He nodded. "Well, that's just about what it smells like. I guess you can get on, now. We're supposed to look in all the cars and things before they leave here, but I don't guess you got no crazy-insane, seventeen-year-old psychopathic killer in there, do you?" Whitey grinned up at me again.

"I'd about guess the same." Hogg looked up too. "But it wouldn't hurt none to check. Boy," he said. (The hand tightened on my leg. I could feel teeth tight together against my thigh, the lips pulled back.) "Run the sleeper curtain back there and let's have a look."

I got up on one knee—the hand slipped to my ankle; and it was shaking again—and turned in the seat. I pushed the sleeper curtain two feet down its runner.

Inside was a piece of gray blanket, and a newspaper it looked like nobody had ever read, though it was wet on one side, and, in the back, some dog turds or something.

Whitey stood on tiptoes to look.

Hogg grinned at him. "Yeah, I would about say we didn't."

Whitey's face wrinkled a little, and his light, light eyes narrowed. He glanced once at Hogg. He was just realizing that not all the smell was the truck. "Naw, you ain't got nothin' in there." He stepped back. (I sat down again.) "You can get on." He turned around, walked away. By the green Chrysler, he glanced back, gave me a sort of sad half-smile, then walked on.

Hogg came around to the driver's side, opened the door, swung up under the wheel, slammed the door beside him, reached down for the starter, turned the key—the motor turned over and Hogg's leg eased up the clutch—and said, looking straight out the windshield, "Denny, you are one lucky motherfucker!" We rolled forward across the lot.

Hogg dropped a hand from the carpet-taped wheel to Denny's head—suddenly, gripping him by the hair, he turned the face up. Light spilled on the stained cheeks. Denny's mouth was wide. His tongue and eyes glittered. The lips were working like a landed fish. "What'd you do? Recognize my truck while I was down on the docks lookin' for the cocksucker, then sneak in and hide?" Hogg let go.

Denny's head fell over against my hip. Denny's hand moved up to my knee again.

"Naw," Hogg said, "you just better stay down there out of sight till we get away from here."

"All right, Hogg...." Denny sounded like he had a really bad sore throat. Or maybe somebody had hit him there. "That's all...all right."

A passing street lamp dragged slow light across our laps.

Denny put one hand on Hogg's leg. Breathing hard, he slid it to Hogg's fly. Hogg's leg moved on a pedal. The light pulled away as we turned for the lot exit.

"Shit," Hogg drawled. "You know you *still* got a nice touch, motherfucker? I guess that's 'cause you take so much practice shuckin' on your own. Do what you want. Just stay down."

"...all right." It sounded pretty hoarse. "I just wanted to feel it..."

As we came to the gate, half a dozen policemen started toward us. One waved us to halt.

"Oh, shit..." Hogg whispered, hardly moving his lips. As he slowed, though, Whitey came up the other way:

"He's all right," Whitey shouted. "Let him go. I just checked him out."

Hogg gave the cops a big grin. "Go suck on some mule shit," he said, too low for them to hear and still smiling. We bounced down onto the street.

Fifteen minutes later, when we'd been on the highway for maybe eight or nine miles, Denny said: "Can I come up now?"

We leaned as Hogg pulled around another curve.

"Can I come up? Is it all right, Hogg? It's all right if I get up now, huh? That's all right, ain't it?"

"Yeah," Hogg said.

Denny scrambled up between us. He kept trying to get comfortable, pushing the heel of his hand down against his crotch, then squirming, grimacing, and grunting. Hogg drove and didn't look at him.

"Just a second, lemme..." Denny pushed up on the seat to pull at the bottom of his pants, then sat again, still squirming. "That's all...yeah, I guess that's right. Shit! You should of... Hey, man! Hogg? That was something, huh? That was...yeah, you know how I got at the motherfuckers! Yeah, I really did. I'm not kidding. That's all right. Zap! Zap! Not like zappin' people in the street. Zap! I really... Oh, shit! Yeah! I really killed some of them. With a gun, you know? For a while. I had a gun: I beat one motherfucker in the head with it."

"That was my gun." Hogg was still looking out the windshield.

"Huh?" Denny looked sharply at Hogg. "Yeah, I...maybe." His head drifted back. Frowning, he dug at his stomach with the fingers of one hand. The other had gotten wedged between his leg and mine, like he'd forgotten it there. "Yeah. I guess that one was...." He looked at Hogg again. "But some of 'em, I used a screwdriver in the eye, man! Shit!" Denny screwed up his face; his hand pushed at his groin. "...all right. You said that was all right. You don't have to kill the... In the grocery store...in the supermarket, I didn't kill 'em *all*. But it's all right, huh? It's pretty easy...rip!" His hand swung up, dropped in his lap again. "Just like that—Rip!—right in the throat. That wasn't bad. Beatin' 'em to death is hard, though. 'Cause you ain't sure when they're dead so you just have to beat some more. But mostly it's easy. I could show you. Sure. It's all right—"

Hogg took one hand off the wheel, turned in the seat—his arm went way back into the sleeper curtain—and hit Denny upside the head, about as hard as he could.

Denny gasped and rocked forward against the dashboard, both hands spread on the windshield.

Hogg was back driving when Denny's hand jerked across the glass, jerked again, then came back to his cheek to rub. He swallowed, swallowed again; he was breathing hard.

"You cut out that kind of talk now," Hogg said, looking out for another curve. "Somebody other than me or the cocksucker hear you going on like that, they might just think you were crazy."

Denny gasped, pushed himself back in the seat. "All right... that's—" He gasped again, his face all twisted like crying. He kept rubbing his cheek. But he didn't squirm so much. "Yeah..." he got out. "All right."

We took a curve close to the shoulder.

Hogg dropped his hand from the wheel again, this time to Denny's knee. He slid his hand toward the boy's groin and back. "Now if I'd'a hit you on the *ass* like that, you'd'a shot your wad." He grinned. His big fingers closed on Denny's crotch. "How's it feel?"

Denny's knees fell apart. His mouth opened. His face wrinkled around it. "...all right."

"Hey, cocksucker—" Hogg glanced at me—"take it out for him and let's get a look. Denny, when's the last time you come?"

"I...I killed 'em...." Denny looked at Hogg's hand in his lap and shook his head. "I kept on killin' 'em... But I didn't come, you know? It hurt... But it didn't make me shoot...."

"Best reason in the world I know to give it up." Hogg flexed his fingers in the stained, stiffened cloth. "You ain't gonna kill nobody no more, that right?"

"Huh...?" Denny asked.

"You ain't gonna kill nobody no more. All that stuff you did was just a mistake. Didn't even make you shoot your load. So you ain't gonna do it no more. All right?"

"I...yeah, I...no more." Denny pulled his hand loose from between our legs and put it on top of Hogg's. "Yeah, I won't...do that no more. All right." He looked puzzled.

Hogg grinned at me. "Go on, cocksucker. Take it out." He took his hand away.

Denny's fell back on his thigh like a muddy claw.

I turned on the seat and pulled open Denny's fly.

It looked awful. It was all swollen, and a funny color, even in the half-dark. When I took it out, it was stiff, but not like a hard-on. It was just leathery; it wobbled on his groin. The head was bulged up around the nail so there wasn't any space left. The foreskin was stretched tight and didn't move at all.

Denny, his tongue-tip in the corner of his mouth, watched.

I took his balls out too. They were very hot. His cock was almost chilly.

I opened my mouth and bent.

"Yeah...!" Hogg grinned.

I felt the truck slow, heard the wheels grind on the gravel shoulder. We stopped.

Denny's cock tasted cold and salty. Denny moved his hands to my hair, jerkily, shifted his buttocks on the seat, lifted them a little. The bent nail clicked my back teeth. I reached under his ass with one hand and found Hogg's already kneading a scrawny buttock that seemed like it had too much bone in it.

Denny grunted. His fingers closed. His knuckles ground my scalp. As I moved my mouth up and down, his cock swelled...then something, neither piss, nor cum, nor blood, spurted—and from two places. And his cock was still getting bigger.

Christ, it was bitter.

I got my other hand under his nuts, into the fine hair between his legs.

"That's right...." Denny whispered. "Yeah, that's all..." He pushed himself up again. Hogg and I were both digging for his asshole.

"Come on," Hogg said. "Get up, boy. I'm gonna beat you across the butt. Then I'm gonna fuck you. Then I'm gonna beat your butt some more."

"All right—" Denny tried to stand without pulling out my face.

"Yeah. All right."

Holding his hips, I slipped to the floor. The grit on the rubber pad ground my knees. The dashboard pressed my back. Denny, half-standing and leaning forward, had one knee on the seat and one sneaker on the floor.

Hogg's buckle clinked. The belt hissed from its loops.

I took Denny's cock to the clotted hair.

Hogg grunted: "Here you go, motherfucker!"

Crack! and Denny swayed. "Shit...!" he whispered. His thigh tensed under my hand.

"Get your fuckin' pants down!" I felt Hogg pulling at them. *Crack*!

"Shit..." and Denny swayed once more.

Crack!

"Oh, shit..." Denny hissed.

"Go ahead, shit if you *want*." Hogg chuckled. "Don't make no difference to me." He brought the belt back again; and again; and again. I could hear him grunt with the effort, each *Crack*!

Denny's fingertips, against my face, danced like bugs at Hogg's strikes. Sometimes, his palms collapsed against my cheeks. I could feel his arms shaking. *Crack*! and he sagged forward again. I chewed his wounded meat.

Then Hogg was up behind Denny, pulling his pants down more. Denny let go my head. I reached between Denny's legs and found Hogg's cock butting around on Denny's ass.

"That's it, cocksucker. Feed it in for me!"

I wedged the wide head between Denny's buttocks. It didn't go easy; but it went. Denny sucked in a breath and held it. Against my face, I could feel Hogg begin to hump. Denny's breath came out a little at each thrust.

I came off him and looked up.

Denny's head hung down between his shoulders, eyes closed, mouth open. He held himself up with one fist wedged between the left and right sunshades above the windshield. Passing headlights lit the places thumb and splayed fingers on his other hand had smudged the side window, like frost. Under the sounds of Hogg's grunts—Denny was holding his breath again—I heard Denny's urine trickling on the seat.

Hogg's hairy arms were locked around Denny's chest. Hogg's thick thighs moved outside Denny's thin ones. Hogg's head was a lot of loose hair, shaking beside the matted shocks of Denny's. Hogg's hams hammered.

Denny swayed.

Hogg was a furious blond beast on his back.

I went down on Denny's cock.

Hogg's hands slid down Denny's belly, slipped under my face. My nose, going in, pushed between his knuckles. He turned one thumb in my mouth, then put in two of his other fingers, with Denny's dick, so that I lost most of the piss down my chin. But Denny began to gasp. He took his hand off the windshield to hold my head. When he came, he gave a hoarse moan and nearly fell on top of me.

I was trying to get out from under him when Hogg got hold of my hair and pulled me across the seat. "Come on, finish me off, cocksucker!" He was sitting back with his knees wide and his pants open. Chin back in his neck, he grinned down at himself. Out of tangled blond, bright with slime and stuff from Denny's ass, his cock jutted across his thigh. One ball was out the zipper, the scrotal skin loose as a chicken's wattle. The hand he wasn't pulling my hair with lay, palm up, beside it, callused fingers curved so I could see the dirt-wedged wrecks of his gnawed nails. His belt lay across one knee.

My head hung from his other hand. My mouth was open. Some of Denny's cum trickled my chin. I stuck my tongue out and down to try and catch it, but it wouldn't reach.

Hogg's legs and belly tensed.

His cockhead lifted two inches.

He pulled my head into his lap.

I caught hold of his hand with mine and began sucking it. His dick was a bar beneath my chin. "Oh, shit," Hogg hissed when I began to go back and forth from his little finger to his thumb to his dick. He swabbed the back of my throat with his shitty foreskin. "Stand up, Denny, and turn around again!" I heard Denny moving on the other side of the seat. I felt the belt slip from under my chest. Then Hogg's body jerked; there was another *Crack*! Then a couple more.

Denny's breath hissed, each whack.

Still sucking, I crawled around to get Hogg's leg between mine, so I could rub off. "Yeah, you son of a bitch! Come on you little shitface bastard!" He stopped whacking and, with the hand I'd been sucking, began to jerk. His fist beat me back.

Still humping his leg, I looked: His chin was up. His shoulders shook. Between the flaps of his shirt, darkened on the flanks with sweat, his hairy chest heaved out, collapsed and heaved again. He thrust two fingers into my mouth with the hand that still clutched the belt. Brass and old leather ground my chin.

Denny was sitting over in the corner of the seat again. His head lay on the glass. He was breathing hard too. His hand was a loose claw at his violated genitals. His fingers twitched.

Hogg's chin came down. His teeth were tight. His lips were back. Another passing car lit the wrinkles scored out from his squinting eyes. His fist blurred up and down his cock. His thighs tightened and relaxed under my arms.

The fingers pried open my mouth.

From the corner, Denny, who'd opened his eyes, whispered: "...Yeah...in the motherfucker's face!"

Hogg's fist rammed into his crotch hair and stayed, grinding.

The first spurt hit my upper lip.

Hogg's hand rose to grip and close over the head.

The second dribbled between his knuckles. He gasped. And his fist, wet now, thudded back against his groin.

The third and fourth went into my mouth and dripped from the roof on my tongue. I swallowed.

The fifth got lost in his fingers again, because his hand went up. It slipped back, and I got the sixth. The seventh just welled up, overflowed his foreskin, and ran down the shaft, over the veins, to disappear under his flexing knuckles. I went forward and began to lick. His fingers loosened, to let me get under them and between.

He dropped the belt. I heard it hit the floor.

"Hey, cocksucker," Denny said from the corner and laughed, weakly, "he's pissin' again and you're missing it."

I looked up.

From the split helmet, in its wet, wrinkled collar, glittering yellow arched away, splashed the dashboard. Hogg's head was back against the seat. His eyes were closed. He was taking great, gasping breaths. Piss ran along the dashboard's underside, dripping—onto Hogg's knee, onto Denny's. Denny ran his hand down his stained pants leg to where it was wetting, then put his fingers in his mouth.

Piss dripped the dashboard onto my back.

I opened my mouth and moved it into his hot water. It broke, warm, on my face. I dropped my mouth. Hogg's hands locked behind my head and pulled me down.

I clawed down into his fly with one hand and felt around under the nut still inside. There was a warm puddle in the seat of his pants that he kept easing around in. As his pee ran out, I shot against his leg. Cum rolled down my thigh to blot in the cloth at my knee.

"Yeah..." Hogg grunted.

His hands slipped apart in my hair.

I lay with my cheek against Hogg's wet groin, his cock shrinking in my mouth; without dropping it, I looked at Denny.

Hogg was looking at him too.

Denny sat with his back against the door, one foot up on the seat. His sneaker was all blotched with brown. His pants were torn both at the seams and across the cloth, and covered with big, stiffened patches that were almost black in the dashboard light. (One arm lay up along the seat back.) The fly was still open, flapped back from his bony hip. One hand moved down and back on his cock, first overhand, then underhand.

Suddenly Hogg grunted, leaned over, pushed Denny's fingers away and lifted the discolored penis. "Hey, now. Don't look quite so swole up no more." He turned the pierced head. The flesh no longer filled the looped nail. Hogg pushed the crown of his little finger between the flesh and the metal arc. (Denny's face squinched: "*Ehhh*...") "Looks like the pus done mostly all run out." Hogg grinned at me. "I guess workin' on him did him some good, cocksucker."

"It's..." Denny blinked. "It'll be all...right, I guess." He spoke haltingly, looking down at himself; but his voice had lost some of its glassy quality. "Yeah, I...I guess it's okay."

Hogg sat back. His grin became laughter. "Hey, Denny! Hey, maybe we just gonna get you back to your old self again. You know?"

Denny smiled, uncertainly. "Yeah...it's all...okay. Sure." His hand drifted back to shucking.

Hogg sat forward and looked out the window. "We're only a few yards off the water." He pointed out Denny's window toward trees and bushes. "It's right down beside the road through that brush there. I didn't think I'd ever hear myself say this to anyone, boy—" Hogg's cock had pulled out my mouth and was a sticky roll of flesh under my cheek—"but I want you to get down there and wash. I want you to get yourself just as scrubbed and shiny and squeaky-clean as you can. You hear?"

"Huh?" Denny asked. "What…?" He looked down at himself.

"You all covered with piss and shit; which is fine. But the blood is gonna get you in trouble. Come on. Take your clothes off."

Lights from another car brightened and faded on Denny's streaked face.

"Go on. Take 'em off."

Denny began to pick at the buttons on his shirt. "All right." Button by button, his shirt fell open across his narrow chest.

Again Hogg reached over. He felt around the shirt till he found the breast pocket, stuck two fingers in, and came out with a wad of bills. "I didn't figure you had time to spend any of this since this morning. Good. I'll just keep it for you till you get back up here."

"Hey," Denny said. "That's my—"

"I'll give it back to you," Hogg said. "You just get down there and get yourself cleaned up."

"But—"

"You do what I say, motherfucker. Or the police gonna get you and gas your ass. That's if they don't just lock you up in the nuthouse basement and throw away the key."

"I'm okay," Denny said. "I ain't nuts."

"Right," Hogg said. "And you ain't gonna kill nobody anymore, neither." Hogg hit the heel of his hand against Denny's shoulder when Denny didn't answer. Hard. "Right?"

"Yeah. All right." Denny nodded, blinking. He began to untie his sneaker.

"All right," Hogg repeated. "Now let's just see you get your redneck ass down to the water and scrubbed up good."

Watching Denny pull off his pants, Hogg put the money in his own pocket, reached down and rubbed my cheek. His fingers were tacky with half-dried scum. "The other sneaker too, stupid."

"Oh." Denny said. "Yeah."

"Shit, cocksucker." Hogg glanced down at me and shook his head. "I'd'a' thought hell would'a froze over before you'd hear me tell somebody to take a bath. I mean, Jesus H. Fuckin' Christ!"

Denny, naked, scrawny shoulders hunched, legs together, hands wedged between them, sat beside the soiled pile, staring at the dashboard. Another drop fell on his knee. His mouth hung slightly open. Another passing car lit his stained arms and sides. He pulled one hand into his lap to scratch; it stayed there, moving a little. "You got some soap?"

Hogg laughed. "You get yourself a handful of sand and scrub yourself off with that. When you come back here, you better be pink all over!"

Denny nodded, pushed up some of the matted hair stuck down on his forehead, opened the truck door, and jumped.

I raised my head to watch him, out the open door, walk gingerly over the shoulder's gravel.

At the bushes he lifted his arms to wade into the high brush. Among the trees I could see the moonlight a-glint on the water.

"Sit up, cocksucker!"

While I got up, Hogg pulled Denny's clothes over and began to stuff them back under the seat. "We can burn these fuckers later." He shook his head. "The poor scumbag, I just hope he don't flip out again and try to act up with me. 'Cause I'd hate to be the one to kill him myself." I handed Hogg the other sneaker and he wedged it back under with the rest. "Yeah, I think you better suck him off once more when he comes back. You seen how it calms him down. Besides, it sort of tickles me to watch." Hogg sat back again. "Maybe that thing through his dick is gonna heal up after all."

A siren sounded down the road, grew louder.

Hogg frowned at me, then looked out the window.

Two police cars came up behind us screeching—and went past.

"Shit!" Hogg bent down again to push Denny's clothes further under. He sat up, bit on his lower lip a moment, then turned on the radio:

"...feet-seven-inches tall, blond, blue-eyed, about seventeen years old, in dirty, blood-stained clothing. It is unknown whether or not he is still armed, as weapons were found discarded at the scenes of his last crimes. Nevertheless, he is extremely dangerous. This psychotic killer is, allegedly, responsible for the deaths of thirty-one people in some of the most brutal and bloody slaughters this state has known, including a pregnant woman and a year-old baby, whose throat he cut and then dropped the tiny, mutilated body in the water by the barge where the murdered parents lived. The police are certain that he is still in the vicinity of Crawhole waterfront, as no cars are missing and Harkner, by report, does not drive. Over seventy-five policemen, from Ellenville, Rye Hill, and Frontwater, are combing the area in a systematic search. Inspector Haley says he is certain his men will bring results before dawn.

"As for a wrap-up of the local news, the Harris County Flower Show will open tomorrow on schedule at ten o'clock with entries from Rockney, Fairhaven, Maple Grove, and Whitbey.

"Last night, several men broke into the hardware store of Mrs. Alberta Ellis and her fifteen-year-old daughter, Judy. Mother and daughter were repeatedly sexually molested and Mrs. Ellis was severely beaten with sticks and chains—she is in serious condition at Frontwater District Memorial Hospital. She was able to identify one of her assailants as Jimmy Goofrin. Goofrin's body, shot to death in the head, was found late this afternoon beside the highway where it had been clumsily hidden in the bushes, some seven miles away.

"Mosely Harwood, of North Cedar Vale, was named the new chairman of the landscaping committee started last fall by Reverend

Robert Hobart and Mrs. Fitzhugh Jamison. He has already scheduled a checkup from tree surgeon Frank Jahovey for the seventy-year-old oaks along Cliff Walk. Other projects will be announced.

"A fatal accident this afternoon on the Ellenville Highway, when a limousine went out of control and leapt across the divider, running motorcyclist Vernor Hawkins and his two passengers off the road. Cyclist 'Hawk' Hawkins, vice president of the Phantoms, a local bike club in the news earlier today in connection with the first of the alleged Harkner slayings, drove away from the accident unhurt. But the car, the driver of which still has not been identified, went up in flames, as the police reported, on impact.

"This coming Tuesday, the Ellenville Relief Fire Brigade will sponsor a bazaar for the benefit of the Ellenville Daycare Center, which was so severely damaged by a snowstorm last February. There will be a fashion show of clothes from Grandma's time, coffee and sweet-rolls. Your contributions will be appreciated.

"Once again, our major story: police from three counties have gathered this evening to help search the Crawhole waterfront for seventeen-year-old Dennis Harkner, whom witnesses claim they watched shoot and club to death five people at a Frontwater Bar this afternoon and who, allegedly, over the rest of the day and evening shot, stabbed, battered and strangled to death more than two dozen other victims, men and women, child and adult. Harkner is about five-feet-seven-inches tall, blond, blue-eyed, about seventeen years…"

Hogg had closed his pants, settled his arm around my shoulder, and I was sort of drifting in the smell of him when Denny climbed back up into the cab, closed the door and sat down.

He was dripping and shivering a little. His hair was flat over his forehead. His breath hissed sharply. Water rolled down his face, around his parted lips. His shoulders were hunched and his knees pressed together. Three-quarters of the nail's arc, visible at the head of his cock, gleamed dully beside the drops glittering between his thin thighs. Water tracked his belly into his crotch hair. Hogg glanced at him, but Denny was listening, too:

"...creature who has terrorized a town for eight whole hours now. No one within the sound of my voice will be truly comfortable until he is taken. Who is Dennis Harkner? Martin Sells, the manager and chief producer here at the station, has been on the phone long distance to Womack County, Pennsylvania, talking to Miss Addie Bowley of the Womack Correctional Institute for Boys from which young Harkner several times ran away, to find out for you. Miss Bowley gave us this statement: 'He always struck me as a bright, if occasionally sullen boy, who alternated between being very friendly and fits of temper. He was disciplined several times for minor infractions of a sexual nature. And he once helped organize his fellow inmates in a civics program for forestry protection during the winter of...'"

"Sure are talkin' about me a lot." Holding his cock, Denny just rubbed the head with his thumb. Water glittered on the red thumbknuckle.

"Ain't been talkin' about much else," Hogg said. "You know the lady that they're tellin' what she said about you?"

"Miss Bowley?" Denny looked over. "I heard of her. But she was in the upstairs office and I don't think I ever saw her to speak, you know?" He looked back at the radio. "Guess they gonna get my ass pretty soon."

"...cordon of roadblocks completely enclosing the Crawhole area within miles—"

Hogg switched off the radio. "We're thirty-six miles outside of Crawhole already." He sat back. "And they still don't know you got wheels under you. They probably think you're hoofin' from warehouse to warehouse around the docks. The fuckers ain't too smart, you know. I been stayin' out from under them for a while now myself. You just got to use your head." Hogg took his arm from around my shoulder, turned, and reached into the sleeper. He pulled up the gray blanket and from underneath took out a shirt. It was a Sweet-Orr blue, wrapped on a rectangle of cardboard with a white-paper cleaner's band around it. "Ain't new, but it ain't bloody either. If you roll up the sleeves it'll be okay. Think it's got a tear in the elbow. But at least it ain't got killin' marks all over it." He leaned the shirt against the back of the seat, reached under the blanket again and brought out a folded pair of gray khaki pants. "Damn wop was sleepin' all over these last night, but other than that there ain't nothin' wrong with 'em." As Hogg held them up, the legs came unfolded. There was a new denim patch on one knee, the kind that irons on and, if you don't sew it too, usually comes off in a few days. But I guess it was all right. Who'd ever pressed them last had got the crease in one leg about half an inch off the one that had been put in by the factory. There was a belt around the loops, the kind with three rows of steel studs all along it and a big, fancy buckle with turquoise inlay and a metal cow's skull with long horns—another car passed. The buckle gleamed and the studs flared and died like electric lights. "I guess they may be a little baggy on you," Hogg said, "but that's better than bloody. Damned if I'm gonna give you my new belt though—I paid nine dollars for that six months back and I ain't had a chance to—" He stopped, frowned down at his own scuffed, brass-buckled garrison, back on his pants now. He squinted at the pants he was holding up. "Shit—you might as well have that too." He lay them carefully in the sleeper so the legs hung out down the seat back. "Maybe you'll find somebody who'll give you a workout with it." Hogg narrowed his green eyes at the clean clothes. "They gonna be big on you, ain't nothin' you can do about that. And you gonna look funny. But you *ain't* gonna look like what *they're* lookin' for."

"Shit...." Denny said softly. He looked at Hogg. He looked at the clothes. He looked at me. He looked at the clothes again. He swallowed. He looked at Hogg again. His eyes were wide and his face seemed like he was tasting something faintly bitter. He looked at the clothes—again—and whispered: "Oh, *shit*...!"

"Hey—" Hogg leaned forward and turned the ignition. The motor thrummed and we bounced a little. "I wanna see the cocksucker here do you in one more time, huh? Before you get dressed. It tickles me." The truck crunched forward on the gravel.

"Hey, cocksucker, move the duds out from behind my shoulder so I don't lean back on 'em and mess 'em up." I did. "Now go on and suck him off again. I wanna watch." We rolled onto the highway.

Denny looked at me with that same look on his face, that I guess was just wondering confusion. He let his knees drop open and slid his hands forward on his thighs. With the nail hanging from it, almost loose, his cock rose a little. I got on my knees on the floor again, crawled between his bare ones, and put his cock in my mouth. The nail was cold. The bay water was bitter with salt. I couldn't help thinking, as I bobbed, it was the cleanest dick I'd sucked all day. Denny put his hands on my head now. His heels hooked behind my knees. I held his wet, bony hips, and felt small muscles flex. Because he'd just shot ten minutes ago, I figured it would take awhile. He splashed pretty quick though.

But then, with Denny, it never did take that long.

"Come on," Hogg said when I got back up on the seat. "Give him a hand with his clothes—" He pulled the wheel around, glanced over—"if he needs it." We were speeding along the highway.

"That's...all right," Denny said. He was unbuttoning the shirt. "I can do it." He slid his arm into the sleeve. It was stuck together with starch and hissed coming apart. After he got the pants on, he sat with his bare feet on the floor, watching the night outside. Once in a while he'd look down and finger the studs on the belt around his waist. He'd fastened the buckle at the last hole, but it still hung pretty loose in his lap. His fly was still open and, looking back out at the road, he reached in to scratch. His hair, drying, was getting curly. Like mine.

We drove a long time.

Sometimes Hogg would wiggle around and gouge at his crotch with his thumb, like he was really itchy. Once I reached between his legs to take his dick out, but he pushed my hand away and told me to cut it the fuck out before he broke my neck.

I guess we drove three-and-a-half, four hours.

The truckstop where Hogg finally turned in had maybe half a dozen cabs with their vans parked over the gravel between the gas pump and the all-night diner.

"This ought to do it, if anything does," Hogg grunted, yanking back on the break. He looked at Denny. "We're over a hundred-fifty miles out of state. Most of the folks around here probably never even heard of Crawhole...except for on the radio tonight." Hogg sat back in the seat; the shadow from the top of the windshield slid down over his eyes. "Okay, now: What's your name."

"Huh?" Denny started a little, looked at Hogg; he hadn't really been listening. "Dennis..." he said. "Denny Harkner."

"Naw, it's—" Hogg dropped his head a moment to gnaw at his thumb: "It's Bo Jonas. Bo is short for Beauregard. Can you spell Beauregard?"

Denny frowned. "B-o-r-r..."

"It's short for Bobby," Hogg said. "You can spell Bobby."

"B-o-b-..." Denny frowned again: "...y."

"That's right: Bo Jonas. You got that?"

"Yeah," Denny said. "Un-huh."

"You come from Plattsburgh, New York," Hogg said, "and you're hitchhiking to see your Aunt Ruth Jonas down in Lakeland, Florida."

He looked out the window. "Lots of fruit haulers when their carryin'-licenses lapse, come by this way 'cause they're scared of the big highways—Now *what's* your name? And where're you goin'?"

"Eh...Bo Jonas," Denny said. "Bobby... And I'm going to Florida...where in Florida?"

"Lakeland. That's about fifty miles east of Jacksonville."

"Yeah. Lakeland. And I'm coming from Plattsburgh. To see my aunt."

"Ruth Jonas," Hogg said. "There's a big Air Force base in Plattsburgh, and it's just twenty miles south of the Canadian border, across from Montreal." Hogg dug in his shirt pocket and took out the money. "Here's your dough from yesterday. Put it in your pocket, close your fly, and keep your hands off your pecker."

"Yeah." Frowning, Denny took the money and tried to slip it in his own shirt pocket. Starch stuck the square of cloth to the cloth beneath and he had to slide two fingers in and then spread them to get it open. He put the money in. There was a button on the top of the pocket and he closed it. "Okay. Yeah, all right."

"Your pants cuffs rolled up?"

Denny nodded. "I wish I had some shoes."

"They'll just feel sorry for you and give you a ride that much faster."

Denny took the door handle, then looked back. "I don't want nobody feelin' sorry for me. I'd kill a motherfucker for that."

"That's all right," Hogg said; but he gave me a half-disgusted look and shook his head. "You just get on out of here."

"Yeah," Denny said. He looked at me too. When he put his hand on my knee—the skin at the sides of his nails was still white and translucent from the bay—his face did a small, bitter twitch. "Hey, so long, cocksucker." He was trying to smile. "Hey, Hogg?" He blinked, and the twitch flickered again among his thin, acned features. "Goodbye and…thanks."

"You're very welcome," Hogg said. "Now get on out."

Denny pushed on the handle, jumped down to the asphalt, slammed the door, and walked toward the lighted truck stop. His pants were awfully big. Rolled up around his ankles like that they looked pretty strange. The belt—the studs glittered across his butt as he passed under the tin-coned lamp on the phone pole—was pretty far down, and lopsided. The sleeves rolled up above his elbows were like bags hanging off his shoulders. But I've seen guys in funnier clothes. When he got to the gravel, his step got a little more ginger to it and his hands started bouncing around his hips.

Four men came down the concrete steps of the restaurant. Denny went straight for them. I couldn't hear what he was saying but they stopped to listen.

Once one of the men thought something Denny said was really funny and laughed.

Eight soiled knuckles in a row on the top of the carpeted wheel, Hogg watched through the bug-specked windshield.

They talked some more. Once Denny pointed back at Hogg's truck.

The center knuckles rose.

The man who'd laughed put his hand on Denny's shoulder and laughed again.

Two of the men walked away. Denny went with the man who'd laughed, toward one of the smaller trucks.

"Shit," Hogg whispered, reached forward and started the motor.

We pulled around onto the highway, going back the way we'd come.

"He must be one lucky motherfucker, you know? The dumb-ass scumbag just might make it!" Hogg shook his head. "Guess I should've taken my clippers out and cut that damned thing off his dick—but, hell, he went through so much gettin' it *in* there...." He shook his head again. After awhile he said: "He might make it. Be his luck. I don't see how he kept alive all *this* time."

I fell asleep during the drive back.

Once I woke when we'd stopped at some all-night filling station. I looked up over the window edge to see Hogg, outside under the highway light, joking with the pump-jockey in his red baseball cap with the visor turned backward and a dirty blue collar open at his neck—like Hogg was any old trucker, bob-tailing it home after a run.

A couple of hours later, I woke again.

Hogg had stopped the truck. In his lap, he had a wax paper full of French fries. When I blinked and raised my head, he said: "Here..." and fed me a couple of handfuls. I ate right from his fingers—only I was so tired, I fell asleep licking ketchup off his thumb. When I woke again, my head was against Hogg's big arm, shaking with the road. First I thought it was just a few minutes later. But the radio was on. (Some guy was singing about MacArthur Park, and how it was melting in the dark....) Outside, swatting at the new blue like rags of black lace, trees flipped by.

As I sat up, between them I saw the gun-gray bay dragging back beside us.

Hogg glanced at me, grunted, then pulled the truck over to the shoulder. "Christ, I gotta take me a wicked shit! An' my fuckin' kidneys been workin' overtime." He reared back on the hand brake, opened the door, dropped to the road, and came around to my side of the truck. (The French fries paper was balled up under my hip.) I leaned out the window to watch. Hogg put both hands on the dusty fender, bent a little forward, and gave me a grin.

I heard what sounded like a fart—that got swallowed in something wet. Now he lifted the heel of his bare foot and shook his leg. Something fell loose inside his pants, dropped down inside to catch behind his knee. He shook his leg again.

I pushed down the door handle, jumped out, lunged forward, and flung myself on the shoulder's dirt, a hand each side of his feet. The turd's end, like some big nigger's dick out at Crawhole, dropped from his cuff to lean against Hogg's blackened heel.

"Shit," Hogg drawled. As I was trying to push it in my mouth, he rocked his foot back on his heel, turned it—the hard cracked rim pushing my face aside—and mashed his foot on the turd. Shit wedged up through his grimy toes. I caught his ankle with one hand, tried to pull his foot over with the other, jabbed my tongue between them, tried to push them into my mouth.

Above me, Hogg chuckled. "That's right, cocksucker. You're a nasty little bastard...."

His toes came up and clawed my tongue, gray with grit and shitpaste. Under the shit they were salty. He laughed again and let me get his foot up. I rolled almost to my back, gnawing on what crusted the ball, with dirt in it now, and small stones.

"Cocksucker," he said, "I'm gonna fuck your face like a goddamn asshole. Get that shit all wet for me, that's right—"

I scraped to the horn with my teeth.

"You ain't nothin' but a fuckin' scumbag asshole anyway."

He kicked my face away with spread toes. When I went forward again, my tongue wagging, he hit me back, across the mouth with his foot's crusted rim.

"Get on up! I got somethin' comin' to wet it down!"

I heard his water and pushed back.

Urine ran on the truck tire, darkening the rubber and turning the clotted nuts on the capless hubs black. The loose hank of foreskin made his piss splatter.

Working my mouth, I crawled in front of him. His water wet my ear, my cheek. I held my mouth wide. It bubbled hot at the back of my tongue, tickled and dripped from my pallet, ran out over a place where there was no shit on my lower lip.

"Make it wet...that's it. Nice and wet. Wet that shit up. Yeah! Just like ol' Hogg likes it."

Pee ran down my chin, my neck, under my shirt and down my stomach.

Hogg put his middle finger in my mouth—water splashed the ham of his thumb, dripped off his fingertips—and scraped something from the back of my teeth and under the side of my tongue. Then he brought his hand back to milk his dick forward, rubbing it, and rubbing it in. "Yeah...!" Veins bulged, disappearing under his thumb and forefinger. "That's right, cocksucker! You got it!" With his other hand on the truck above me, he leaned forward. His dick went into my mouth. I closed my lips around it, wallowed my tongue under it. His hand came down from the truck and caught my head; then his other hand. He grunted, slid in, pulled back, slid in again.

I heard a car pass.

But it was still half dark. And we were on the far side of the truck anyway.

He took a lot longer than Denny, me hugging his hips with my elbows, Hogg clutching my sides with his knees. But when he shot, snot-thick and slimy, it sloshed into what was already there. I sucked and swallowed and sucked. He took one hand off my face and leaned again on the fender. His other hand flexed and relaxed on my cheek. "Goddamn, boy! You just found another one of my things. Suckin' on my fingers and toes is number two after suckin' off my dick. But fuckin' a mouthful of shit—my own shit, now—I'm damned if you ain't found number three as well." He took a deep breath. Then he bent, put his hands under my arms, and lifted me off the ground.

I put my arms around his neck, my head on his shoulder. I was breathing hard too.

He got one arm under my butt. I had a knee on either side of him. My pants had come open. My dick was hard, out, and up against his belly, all piss and sweat wet between us. I started to squirm off.

Hogg said: "Let's get up in the cab."

I held his neck. With one arm around me, he pulled himself up into the cab by the other, then lay back across the seat with me on top of him. I was still squirming. "That's it, boy! Come on, you two-bit cocksucker! Shoot that shit all over ol' Hogg's hairy belly! That's right! I want your gunk, cocksucker. I want your cum all over me! I want your spunk! I want your mess! Shoot it out, boy!" Whispering against my face, his breath was like hot whiffs from a pan with a piece of bad meat you say hell, I'll fry anyway. "Shoot me up with that fuckin' greasy cum, you lowdown, pissed-up scumbag!" He held one arm tight around my shoulders. He wedged his other hand between us so that his horny nubs were right against my moving penis.

I rubbed on him with my mouth and my eyes wide.

While he whispered, I watched his tongue gleaming and moving behind his moving teeth. Suddenly it slid out. His mouth came up against mine. His tongue began digging inside my face. I shot all over his belly and his fingers.

He squeezed me and laughed, without taking his tongue out my mouth.

After maybe a minute, he did—and a deep breath. His face trickling with sweat, he pushed me back and elbowed himself up to sit.

I sat too.

One after the other, he made me suck his hairy fingers off for my scum. Then he sucked them too, for what I'd missed. For a while, then, he just rubbed his heavy stomach between the sweat-blotched edges of his shirt. Under the hair, the shiny film he spread over himself dulled.

"Man!" Hogg's rubbing hand joined his other in his lap. "I think that was the one we both needed. Always been sort of partial to shit, 'specially my own. But you don't get much of a chance to fuck in your own, less you got a cocksucker who likes a face full of it now and then." He grinned at me, then closed the door beside him. "Shit...I'll get drunk and eat me some fuckin' dog turds off the street, sometimes—if it ain't some drunk old nigger's shit the black bastard pooped when he was squattin' in the back alley. Sometimes dogshit's better. Sometimes nigger shit. It depends on how you're feelin'. But I wouldn't ever eat no white guy's shit—it ain't low enough; unless I was a nigger myself, maybe; or it was maybe yours...just like you'd eat mine. You can't get lower than eatin' your own nigger cocksucker's shit, now, can you? An' I wouldn't even eat yours a *lot*—not like you eat mine. 'Cause that's the way we're set up, us two. I'm the shit machine, and you're my personal shit bowl and pee pot, right? I'm just tellin' you, see, so you know I know how it is with you: a dog, a nigger—or somebody real close, like your own shit machine. That right?" Hogg grinned. "That in there—" He thumbed back toward the sleeper— "is some I couldn't finish. You want it, later, go on...Real low—or real close. An' that in there, that's the *lowest* shit you could chow down on! Trust me. But then, I guess you know all about that already, don't you? Man, I'll tell you, cocksucker, I ain't really too much better than fuckin' Piper! He's the one who taught me all this."

I closed my door.

Hogg started the truck.

I kept rubbing one eye with my wrist because it itched.

Outside, the water and the sky just above it ran with gold.

Trees flashed between us and the bay.

"Think we gonna get us some breakfast soon. We almost back to Frontwater. Remember that diner we stopped in yesterday, or the day before, when I first got you? That ain't too far." Hogg chuckled. "I'm about ready to see what they'd do if we came in there again. Get ourselves a few handfuls of scrambled eggs and syrup and pancakes!" Ten seconds later, he glanced at me. "Boy, you know I'd been thinking about getting' out to *take* that shit at least an hour—while you was curled up against me, asleep. Even stopped the truck once and got out...you was just snorin' away. So I said, fuck it, I might as well wait. 'Cause I *knew* what you was gonna do." He looked at the road, looked at me, looked at the road. "Just like Piper, man. Like you was my own kid brother. So I figured I'd get back in and go on till you got to stirrin'. I mean I ain't worth a fuck if I can't hold my gut for another half hour or so, right? And you were pretty sleepy."

On runneled gold, with a tug either side and piled between with refuse, a Crawhole scow moved on the bay's far waters.

"You ever been on a dog leash?" Hogg was still looking at the highway. "In the glove compartment, I got me a dog collar I always keep around. Came off an old dog I used to have—well, now where the hell *else* would a dog collar come from? I'd like to give you a workout on a fuckin' leash.... With all this shit about Denny, I'm just about ready to relax for a couple of weeks and not do nothin' but lay around. And I wouldn't mind you layin' around with me. A couple of weeks? Even a couple of months. About forty miles above Ellenville, I got me a shack in the woods I go to sometimes, when I want to stay out of the way, you know? Nothin' but a bunch of niggers livin' up around there now and the law don't come in much—Nigg's got a kid brother up there, shacked up with two wives, too." Hogg looked at me and nodded deeply, like I might not believe him. "You'd probably have yourself a good time up there—man, them niggers don't do nothin' but fuck each other's kids, fuck each other's women, fuck each other's mules. Nigg, last time I saw him, he say he's maybe goin' up there soon. You'd like that, too, wouldn't you?" He grinned at me again. "I usually have me a pretty good time when I go. You know, I been at just about everybody in Nigg's family, one time or another—except Lee-Ann, who is one of his sister-in-laws, 'cause she say right out she just don't fancy me at all! And since I'm a visitor to the neighborhood, I got to be polite. You know what she say, too? She say, if I don't bring *somethin'* up there soon for them niggers to fuck—even if it's just a damned sheep—they gonna stop bein' so sociable with their own after a while. So maybe I'm just gonna take you along, huh?" Hogg laughed. "Get us some whiskey. Put them chains on that collar. Stake you down by the outhouse, cocksucker, and I could nail the outhouse door shut; and me and anybody else who come to visit would never have to go inside it again. You could lap and lick and waller and be happy as a little mud puppy."

At the scow's back was a cabin.

A nigger wandered out on deck, punched his fists into the air to stretch, then climbed up the garbage pile to look around. A few seconds later, a white man came out and ambled to the back rail. I couldn't be sure, but I think he was taking a piss in the bay.

The way Hogg had been fucking on my mouth with his shit, then him going on about the dog collar, had put me in mind of the two garbage men for a time now. They'd been on my mind, actually, from when I first woke up.

On the barge's back, the white guy's hair, as he stood at the rail, looked as red as the water around him—it could have been blond. But in the sunrise, it *looked* red.

More trees came between the truck and the bay.

"I just don't know, cocksucker. Somethin' about you." Hogg tugged at the wheel, and we came around the inlet and straightened out. "Now when Nigg and that bikey run off with you, I

could just as easy've said, good riddance and fuck the little bastard, you know? I ain't worried about no little cocksucker like
you spillin' off his mouth about what we done. Naw, that ain't
your style. But I don't know. There's just somethin'."

What I was thinking was that I could probably get off as soon
as we stopped at the diner—slip out through the bathroom window, maybe. Or just run when he wasn't looking. It wouldn't be
hard to hitch out to Crawhole soon as the morning's work traffic
started. I wondered if Big Sambo would take me back on his tug.

He'd paid out fifteen dollars for me, after all.

Of course, after the beating Hogg had given him, he might not
be so interested. And even though he had the skin for it, Hogg
pumped out his dick so much—eight, nine times a day—there
was no way he could leave it long enough to raise a crop of
cheese like Red's. (I still wondered if Red's dick had freckles on it
like the rest of him. It had been so dark most of the time I was
sucking him, I didn't know.) Rufus wasn't so bad in the cheese
department, either. Red and Rufus had said they'd leash me up
inside the scow cabin. I wondered how they'd feel when they
finally noticed I was a nigger. (That's all the two guys who'd got
me off in the burned-out place on Federal Street had been interested in—calling me "nigger that" and "nigger this." I kind of liked
that part. One of them was black, too. But the rest of it hadn't
been fun at all. There was no rough stuff in it, both of them were
cut, and they were all into talking 'bout how they really loved me
and only sucked on me and wouldn't let me suck them off or pee
on me or fuck my ass or nothing. For three days, I mean, before I
could get loose! It made me feel all dirty and helpless and really
scared.) It might make Rufus raise an eyebrow, but I didn't think it
would bother Red. And though they'd probably been nice people,
Mona and Harry wouldn't be around now to guess what them
guys were doing with me and get all twisted out of shape.

"Shit, cocksucker," Hogg said, "when you were gone, though,
I just got so fuckin' angry I could've gone rampagin' off like
Denny—might have, if he hadn't a' done it first! Then I said, well

if you're *that* fuckin' angry, go *get* him! Just the way you're always reachin' in between my legs for it and don't care what
comes out of it... I don't know, but it makes an old shit-tub like
me feel kinda..." Hogg shrugged. He grinned over at me. Then
he looked at the road again. "Don't know *what* it makes me feel.
But I like it." He gave a sort of grunt. "Guess I'm still wonderin'
why I came out to Crawhole for you. Probably my sense of
duty... I mean I'm *glad* I did, if only 'cause maybe we helped
out Denny. But it ain't *that* hard to get some faggot to swing on
my joint, dirty as it is. Most of 'em just like it all the more—well,
maybe some of the *old* ones do." Hogg pushed out his lower lip
a moment, frowning. "Some of the young ones's still pretty squea-
mish about that stuff, unless they're just freaks. Like you. Well, I
guess it ain't all *that* easy, either." He took a slow breath. "And
keepin' a kid around in the kind of work I have—and that ain't
mentioning the kind of fun—some people would call that about
as crazy as ol' Denny there—Christ, I hope that crazy fucker
makes it!" The next laugh was just a snort out his nose. (Yeah, I
was thinking, the best thing out of a dick, no matter how dirty, is
the cheese.) Hogg took one hand off the wheel to scratch under
his arm. "I guess I'm funny, huh? Wantin' to see *him* running
around loose—and *you* on a goddamn leash!"

Through the trees, I watched the scow drag its fan of copper,
toiling between dark tugs.

Was one tug Sambo's...? But then, Big Sambo's tug had been
all broke down.

"Hey, cocksucker?"

I looked around.

Hogg crooked his thumb in one bulldog nostril, took it out,
slid it in his mouth, and sucked at the snot, watching me. From
the way his jaw was working, I could tell he'd started biting at
what was left of the nail. (I'd seen Red eat his snot once; but I'd
probably have to fight him for it if I wanted to get it from him,
where Hogg would just finger-feed me from his own nose right
out...) Hogg turned back to look at the road, stopped gnawing,

and put his hand on the wheel again. A smile opened in the gold stubble. Wrinkles scored around his green, green eyes.

"Hey…"

Flickering with leaf shadow, dawn fled over his face. In the middle of the rush of light, his lips put a blue shadow aslant his yellow teeth. Between the rags of his shirt, wide open with most of the buttons gone, sun shook in his sunburned chest's hair.

"Hey, cocksucker…tell me what you're thinkin'."

Holding the wheel with one hand, he dropped the other to tug at the crotch of his pants, getting comfortable, and lifted his butt to let an ass-flapping fart. His forearm filled the rolled-up sleeve like a ham with hair. His elbow, through the tear, and his knuckles, on the wheel, were dark as wrinkled fruit skins. (If we stopped soon, I could make like I was going to the bathroom or something and get away and be back to Red, Rufus, and Crawhole in an hour….) Hogg put his hand back on the wheel. His thumb lay up over the taped plastic. His gas, rising, made the cab smell rich and good. I looked at the grime-rimmed nail gnawed back on a nub like an oversized acorn of callus.

"Come on, cocksucker—" Hogg glanced at me again. Then a frown tried to fight its way in among the lines in his three-day stubble, into the lines around his close, green eyes. But a bigger smile kept it out. "Hey…is everything all right?" He looked at the road. "What's the matter?"

I turned to watch the fleeing trees. "Nothin'."

—San Francisco, New York, London
March 1969–October 1973

A NOTE ON THE TEXT

This edition of *Hogg* by Samuel R. Delany incorporates stylistic revisions by the author as well as corrections of earlier editorial and typographic errors. Wherever this edition deviates from earlier ones, the present text is correct.